REDWORK

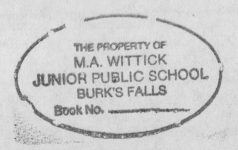

MICHAEL BEDARD
REDWORK

LESTER
PUBLISHING
LIMITED

The author gratefully acknowledges his debt to the words and wisdom of the older people whose personal histories appear in the pages of Ronald Blythe's *The View in Winter*.

Canadian Cataloguing in Publication Data

Bedard, Michael, 1949–
  Redwork

ISBN 1-895555-23-X

I. Title.

PS8553.E32R43 1992   jC813'.54   C92-094420-5
PZ7.B43Re 1992

Lester Publishing Limited
56 The Esplanade
Toronto, Ontario
M5E 1A7

Printed and bound in Canada.

92 93 94 95   5 4 3 2 1

This one's for you, Dad

True it is, without falsehood, certain and most true.
That which is above is like that which is below,
and that which is below is like that which is above,
to accomplish the miracles of the one thing.

The Emerald Tablet
of Hermes Trismegistus

PART ONE

Raven's Head

Does the eagle know what is in the pit?
Or wilt thou go ask the mole?
Can wisdom be put in a silver rod?
Or love in a golden bowl?

William Blake
Motto, The Book of Thel

— 1 —

ROACHES. There must have been fifty of them crawling around in the bottom of the empty jam jar, a tangled mass of legs and feelers.

For the past week, he and his mother, Alison, had been hunting them in earnest, setting out the traps around the apartment at night, shaking out the catch come morning, like a pair of trappers tending their line.

They had just made the morning rounds. Two of the sticky homemade traps sat on the counter beside the jar. Cass was trying to get a count. He'd get so far, and then one of the revolting creatures trying to scramble up the inside of the jar would stumble, the pile would shift, and he'd have to start all over again.

Alison was sitting at the kitchen table with her battered copy of William Blake's poems and a second cup of coffee, waiting for consciousness to dawn. When it finally did, she sprang into action. Without warning she scooped the jar up off the counter and headed for the door.

"Be right back," she called over her shoulder.

"Hang on. I'm coming too."

By the time he kicked on his shoes and pulled the apartment door closed behind him, she had already started down the stairs. The sound of Saturday morning cartoons and screaming kids spilled from the neighboring apartment.

He caught up to her at the bottom of the stairs. They walked briefly into a late winter storm, then swung open the door of the restaurant under the apartments and went in.

The smell of home fries and bacon fat hit him in the face like a wet rag. His eyes drifted down the line of battered booths. A couple of blank faces glanced up briefly and went back to their breakfasts. A hand holding a cigarette drifted up from a booth near the back, punched out a song on the juke-box, then dropped out of sight. The smoke curled to the strains of the country tune that started up.

Alison marched along behind the row of stools at the lunch counter. A pale waitress piled dirty dishes into a rubber tub behind the counter, while a man with string for shoelaces huddled over a cup of coffee, watching every move she made.

At the far end of the counter the restaurant owner sat at the cash register with a toothpick wedged between his teeth, poring over the morning paper. In addition to being the restaurant owner, he was the landlord of the apartment they'd been renting for the past few months.

They'd seen signs of the roaches when he first showed them the place: brittle corpses in the kitchen cupboards and under the sink. No problem, he said. He'd have the place fumigated before they moved in. He hadn't, and every first of the month when he came like clockwork to collect the rent, Alison would remind him about the roaches. He would smile and nod sympathetically while he folded the money into his pocket.

Finally, last week Alison had found a family of them in the fridge. That had done it.

Now she walked over and planted herself in front of the cash register. He glanced up and the toothpick twitched a little.

"Well, good morning, Mrs. — "

Alison brought the jar down hard on the counter. Every head in the place looked up. For a long agonizing moment only the country tune kept on. Then the waitress caught sight of what was in the jar. A plate shattered at her feet.

"We have a slight problem upstairs," said Alison in that

terrifyingly calm voice she saved for moments like this. "We were wondering what you intended to do about it?"

What he did was give them notice.

Every night for the next three weeks the two of them sat at the kitchen table after dinner combing through the classifieds. What they were looking for was another place over a store, or maybe a flat in a house. What they were really looking for was someplace cheap. With Alison currently working for the Miss Maid Housecleaning Service while she banged away on her Blake paper at every free moment, they weren't exactly rolling in cash. The hours were long, the work was unsatisfying, and the pay was low—which made it sound suspiciously like every other job he could remember Alison having had. But it put food on the table and a roof over their heads. Someday she would finally finish this M.A. thesis she had been working on seemingly forever, and then— What exactly would happen then was never really specified, but whatever it was it would presumably not include sifting through the classifieds and catching cockroaches in jam jars.

It was a small ad in the Friday paper that caught Cass's eye.

"Listen to this one: 'Second floor flat for rent in quiet old house. Would suit couple. Deer Park area. Reasonable.' It gives a number to call."

"Deer Park. That's a nice old neighborhood. We have a couple of clients around there. I wonder what they mean by 'reasonable'?"

"Only one way to find out."

It was just past nine the next morning when they stepped off the bus on the edge of a large park. Yesterday's storm, no doubt winter's last stand, had spread a thick icing of snow over the park. A tenuous path had been tramped through it.

"It's over there, I think," said Alison with a vague nod across the park. She started along the path with Cass following behind in her tracks. They had been given directions by the old man Alison had spoken to on the phone the night before. He apparently lived on the ground floor of the house. He explained that it was a two-bedroom flat on the second floor that was for rent, told them where they could find the key if they wanted to look at it, and quoted a price for the place that Alison still couldn't believe.

Here and there solitary tracks veered off the main path, launching into the white wilderness. Toboggan tracks scored a hillside: rumors of children, though none were now in sight.

They trudged past the white crater of a wading pool, a playground where swings and slides stood like prehistoric beasts blanketed with snow, a deserted tennis court. It was so quiet he could hear Alison's breathing as she labored along the narrow path. A far cry from life above the Bluebird Bar and Grill with the steady drone of traffic and street noise and the streetcars rumbling past day and night. Here the cars seemed to have gone into hibernation, huddled quietly at curbside under coverlets of snow. The only noise was the squawking of starlings fighting over frozen crusts in the tennis court.

"What was the number again?" asked Alison. She was standing at the edge of the park staring at the houses across the street.

"Fifty-five, I think." He checked the note she had scrawled in the margin of the paper. "Yes, fifty-five Woodlawn Crescent."

So this was Woodlawn Crescent, this string of narrow brick houses facing the park on this side. Directly across the street was number thirty-three, sleek and fashionably thin, with teal blue trim and tall, curtainless windows. A white BMW slept in the drive. Its friend on the right, number 35, had been recently sandblasted by the looks of it. It had a Victorian-style lamp at the head of the walk and stained glass sidelights flanking the front door. The rest were variations on a theme: old houses with new faces, like old people desperate to look young, one face-lift trying to outdo the next. It was all vaguely depressing. He could smell the money clear across the street.

They walked slowly along the fringe of the park, Alison rhyming off the numbers as they went, with barely concealed enthusiasm.

It was he who first saw the house. It was set back farther than the rest and surrounded by a high, ragged hedge. Even the frosting of snow could not disguise the fact that the place was in rough shape. It looked like an old farmhouse that had wandered into the neighborhood and forgotten the way back to the dirt road it belonged on. It was painted red with dull green trim and roof. But not a pleasant red, more the dark, disturbing color of blood. The paint was cracked and fissured like the wrinkles on an ancient face.

"Forty-seven, forty-nine, fifty-one—" Alison stopped dead in her tracks. Her eyes widened. "Oh, no," she said. "It can't be." She took the paper from him, read the address in the margin, then stared at the number nailed to the fencepost at the front of the property. Her face dropped and her arms fell slack to her side. It was as if the air had gone out of her.

He guided her to a bench nearby under a large tree leafed with snow. He brushed the bench off with the paper and spread it out on the seat. She sat down with a thump. In the long silence that followed, he happened to look up into the latticework of snow and branches above them, and suddenly he remembered the story of Blake and the tree of angels.

Blake was twelve at the time and was walking home across the fields when he lay down under a tree to rest. He was looking up at the sunlight on the leaves when suddenly he saw an angel sitting in the top branches. Instantly the tree was full of angels, their wings flashing in the sun.

He ran home and told his mother. She didn't believe him, of course, but from that day on, Blake continued to have visions of the spirit world. He became an engraver, and for nearly forty years he engraved his visionary poems on copper plates with pictures in the margins, which he would later print and color by hand. Nobody was much interested. In fact, most people thought he was plain crazy. It was no wonder Alison was a little strange, considering the company she kept.

"It's not really that bad," he said finally. "From here, I mean."

"It's awful." She was bent over, lacing her boot. "'Quiet old house.' I should have known." She stamped the other boot down in the snow and attacked that lace as well.

"Well, it *is* old." He let his eyes drift over the house. An enclosed porch was set to one side at the front, with a windowed sun porch above it on the second floor. A small round window set in the gable of the attic was boarded over with a weathered piece of wood. There were gaps where the wooden shingles that dressed the upper half of the house had fallen away. Something had been chewing on the chimney bricks. It looked like a strong wind would send it toppling to the ground.

"Who knows," he said. "Maybe it's nice inside."

Alison gave him a withering glance.

The front door of the house next door opened, and a small gray woman leaned out, looked over at them, and plucked a folded paper from the iron railing. She looked briefly up at the sky as though she were expecting something, then disappeared quickly back inside and closed the door. Her walk was swept clear, as were those of all the houses to either side of number 55. It sat alone among them on an island of snow.

The longer Cass looked at the old house from the vantage point of the bench, the more intrigued he became by it. It seemed a house that held secrets. Something about it struck a dim chord inside him, like a half-remembered dream. He could almost imagine what it would look like inside.

"Well," said Alison finally, "I don't know about you, but I'm getting a frostbitten backside sitting here. Let's head home."

"You mean you're not even going to look at it? We came all this way, and you're not even going to look?"

"Come on, Cass. I've seen all I need to see from right here. The Bluebird begins to look good beside this place." She got up.

He stayed sitting on the bench, determined now to see the inside of the place.

"Oh, so that's it, is it?" said Alison. "Passive resistance." She glanced over at the house again.

"Okay, you win. If it's that important to you, I guess we can give it a quick peek. But I'm warning you, Cass, I'm not going to like it."

The gate was anchored shut. It took a couple of good kicks with their boots before it relented and let them in, scooping a fan-shaped swath in the snow. It wasn't exactly as though people were beating down the door to rent the place.

They made their way up what they thought must be the walk, hidden under snow, and picked their way tentatively up the porch stairs. It was obvious that no one had been in or out of the house since the storm.

Cass glanced in the ground floor window on the way by. A strange collection of creatures lined the sill, all of them dusty with neglect. There were a large china dog and cat separated by a set of wooden monkeys with steely eyes, a band of ivory elephants trudging across an ivory bridge, a small glass frog with gaping mouth, a stuffed bird perched on a dusty piece of branch, a delicate crystal unicorn. A dead moth lay among them as if attempting to belong. Beyond the sill lay darkness, webbed with lace.

Alison banged the snow off her boots onto the coco matting inside the porch. The old man on the phone had said they would find the key on a string in the mail slot. There was a thumbtack with a loop of string around it stuck into the wood above the slot. The string disappeared through the hole.

Two buzzers were set in the wall by the door. In the small window beneath the lower of them was a piece of paper with a name written on it. The key bounced up lightly against the inside of the door as Alison reeled it in. He struggled to decipher the name. It was done in a small, crabbed script. It looked like Magnus, A. Magnus, though it might well have been something else.

Alison looked over at him doubtfully, slid the key into the lock, and opened the door. An odd smell greeted them as they came in; the sharp, acrid smell of things shut in too long.

"There must be a light here somewhere," said Alison, running her hand warily along the wall inside the door.

He reached up instinctively, and his hand immediately closed on the switch. A dull yellow bulb in the ceiling snapped into life.

"Charming," said Alison.

They stood in a narrow entranceway. To their left was the door to the ground floor flat, a dark wooden door with a dull brass knocker. Beside the door on a dusty boot tray stood an old wicker bundle buggy and a pair of rubber boots. The back of the buggy had been bashed in.

To their right a short flight of stairs led to a landing, then turned and launched off to the second floor. He left his boots on the landing, and while Alison struggled with her knotted laces, started alone up the stairs.

The door at the top was slightly ajar. Light spilled down the top few stairs. He pushed open the door and entered the empty flat.

The room, apparently the living room, had a fireplace on the wall opposite the door, with a mantel over it. Beside it was another room. Both had recently been painted. The smell was still in the air, along with traces of that other, darker smell.

Cass walked slowly through the empty, echoing rooms, the sound of each footstep unnaturally magnified. Despite the painting, there was a feeling of age to the place. It was in the dark wood around the doors, the plate rack running along the wall of the second room, in the worn hardwood floors and the bits of furniture that had been left behind. Though empty, it was not unoccupied. Ghosts observed his every move.

He came to rest in a small bedroom at the back of the house. From the moment he stepped through the door he knew that this would be his.

Somehow this room had escaped the painter's brush. It was papered in an old floral print. Here and there were darker patches where pictures had once hung. A tall, bare window looked out onto the rear of the house. An old dresser with a dusty mirror mounted on it stood alone against the wall the door was on. He ran his finger in a slow circle through the dust. That strange sense of familiarity he'd felt on the bench was much stronger now.

He could hear Alison prowling around the apartment, opening and closing doors. He was standing at the window when she came in.

"The kitchen's nice," she said. "Plenty of cupboard space. And these floors—with a little work this hardwood could be gorgeous."

"Mmm," he said, only half listening. The window overlooked a small yard bounded on both sides by a weatherbeaten wooden fence and at the back by an old clapboard garage with a flat roof. The yard lay quietly sleeping under the snow, but here and there weathered stakes and the shriveled remnants of plants pierced the whiteness like a brief disturbance of the dream.

"Mouse droppings," said Alison, inspecting the closet. "Likely coming up through that heat register there."

"Just lay a few traps, that's all."

"I suppose. How's the view? Oh my, not much to look at, is there? I wonder what the bathroom's like?" She wandered off.

At one corner of the garage a short length of stovepipe protruded from the roof. The snow directly around it had melted down to the tar. A slight trickle of smoke spilled from the lip of the pipe, vanishing instantly into the air.

He noticed now that the snow between the house and garage was broken by a single set of tracks. There was someone in there. But why the fire?

"Come here for a minute," called Alison. "You won't believe this."

This turned out to be the antique bathtub, deep and narrow, supported on squat porcelain legs shaped like lions' paws.

"My grandmother used to have a tub like this when I was a little girl. I haven't seen one like it in years. I used to be a little afraid of it, I remember. I thought it might run off with me while I was sitting in it. My, my—memories."

In the end, it was probably the tub that did it. That and the fact that not a trace of a cockroach could be found under the kitchen sink, in the cupboards, or in the fridge.

Of course, when they made a second run through the place they noticed the switch that sparked and would need replacing, the bubbling of the plaster above the bathroom sink, the deep crack running through the ceiling of the back bedroom. But Cass could tell that the decision had already been made.

They stood together in the front room, leaning against the sill.

"Well, what do you think?" asked Alison.

He looked out over at the park, following their tracks to the bench and back.

"I like it," he said. "How about you?"

"Well, it needs work. And the outside of the place is a shambles. But there's something about it." She followed his gaze out the window. "It would be good for you, the park and all. A chance to meet some other kids."

He nodded noncommittally, hoping she wouldn't start in on that right now. A car inched down the street, halted briefly at the curb in front of the house, then quickly drove off. Another prospective tenant, no doubt.

"Well then," said Alison, "I suppose we should leave our name and number for Mr. What's-his-name."

"Magnus," he said, remembering the crabbed signature below the bell.

"Right." She was rummaging through her purse. "I don't know why I drag this thing around with me. I can never find anything in it when I want it. Ah-ha, I knew there was a pen in here somewhere. You don't happen to have a piece of paper, do you, love?"

"Not likely." He tapped his pockets. "Wait, here's something." He pulled a folded piece of paper from his back pocket, then remembered what it was. That chemistry test: B— needs improvement! He handed it to Alison. She looked at it briefly, then turned it over without comment.

"Borrow your back?"

He squirmed under the dance of the pen as she wrote the note.

"There, that should do." She read: "Dear Mr. Magnus, We are interested in the flat. You can reach us evenings at the following number. Sincerely yours, Alison Parry."

They closed the door behind them and made their way downstairs. Alison slid the note under the door of the ground floor flat as Mr. Magnus had instructed they do if they were interested.

As he pulled his boots back on, Cass's eyes wandered to the dark wooden door, the dull brass knocker, the old wicker buggy. What secrets lay beyond that door, he wondered, beyond the dusty windowsill and curtain of lace?

Alison had already crossed to the park by the time he caught up. As they walked past the bench, a host of starlings flew in a sudden flurry from the upper branches of the tree and scattered over the park. He watched as they whirled through the still air and landed lightly in the snow of the wading pool.

It was on Monday that the call finally came. He had just got in from school, dumped his books in the bedroom, and gone to the kitchen to fix something to eat. Alison wouldn't be in for at least an hour. He was ferreting through the cupboards as he browsed on bread and peanut butter, wondering what to fix for dinner, when the phone rang. He picked it up.

"Hello?"

"Hello. May I speak to Alison Parry, please?" The voice was thin, brittle, like ice just forming. He had to strain to make it out.

"I'm sorry, she's not in right now. Could I take a message?"

"Is this Mr. Cass Parry?"

"Yes, that's right. Who is this?"

"My name is Arthur Magnus. You left a note under my door regarding the flat for rent."

"Oh, yes."

"Well, the flat is yours if you wish. Provided, of course, you haven't changed your mind."

"No, we're still interested."

"You may move in anytime. The rent is due at the beginning of the month. You can put it under the door as you did the note. If there are any other questions, you could have your mother ring me up. And, young man?"

"Yes?"

"You may tell your chemistry teacher for me that this test is a load of rubbish." There was a dry cough, a faint click, and the phone went dead.

2

BOXES. There were boxes everywhere.

As always, the move had been traumatic. Friends who had promised to help had developed dire illnesses at the last moment, or had simply gone into hiding. That had left the two of them, along with Alison's friend Murray and his battered pickup, to lug the entire mess down one flight of stairs at one end and up another at the other end. Murray, who had helped with the last two moves, had been a little less than pleased, and not at all hesitant to let them know it.

They had finished well after midnight, and the three of them had sat in the darkness of the front room eating cold pizza by candlelight and listening to the mice run sprints in the kitchen. Before he left, Murray had made Alison swear on her word of honor that she would never, ever move again.

The following day had been spent in first blasting a path through the chaos, then opening and carrying boxes to their appropriate places, with Alison all the while vowing that if she ever did move again she would at least take the sensible course and label the boxes as she packed them.

By the end of the day they had succeeded in breaking the one huge mess into several smaller messes scattered throughout the flat. They had assembled his bed, made a space for her mattress on the floor of her room, and put their few sad sticks of furniture in place. They looked a little pathetic beside the several old pieces that apparently came with the flat, as though theirs were only temporary intruders, tolerated at best. The posters and impressionist prints Alison had thumbtacked to the wall looked hopelessly lost. Only the plaster bust of Blake she had enshrined on the mantel seemed at all at home.

Rather than go through the upset of a transfer in the middle of term, they had decided that Cass should finish up the year at the same school. The bus route was direct and the trip took less than an hour. Since Alison was rarely home before six, it still left him plenty of time to get the dinner going and to muddle his way through the mess a little before she got in.

It was then, when he was alone in the flat, sifting through seemingly endless boxes, that Cass first felt the ghostly presence moving about below him. Strange, disembodied sounds snaked through the heating ducts and drifted from the air registers on the walls: the low rumble of a radio, the occasional clatter of dishes, the eerie creak of floorboards, the thin keening shriek that only reluctantly resolved itself into the whistling of a kettle.

Save for these small sounds, one might easily have imagined that no one lived in the lower flat at all. The windows were always dark, the door always shut, and the old buggy never budged from its spot on the dusty boot tray. It was like living over a tomb.

By the end of the second week life was once again nearing normal. With the sad exception of the kitchen, the chaos that remained was now confined to the backs of closets and to the small sun porch at the front of the house. The sun porch, isolated as it was from the rest of the flat and unheated, had rapidly become the resting place for all the troublesome things still left to sort through after their initial burst of energy had fizzled out.

In time, the small windowed room would be a study. Right now it was a disaster zone. Alison's three battered green filing cabinets, bursting at the seams with notes and papers of elusive importance, stood in the midst of the welter of boxes, like weary soldiers surveying a battlefield. A desk, dismantled to maneuver up the narrow flight of stairs, lay buried beneath boxes of books and an intimidating pile of odds and ends.

Despite this, the room drew him, and barely a day went by that Cass did not pull on an old sweater of Alison's and head out there for a least a little while. He told himself it was to chip away at the confusion, but not very deep down he knew well enough the real reason. It was to watch.

It seemed as if he had spent most of his life living over stores, stationed invisibly at windows, watching. It was as much a part of him now as the ragged scar on his forehead, the intricate whorls on his fingertips. It was what he missed most here, the endless flow of traffic to and fro, the constant coming and going of people, the anonymity of noise. The residents of Woodlawn Crescent had paid for their quiet. They had paid for it just as surely as they had paid for their garbage pickup and their snow removal. And, heaven knows, they had it.

It nearly drove him crazy at first. He would walk up the street in the morning to catch the bus practically tempted to tiptoe. At night he would lie in bed longing for the low, comforting rumble of a passing streetcar, the purr and yowl of car engines, the hiss and crackle of the neon sign outside his window—all those many night sounds he hadn't even realized were there, until they weren't.

And yet for a brief time each day even Woodlawn Crescent woke up, dragged itself from its bed, and puttered about a bit before settling back to sleep again for the night. It was then that he pulled on the sweater and went to work on the sun porch.

From here he commanded a view of the entire neighborhood. To his left he could look down the street and follow the slow curve of the road as it wound itself snakelike around the park. To his right he could see as far as the top of the hill where the small grocery store stood and the bus stopped. And directly ahead, like a vast picture book spread open on his lap, lay the park.

Most of the snow had finally melted, leaving the park a boggy mess. The refuse of winter, hidden until then, lay scattered over the dull wet grass between dirty islands of ice. Except for a handful of boys on bicycles who seemed to make a game of churning up the wet ground with their tires, most people avoided the park, keeping instead to the fringes with their dogs, or jogging alongside the curb.

Now and then, as he sifted halfheartedly through endless books and boxes, a car would round the bend in the road, purr quietly down the street, and turn into one of the driveways. Doors would open, people appear briefly with briefcases and children and quickly scurry for their steps. There would be the dull thud of a door, and that would be the end of them. The neighbors next door were young, childless, and bore an uncanny resemblance to department store mannequins. In all the time he had watched them make the short trot from car to house he had not once seen them so much as glance in his direction. It was as if the old red house directly to their right simply did not exist, as if the world ran up against the bare, ragged branches of the hedge between them, and stopped dead.

So did the girl on the tricycle two doors down. She must have been about six. Short, well fed, and overclothed, she patrolled the brief stretch of sidewalk in front of her house every day from the time her mother took the tricycle down from the porch until her father arrived home from work. Back and forth, back and forth she went, as if engaged in some operation of vital importance, pausing every now and then to peer over longingly at the park, chattering to herself all the while.

Occasionally in the course of her travels she would bypass the boundaries she had been set. The tricycle would suddenly slow to a crawl, and she would inch up as far as the crack in the sidewalk that ran even with the end of the hedge in front of the old house. Cautiously she would lean forward in the seat and stare through the webwork of branches toward the house with wide, searching eyes. Then without warning she would suddenly spring up in the seat, whirl the tricycle around, and pedal away for all she was worth. Though he had observed this performance several times, each time it happened again Cass found himself watching with the same strange fascination. Clearly something about the house frightened the little girl and sent her scurrying back to the safety of her walk. But what?

Certainly the place was a sight, especially now, without the luxury of snow. Bare branches of ivy gripped the walls in a chill embrace; the garbage of years had gathered at the base of the hedge, and the lawn was thick with the matted brown leaves of last and likely other falls. But surely that could not explain it. Nor could it explain the guarded distance in the eyes of people he passed on the street or the way some kids would almost automatically veer off the sidewalk and onto the curb as they walked by on their way home from school. No, there was more to it than that.

One girl stood out from the rest. She was tall, thin, perhaps a little older than he. She came by about the same time every day, and it got so he would look forward to seeing her, the way he used to watch for the old woman who sold flowers on the street corner across from the Bluebird.

She was always by herself. He would see her get off the bus at the top of the hill and come shuffling down the street, her head invariably buried in the pages of a paperback book. She wore a ratty old coat that must have been her father's. It hung down past her knees and was rolled up at the cuffs. She carried her stuff in a weatherbeaten backpack slung over one shoulder. Her hair was cut short and blunt, and hooked behind her ears. Now and then, as she was walking, it would pop loose and she would reach up and flick it back impatiently as if she were shooing away a fly, and knuckle her small round glasses back up to the bridge of her nose.

What he liked about her was how completely oblivious she seemed to be to everything. It was as if she were on another planet. Yet without so much as a glance up from the pages of her book, she always managed to skirt the terror on the tricycle or whatever else might happen into her path. And invariably as she passed the house she would suddenly look up and stare fixedly at the ground floor window, as if she expected to see someone standing there staring back.

It was little enough time before Cass understood that the someone she glanced up from the book expecting to see was the same someone that sent the little girl tearing off on her tricycle and the schoolchildren weaving onto the curb as they walked by. It was the someone whose voice on the phone had been as dusty and fragile as the figurines perched on the windowsill, whose presence in the house was as steady yet as insubstantial as the smoke that drifted from the chimney out back—the mysterious Mr. Magnus.

Alison was standing barefoot on the kitchen counter sliding a quart jar of dried beans onto the top shelf of the cupboard.

"Why on earth do we keep dragging these stupid things around with us?" said Cass as he handed yet another jar up to her from the open box on the table. "We never use them."

"Now, now." Alison reached up on tiptoe and slid it out of sight. "It's just a matter of thinking of them, that's all. Remember that lovely lentil soup I made a while back?"

Dead silence.

"And what was wrong with it?"

"Nothing, absolutely nothing."

Alison prided herself on her periodic assaults on the kitchen. These usually took the form of huge pots of homemade soup, pulled together from whatever happened to be at hand, and following no apparent recipe. Sometimes the results were surprisingly good, but more often than not they were utterly inedible and the pot would languish on the top shelf of the fridge to the exclusion of all else until one of them worked up the nerve to flush the mess down the toilet.

That had been the sad fate of the lentil soup, a vile concoction with the texture and taste of wallpaper paste. He shook his head at the memory of it as he passed up a large Mason jar of split peas.

The doorbell rang. It was the first time it had.

"I wonder who that could be?" said Alison.

"Probably somebody selling something. I'll go see."

He raked a hand through his hair and tucked in his shirt. The bell rang again as he started down the stairs.

"Hang on. I'm coming, I'm coming."

He opened the door on the small gray woman they had seen coming out of the house next door back on that first day while they were sitting on the bench. He had noticed her again on moving day, watching from her window.

"Hello," she said. "I'm Mrs. Wharton. I live at fifty-seven, next door." She made a motion with the plate of cookies she was carrying in the direction of her house.

"Oh, these are for you. Oatmeal raisin. Just out of the oven." She handed him the plate.

"Thank you."

"Mind you don't eat them all, now. Save some for your poor mother." She was staring past him toward the stairs and showed no signs of leaving.

"Would you like to come in for a minute?" he said finally.

"Well, perhaps for just a minute. I'm sure you're both terribly busy."

He noticed her look back uncertainly at the ground floor door as they started up the stairs.

"There," said Alison from the kitchen as he ushered Mrs. Wharton into the apartment. "I've just set some of those pretty black-eyed peas out to soak. Who was that at the door, dear?"

"It's, ah, the next-door neighbor," said Cass. "She's made us some cookies."

Alison peeked her kerchiefed head around the corner. She must still have been standing on the counter, because her head came nearly level with the top of the door frame.

"Oh," she said as Mrs. Wharton gave a little start. "I'm sorry." She disappeared briefly, then came into the room minus the kerchief.

"Hello," she said, taking Mrs. Wharton's hand. "I'm Alison Parry. How very nice of you. They look lovely."

"Mabel Wharton," said Mrs. Wharton, looking down at Alison's bare feet. "Just a little housewarming gift."

"Would you like to sit down, Mrs. Wharton? I'm afraid things are still rather a mess."

"Well, perhaps for a moment, if you're sure it's no trouble."

Cass quickly swept a stack of empty boxes off a chair. Mrs. Wharton settled herself in, sweeping her small eyes eagerly around the room, devouring every detail. He felt her glance linger on the frayed wicker of the rocker, the bald spot in the rug.

"Cass, dear, would you go and put on the kettle? Perhaps Mrs. Wharton would like a cup of coffee."

"Tea, please. If you have it."

Somewhere in the mass of unpacked boxes in the kitchen there was a tin of teabags. Cass set the kettle on to boil and began sifting through the more likely of them.

"Nice young man," he heard Mrs. Wharton say from the echoing front room.

"Yes. I don't know what I'd do without him."

Then came the inevitable question. He could feel it coming all the way from the kitchen.

"Is your husband—away?"

"I have no husband, Mrs. Wharton. Cass and I live alone."

"Oh." A pause. "I see."

She didn't, of course. Not that it mattered, really. Still, the mere mention of the subject was enough to raise Hegel's ghost again.

Alison had been in the first year of the master's program at the university when she became pregnant. She still had the graduation picture of the guy she'd been seeing at the time. He was in the philosophy program, working on his Ph.D., and she nicknamed him Hegel, after the famous German philosopher.

According to Alison, he was a real genius. He sure looked the part anyway: lean, angular face, furrowed brow, a studied lock of hair falling over his forehead. They had planned on getting married just as soon as they had finished their studies and were settled.

Needless to say, news of the imminent arrival of an un-expected guest threw a fair-sized wrench into the works. Still, Alison was confident they could work it out. Hegel didn't quite see it that way. His solution to the problem was as clear, clean, and clinical as a logical equation—get rid of it. Instead, she had got rid of him. She hadn't had much use for philos-ophy since.

Cass found the tea tin in an unlikely box of odds and ends that had probably been thrown together at the last moment. He reached the teapot down from the china cupboard, unearthed a matching cup and saucer for Mrs. Wharton and a couple of mugs for Alison and himself

In the other room, Mrs. Wharton had launched into her life story. It seemed she had lived on the street since she was a little girl. Somehow it was hard to imagine that Mrs. Whar-ton had ever been anyone's little girl. What was it about her that he didn't like? Something in the way her eyes kept darting around the room, the feeling that she was quietly tucking away information on them for later use. He wished she would go.

"Yes," she was saying as he came into the room with the tea things. "A very quiet neighborhood. Changed a lot re-cently, mind you. Young couples with children have discov-ered us. Been very good for property values. Why, there was a real estate agent round to my place just last month, and do you know what he said I could get for that house?"

"Ah, here's the tea," said Alison with obvious relief.

Cass set the tray down on the cedar chest they had placed below the front window. "Do you take anything in your tea?" he asked.

"Just a splash of milk, thank you, dear." And then to Alison: "Can't take sugar anymore. Borderline diabetic, you know."

"Oh, really," said Alison in her trying-hard-to-seem-interested voice.

Cass poured the tea into the cups and added a touch of milk to each. He picked up the matching cup and saucer for Mrs. Wharton, but at the last instant handed it to Alison instead, giving the guest the chipped blue mug. They sipped in silence for a while.

Suddenly Mrs. Wharton leaned forward in her chair. Her voice dropped to a whisper.

"Have you had any problem with *him* yet?"

"*Him?*" asked Alison.

"Yes." She pointed a bent finger emphatically at the floor. "Him."

"You mean Mr. Magnus?" Alison shot a quick quizzical glance over at Cass. "No. Why? What sort of problem?"

"Well, I'm not one to spread gossip, but some folks around here are starting to wonder if he hasn't gone—you know." And she twirled her index finger in small circles around her ear.

"Senile, you mean?"

She nodded her head solemnly. "Not that he hasn't always been a bit strange. Living by himself in this big old house for all these years, those strange goings-on in the garage. People talk, you know."

"I'm not sure I understand," said Alison.

"Hardly leaves the house at all anymore these past few years. It's a shame the way he's gone, really. I met him on the street a few months back. He was out with his buggy getting his groceries. Hasn't even been doing that recently, since the accident."

Cass's ears pricked up. "Accident?" he said.

"Yes. Most unfortunate. He was coming back with his buggy one day from the store at the corner and a boy on a bicycle ran into him. Completely accidentally, I'm sure. Neither of them was seriously injured, though Mr. Magnus was a little shaken up, I'm afraid. Luckily the buggy took the brunt of the collision." The image of the crushed wicker buggy on the boot tray came into Cass's mind. He glanced out the window at the park. Fresh tire tracks scored the wet grass.

"As I was saying," continued Mrs. Wharton, "I met him on the street a few months back, before the accident. 'Hello, Mr. Magnus,' I said. 'How nice to see you out and about.' And do you know, he looked right through me. Right through me. It gave me a turn, I'll tell you. I don't even think he saw me. And the smell. People are starting to wonder if he can take care of himself anymore. Ah, well, it's just a matter of time, I suppose." She shook her head gravely.

"A matter of time until what?" asked Cass, surprising even himself at the vehemence in his voice. It seemed hardly his own voice at all.

"Well, I don't think I need to go into detail. There are places, people qualified to—"

"Put him away, you mean. Is that it?" The words said themselves.

That stopped Mrs. Wharton dead in her tracks. She looked at Alison, who in turn looked down at the fluted cup in her lap. A minute dragged itself by.

"Well," said Mrs. Wharton finally. "I've taken enough of your time. I should be going now."

"I'll see you to the door," said Alison.

As Mrs. Wharton passed him she shot him an acid glance. She and Alison disappeared downstairs. He sat on the cedar chest, staring into the park, feeling the strange fury fall away, following the tire tracks in the grass as far as the wading pool, where they stopped.

Downstairs, the door closed with a thud. He heard Alison starting slowly up the stairs and prepared himself for an airing out on his manners with Mrs. Wharton. But as she stepped through the door and looked over at him, all she said was: "Nasty old bird, isn't she?"

The soup that night did not taste bad at all.

—— 3 ——

WITH THE COMING of the good weather the park came to life. The trees began to leaf out, and the first flowers appeared. The swings in the playground were rehung, the teeter-totters pulled from the shed where they had passed the winter, the corkscrew slide scrubbed clean and repainted. Children appeared as if by magic from houses up and down the street. Gardens were turned, hedges clipped, and neighbor spoke to neighbor as though they had just returned from long and perilous journeys.

Mothers with children in tow wheeled huge carriages containing tiny blanketed bundles into the park and sat together on benches chatting while the children rode the swings or wound the slide.

The now-familiar gang of boys on bicycles had taken up residence at the wading pool. They usually arrived and departed together. The bicycles were stripped-down black affairs with highrise handlebars and freestyle seats. It was still far too early for the pool to be filled, and they passed the time playing chicken, riding endlessly around the rim of the pool at one another, swerving at the last possible instant to avoid a crash.

One boy appeared to be the leader. He held court at the center of the pool, leaning up against the concrete hub smoking, while the rest milled restlessly about him like electrons whirling around a nucleus.

He was a tall, expressionless character with brooding good looks. With his wraparound sunglasses and his hair sculpted in place, he had the look of someone who spent a lot of time looking in the mirror. Now and then, as Cass was watching them from the porch, he was sure the boy turned his head and stared directly over at the house. There was something in that thin slit of a mouth and those vacant black shades that sent a chill up his spine.

If he saw them there when he got off the bus on the way home from school, he always made a point of walking down the side of the street opposite the park, giving them as wide a berth as he might a pack of stray dogs. There was something about them he didn't trust. They reminded him of the guys that used to hang around the pool hall across the street from the Bluebird, just waiting for something to happen. He kept his distance from them, just in case he might be the something they were waiting for.

Spring had visited the front yard of the house, touching pale pink flames to the old magnolia tree, setting the disheveled hedge afire with crimson leaves, coaxing green life through the leaf mold in the overgrown garden.

Long before he ever set eyes on him, Cass found himself struggling to form some sort of picture of Mr. Magnus. From the cramped, spidery scrawl in the small window below the doorbell, he imagined that he would be thin and twisted too. Like the thorns in the hedge, he imagined that he too would bristle. Like the worn ball of wood atop the newel post at the foot of the stairs, he believed he would be bald. But his first real glimpse of the invisible inhabitant of the ground floor flat came in a strange and unexpected way, on the day Cass finally decided to tackle the bedroom closet.

The six stuffed boxes sitting in the shadows at the back of the closet were in no one's way at all, and it wasn't until the weather turned and he found himself the only one at school still wearing a winter jacket that he finally broke down and decided to drag them out and unearth his windbreaker.

The first box was full of books, books that belonged on the grape-crate shelves still propped against the sun-porch wall, waiting to be put back together again.

It was Alison who had invented grape-crate shelving. In a pinch for a place to put her endless books, she had stumbled on some crates in the garbage outside a fruit store one night and had carried them home. Cleaned up and nailed together end to end they made passable shelves. And you sure couldn't beat the price.

The second box was crammed with old grade-school papers and books that Cass somehow just couldn't bring himself to part with. The third was full of old comic books and bubble-gum cards. With all his harping about her mess, the less Alison knew about these the better. He fed them back to the shadows.

The fourth box was full of summer clothes: T-shirts, shorts, a pair of practically new sandals that Alison loved and he just as much hated, and buried way at the bottom of the pile a wrinkled windbreaker. He shook it out and pulled it on. It was a little snug around the shoulders and the cuffs barely reached his wrists, but it would do. It would have to. To put it mildly, finances were tight.

It wasn't until he had actually crawled right into the closet to drag out the last two boxes, both, it seemed, loaded with more books, that he noticed another, smaller box crouched in the deep shadows in the corner.

As soon as he pulled it out into the light he realized it wasn't one of theirs. For one thing, it was a very old box, not at all like those they had scrounged from the liquor store for the move. For another, the box was full of pictures, each one loosely wrapped in newspaper and tied with string. The few pictures they had owned had been broken one by one in the course of their many moves and sat now in their cracked and shattered frames among the junk on the porch. Packing had never been one of Alison's strong points.

There must have been about a dozen pictures in the box. It was with a delicious sense of discovery that he began to take them out, snapping the frail string and peeling away the old yellowed newsprint. The first few were the standard fare: still lifes with fruit and flowers, dreary landscapes, drearier seascapes, all of them faded with age — distant and ultimately depressing. He was ready to bundle them all up and push them right back into the dark, where they belonged, when he came upon one that gave him pause.

It was an old photograph in a broken frame, of a man in uniform. He was thin, fair, and despite the slight blush of color the photographer had touched to lips and cheeks, he looked a little frightened. Though the short-clipped mustache he wore had initially made him look older, the longer Cass studied the picture, the more he realized that the young soldier was not much older than he. A small cramped inscription in one corner read "For Mother — much love, Arthur."

Arthur? He studied the inscription again. The odd loop of the t's, the way the words sloped backward, bunched up as though blown together. Though the hand now was not as steady and the writing itself was smaller, there could be little doubt that it belonged to the same person who had written the name in the window below the doorbell.

A. Magnus. *Arthur* Magnus. So this, then, this young man

staring so intently into the camera's impassive eye, was none other than the reclusive old man who lived in the lower flat. How strange that this should be his first glimpse of him.

He slid the photo from its broken frame and put it on the bed, then turned his attention to the two that remained. The first was an informal shot of half a dozen people sitting outdoors on wooden deck chairs. An older woman in a dark dress sat shielding her eyes against the sun. The others, men in shirtsleeves and baggy pants and women with bobbed hair and brightly painted lips, were gathered around her, caught in the midst of some conversation. One face was frozen in laughter, another was leaning forward whispering in an ear.

Among them he recognized the young man from the first picture, older and thinner, the mustache now a more natural feature of his face. He sat to the right of the older woman, a glass in one hand, a cigarette in the other, smiling. A cane was hooked over the arm of his chair.

Directly behind him was a wall with a door in it. The door had a diamond-shaped window that caught the glare of the sun. Cass had looked at the picture for some time before he realized with a bit of a shock that the door in the picture was in fact the door to the garage out back, and that these people were actually sitting in the small yard behind the house.

The rose trellis against the wall to one side of the garage still remained, but the yard itself was now almost unrecognizable, the grass gone wild, the garden overgrown, a piece of weathered board backing the now-empty panes in the diamond-shaped window of the door.

He put the picture aside and turned his attention to the one that remained. For some reason the string that bound this one did not snap with the same ease as the others had; the tape that secured the paper had not discolored and come unstuck, though the paper itself was obviously of the same age as the rest. He peeled it slowly away, and uncovered a most curious picture.

It was a painting of a snake, a snake curled into a circle, with its teeth clamped around its tail as if it were swallowing itself. Its outer side was colored green, its underbelly red, and its pale yellow eye seemed to peer directly up at him from the picture. Inside the circle, some words were written in what looked like Greek. The whole thing had a look of extreme age about it. The paper on which the picture was painted was mottled with mildew and rippled away from the underside of the glass.

He must have been sitting there for some time staring at it, noting every detail of the painting, curiously fascinated in a way he could not have explained, because the next thing he knew he heard the sound of Alison on the stairs. He tucked the picture of the soldier into the corner of his dresser mirror, and bundling the other things together, pushed them back into the closet.

That night he lay awake in bed a long time, the image of the snake etched in his mind's eye. Finally he flicked on the light and fetched the picture from the box at the back of the closet. He took down the Blake print from the wall above his bed and put the painting of the snake in its place. It fit the dark patch in the paper perfectly, like a piece of puzzle falling into place.

4

HALF A BLOCK from the store the bag split. Six loaves of 60 percent whole wheat bread spilled onto the sidewalk. Cass cursed as he scrambled to pick them up. The Busy Bee had

had a special—three loaves for a dollar, a real steal. It didn't quite seem like a steal now that he was left carrying the six loose loaves half a mile home.

For the past week he had been scouring the paper every night for the specials, trying to stretch the little money that was left until Alison got paid as far as it would go. The sad fact of the matter was that however reasonable the rent in the new place was, it was still considerably more than they had been paying living above the Bluebird. The old wallet they kept in the top drawer of Alison's dresser, from which he drew the funds he needed for shopping, was running on empty. Something somewhere was going to have to give.

For years it had been Alison trying to shelter him from the sad realities of their financial situation. Now, strangely, the shoe was on the other foot. With the deadline for her thesis looming large, Alison was wrapped in a more or less permanent Blake haze. She had requested and received extension after extension on the paper, but her adviser, Professor Frye, had quietly warned her that there would be no more. She had either to complete the work by the fall or forfeit it and face beginning all over again.

He found that the best way to carry the bread was to hold two in each hand and stick the others under his arm. Now and then he would stop and switch to keep the ones pinned under his arm from getting too squished. He could feel people peering at him through the windows of sleepy pool halls and run-down restaurants as he passed by. A frustrated shopkeeper was struggling with the lock in the iron grille that ran across the front of his store, while two ancient mannequins in fur coats and bare feet looked on encouragingly from the store window. All three of them glanced up as he went by with the bread.

It was as he stopped to make another switch that Cass saw

the sign. He was standing on the sidewalk in front of the
Palace Theater, a run-down movie house that specialized in
double-bill reruns of old movies and Saturday afternoon matinees. The place had definitely seen better days.

The sign had too. It was propped in the curtained window
of the ticket booth. It was chipped at the corners and a coffee
cup stain ran through the words.

USHER WANTED
Apply within

He stood there for a minute, looking from the sign to the
dogeared posters hanging in the display window behind the
booth. Then he picked up the bread and walked slowly up to
the doors of the theater.

They were locked, all of them, and except for the dull
yellow glow from the popcorn machine on the counter, it was
dark inside. He knocked halfheartedly on the glass a couple
of times and was getting ready to go when suddenly a wedge
of white light fell on the lobby floor. Someone walked out
an open door and headed for the flight of carpeted stairs beside
the candy counter.

Cass rapped on the glass again. The figure froze on the
bottom stair, glanced back over his shoulder, then turned and
started walking toward him. It was a tall, heavyset man in a
rumpled gray suit and glasses. The stump of a cigar was hooked
in the corner of his mouth. His hair was dark and slick.

He came up to the door, squinted at him through the glass,
and looked for a second like he might just turn around and
head back to the stairs. Instead, he turned the latch and opened
the door a crack.

"Yeah? What do you want, kid? We don't open for another

hour." His voice sounded like his hair looked. He started to close the door.

"I, uh, saw the sign in the window. About an usher?"

"Yeah?"

"I'd like to apply for the job." He could feel the sweat start to trickle down his arm. This bread was going to be in great shape by the time he got it home.

The man gummed the dead cigar and looked him slowly up and down like a side of beef.

"How old are you, kid?"

"Sixteen," he lied.

"That right?" He looked down at the bread. Something that tried to be a smile crossed his face. "All right, kid, come in. Pull the door closed behind you."

Cass followed the retreating form across a narrow foyer and through a second set of chrome and glass doors. They cut across the lobby toward a door with an illuminated sign above it reading MANAGER. Even in the dim light the carpet looked dirty.

The office was small, hot, and cluttered. The walls were plastered with pictures: movie posters, black and white studio shots of old movie stars, a rumpled dollar bill under glass, a couple of vintage pictures of the Palace about fifty years back.

The desk was a mess. Empty coffee cups and popcorn boxes fought for space with piles of papers and unopened letters. A dirty ashtray perched in a bare spot on the edge of the desk. Below it a space heater buzzed contentedly as the heat rose in visible waves from its red coils. The room reeked of rancid butter and cigar butts, along with a faint chemical smell he couldn't quite place.

The manager hung the cigar on the edge of the ashtray and sat down behind the desk. He looked as if he belonged there.

"Sit down," he said. He began rifling through the piles, gave up, and started on the drawers.

Cass laid the bread down on the floor beside the only other chair in the room and sat down. As he did, the smell registered. Roach spray. Terrific.

The manager finally found what he was looking for.

"What's your name, kid?" he asked, rummaging through a file folder, pulling out a sheet.

"Cass Parry."

"How do you spell that?"

He spelled it. The wastepaper basket was full of crumpled paper napkins and crushed popcorn boxes.

"Where do you live?" The man plucked the cigar from the ashtray and fed the wet end of it to his mouth.

"Woodlawn Crescent. Fifty-five Woodlawn Crescent."

"Ever done this sort of work before?"

"No, sir. But I'm sure I could pick it up pretty fast."

The manager lit the end of his cigar and thought about that for a while. The room filled rapidly with smoke. The heater snapped off with a decisive click.

"The job's three nights a week and every second Saturday for the matinee. Pay's three dollars an hour. You start at six-thirty sharp and finish around eleven. If you're late you're docked an hour. Late three times, you're out. Understood?"

He nodded.

"You're responsible for your own uniform. You need a white shirt, clean. Hair brushed, nails clean. No smoking on the job or you're out. Any questions?"

"No, sir."

"Good. Sign this sheet here. You start tomorrow."

"You mean I got the job?"

"That's right, kid. You got the job."

Dinner that night was Bean Surprise. It wasn't really much of a surprise. For the past four nights the menu had read: beans on toast, scrambled eggs and beans, beans and wieners, and now this. If he never saw another bean in his life it would be too soon.

Alison sat at the table in her Miss Maid uniform with a second plateful in front of her. She had taken off the starched collar and was using it to hold open the pages of her Blake as she dunked another slice of buttered bread in the sauce.

That battered old collection of Blake's poems was as much a part of the kitchen table as the salt and pepper penguins Murray had given them a couple of Christmases before, and the old butter dish that had belonged to his great-grandmother. Barely a meal went by that Alison did not get lost in its stained and sticky pages for at least a little while. Half the time he swore she wasn't so much looking at the book as through it, thinking, gathering all the loose ends together.

"Delicious, Cass," she said, looking up from the book. "Boy, you wouldn't believe the place I was in today. It was weird. The kitchen was completely white. I mean everything. White tile floor, white walls, white cupboards, white fridge and stove, white counters. It was scary. I was afraid to open the fridge in case the food was white too." She closed the book on the collar and pushed it away.

"I spent two hours cleaning this kitchen, scrubbing down the floor, scouring the stove, wiping down the counter and cupboards. I thought I was going crazy. It was like being in one of those sensory deprivation tanks. I had to keep looking out the window to convince myself that the whole world hadn't turned white."

Cass had been gathering up the plates and stacking them in the sink. Now he brought out the pan of brownies he'd made after getting back from the Palace and set them in the center of the table.

Alison had a passion for chocolate. She sat straight up in the chair and her eyes opened wide.

"Oh, my," she said. "What do we have here?"

"Just a little something."

"So I see." She cut out a large corner piece with her knife. "But what's the occasion?"

"I have some news."

"News?" Her eyes closed in ecstasy as she bit into the brownie.

"Yeah, I, uh, got a job."

Alison's eyes snapped open. She put the brownie down on her plate.

"Could you say that again, please?"

"I got a job. Just a part-time job. At the Palace Theater."

"Come on, Cass. Joke's over, all right? Your poor mother's too tired for games."

"No, I'm serious, Mom. I start tomorrow."

"Wait a minute. Did you say the Palace Theater? That's that dump on the Danforth, isn't it?"

"It's not really a dump. Just a little old, that's all."

"You're serious. I don't believe this. You're under age, Cass. You're too young to work."

"So I lied a little. Look, Mom, I can manage it. I do all right around here, don't I? It's just three nights a week, and school's al—"

"Nights? That does it, Cass."

"Look, Mom, we could use the money. It'll be nearly forty dollars a week. I'll be okay. Just let me try it for a few weeks. If it doesn't work out, I can always quit."

"I don't know, Cass." But he could tell she was already weakening. Her eyes had drifted back to the brownies.

"Well, just think about it, okay?"

"All right. I'll think about it."

Alison did a lot of thinking that evening. By bedtime half the brownies were gone.

5

IT WAS 6:25 when Cass walked through the doors of the Palace Theater. The lights in the lobby were on now. It had looked a whole lot better in the dark.

He could see the stains on the rug where people had spilled their drinks or let their butts burn down. The walls were painted a lurid purple, flaking in places to reveal the red that had been there before. It was like being enveloped by internal organs.

A girl was busy over at the candy counter, stocking the shelves with chocolate bars and bags of licorice. She didn't look up as he crossed the lobby to the manager's office.

He was feeling more than a little self-conscious, his hair slicked back, shoes shined. He had even pressed a crease in his pants. He knocked on the door.

"Yeah, come in. Oh, hi, kid. Be right with you." The manager had his hand cupped over the mouthpiece of the telephone. He was wearing the same suit. *His* pants didn't have a crease in them. He turned his attention back to the phone.

"Yeah, George, that's right, three boxes . . . No, that's all . . . Right . . . You too, George . . . Okay, bye."

He hung up the phone and heaved himself out of the chair, making a stab for the cigar sitting in the ashtray at the same time. It looked like the same cigar too.

"Come with me, kid. I'll show you where you change."

He led Cass across the lobby and pushed open a door marked PRIVATE, beside the men's washroom. Cass followed him through a small anteroom with the original red walls, a couple of sad-looking chairs with split vinyl seats and a sand ashtray between them, then through another door.

He found himself in a small room with a mirror and a dirty sink against one wall, a row of lockers against the wall opposite, and at the far end two toilet stalls. It looked like whoever cleaned the theater had forgotten about this room for a while. There was a heavy smell of stale urine and sweat in the air. The manager didn't seem to notice.

"This is where you change," he said. "You'll find a uniform in one of the lockers. Should be a spare flashlight too. If you need batteries, I keep them in the office. Oh, almost forgot." He reached into his jacket pocket and came out with a black clip-on bow tie. "Your tie. Don't lose it." He checked his watch. "The others should be here soon. They'll show you the ropes." He spat thoughtfully in the sink and ran the water to wash it down. "God, this place is a pigsty," he said as he yanked open the door. It closed with a slow *whoosh* behind him.

Cass peeled off his jacket and draped it carefully over the door of one of the cubicles. He started to go through the lockers, looking for a uniform. The uniforms were black with red trim around the lapels and cuffs of the jacket, and twin red stripes running down the outside of the pant legs. Très chic.

The first few he unearthed were filthy, hanging like limp rags from the hooks inside the lockers. The jacket linings were in shreds, and the seams under the arms and up the back were split and held together with sweat and safety pins.

He had just about given up when he came to the end locker.

This locker had a strip of masking tape stuck to the front of it, with something written on it that he couldn't quite make out. He opened the door.

A half-dressed woman smiled down at him from the inside of the door where she was taped. She was not nearly as exciting as what was in the locker itself.

A clean, pressed uniform hung on a hanger from one of the hooks. The red trim actually looked red, and the pants were carefully folded inside the jacket. He took it out and tried the jacket on. A little big, but at this point who was complaining. He slipped out of his pants and hung them on a hook. He had just done up the zipper of the pants when the outer door opened and he heard someone race across the anteroom.

A short kid with glasses and a shock of stiff red hair burst into the room.

"Made it," he said, panting. "The old bugger missed me." He looked up and saw the stranger standing there in front of the lockers.

"Hi," he said, whipping off his jacket. "You must be the new kid. Poor sucker. The name's Zeke. What time do you have?"

Cass checked his watch. "Twenty to seven," he said.

Zeke pushed past him and reached in behind the lockers. He came out with a uniform on a hanger. It wasn't as good as the uniform Cass had found, but it beat the others by a mile.

"Our little secret," said Zeke. "It's dog eat dog around this place." He was pulling the uniform pants on right over his own. Already Cass realized he'd made a mistake. "Speaking of dogs, you'd better get out of that uniform before Fischer gets here."

"Fischer?" he said.

"Yeah," said Zeke, slipping on the jacket, fishing a bow tie from the inside pocket. "The head usher. He won't be too happy when he sees you wearing his uniform." He turned on the tap, wet his fingers, and ran them once through his hair.

The outer door opened, banging up against the wall with a thud. Someone walked across the anteroom, whistling.

"Uh-oh," said Zeke. He quickly reached up under the sink and reemerged with a flashlight. The door opened and a tall kid with bad skin and a brush cut strutted into the room. He had a motorcycle helmet under his arm.

"Hello, Ezekiel," he crooned. "How are they hanging?"

"Fine," muttered Zeke. "They're hanging just fine."

Fischer was wearing a tan bomber jacket and two-tone Italian loafers that must have set him back some. He brought the smell of raw onions and after-shave into the room with him. The hair on his head was like the fine fuzz on a peach. It made his ears look bigger than they were. He turned to Cass.

"And you must be the—"

He stopped dead, and his eyes traveled down the uniform. Behind him Cass watched a look of pain cross Zeke's face.

"Hey, wait a minute. Just wait a minute," said Fischer. He flung open the door of his locker. "That's my uniform you got on there."

"Sorry, I didn't know. I—"

"What's wrong with you? Can't you read?" He pointed to the tape on the locker door. "That's my name, right there. And that," he said, jabbing his finger in Cass's direction, "is my uniform. You've got exactly ten seconds to get out of it."

Cass peeled off the jacket and handed it to him. Fischer took it reluctantly between thumb and forefinger and shook it a couple of times as if he expected something might crawl out. Meanwhile Cass struggled with the pants, trying to edge back unobtrusively against the wall beside the lockers as he undid the zipper and slipped out of them.

Zeke took one look at him standing there in his underwear and his eyes widened.

"Somebody better get out there," he said. "I'll see you on the floor." He practically flew out of the room.

Fischer was combing his fuzz admiringly in the mirror when he caught sight of Cass quietly reaching into the locker behind him for his pants. He whirled from the mirror, mouth open.

"You've got nothing on," he said. He said it very slowly, as if he couldn't quite believe it. "You had your dirty little underpants in my uniform." He made a gagging sound in the back of his throat.

"Now, listen to me, kid." he said. "Tonight when you go home, you take this uniform with you, and you get it cleaned." He was face to face with Cass now. "I want it back here by noon tomorrow, and I want to see the bill. Understand?"

"Yes, I understand." He felt perilously close to crying, but the thought of himself standing in this rotten change room in his underwear with tears streaming down his face was too much to stomach. He snatched his pants from the hook and pulled them on.

Fischer stepped into his uniform pants as if he were wading into a swamp. "Box office opens in ten minutes," he said as he headed out the door. "Be there."

Cass began rifling through the lockers, searching frantically for a uniform. Five minutes later he stepped through the door of the ushers' change room and into the lobby.

The pants he had finally settled on were about five sizes too big, but at least the leg length was all right. The only way he could keep them up was by wrapping his belt around the top and bunching the excess inches of material at the back. It was hard to picture the precise shape of the person who had fit into them.

The jacket wasn't much better. There was a large stain over

the left pocket where something had been left to rot inside it, and a wide tear under one arm, which had been sealed with a series of staples. The whole thing had a most unholy smell to it that made his skin crawl.

He stood there in front of the door waiting for peals of uncontrollable laughter to erupt all around him. But no one seemed to take the least notice.

Fischer was stationed at the door. As people straggled in, he took their tickets, tore them in two, and handed them back the stubs. He dropped the other half through a slot in the tall box beside him. He had a flashy way of taking the ticket and tearing it all in one motion with one hand. His head glowed under the yellow light in the entranceway.

The manager's door was closed. A few people had begun to mill around the lobby, stationing themselves beside the sand ashtrays to smoke, or queuing up in front of the candy counter.

The attendant was busy at the popcorn machine, scooping popcorn into boxes and pumping butter on top. Someone left with an armload of stuff that could have fed a family of five for a week. The crowd shifted and for the first time he got a good look at the attendant's face. His mouth fell open.

It was the girl, the girl with the glasses who passed the house every day. She must have felt his gaze, because she suddenly glanced up from her work. She studied him flatly for a second or two, then the faintest hint of a smile crossed her face, and she turned away.

He caught sight of Zeke standing at the top of the stairs beside the candy counter, motioning to him with his flashlight. He hurried across the lobby and up the stairs, clutching the flashlight he had found in the pocket of the jacket, feeling ridiculous in the uniform. As he passed by the counter, the girl looked through the window of the popcorn machine at him. He made his way up the flight of stairs that led to the theater itself. A walkway with a low wall separated the orchestra seats in front of them from the loges that rose behind.

"Did he see you?" were Zeke's first words.

"Who?"

"Jack—the manager."

"No, I don't think so."

"Good thing for you. He'd have docked you for not being on the floor on time. Okay, I'll take this side, you take that."

"What do I do?"

"Just stand there for now and look like you know what you're doing. If anyone asks you where they can smoke, point them upstairs to the loges. If you catch anyone coming up with food from outside, stop them. Last week a bunch of kids had a pizza party in here and started whipping crusts at the screen. Jack was a little upset, to put it mildly."

People wandered up the stairs from the lobby in ones and twos, balancing soft drinks and boxes of popcorn, and made their way to their seats. Eventually the lights dimmed, the curtain rose, and the first feature began.

A couple of people arrived late. Zeke handled them, guiding them down the darkened aisle with the flashlight beam fanned across the floor in front of them.

The movie was an old black and white picture called *Double Indemnity*. It was about this woman who seduces an insurance salesman into helping her bump off her husband so she can collect on a double indemnity policy. They fake an accident so it looks like the guy fell off a train.

It was all very lean and clean and cold-blooded, and it didn't take too long for it to carry Cass away. He almost jumped out of his skin when someone suddenly tapped him on the shoulder.

"Want some?" It was Zeke, nearly invisible in the shadows, holding out a bag to him. "Sunflower seeds. Go ahead, take some."

"Thanks."

"We're clear from now until intermission. Nobody bothers you. You could die up here and no one would know the difference. The only thing you have to watch out for is people making noise or lighting up downstairs. If you spot someone with a cigarette, you have to go down and tell them to put it out. It screws up the projection somehow. Boy, you'd better do something about that uniform. It smells like something died in it."

He popped a sunflower seed into his mouth, then ambled over to the top of the stairs and leaned down to look into the lobby. Over his shoulder Cass could see the girl working the candy counter, popping a new batch of popcorn and filling cups with ice for the intermission. Over by the door Fischer was counting stubs. Zeke straightened up and leaned back against the wall in front of the smoking section.

"Too bad about the uniform," he whispered. "Fischer's a real fanatic about stuff like that. He's been here forever, so he figures he owns the place. Jack thinks he's a real fine young man, if you can stomach that. The two of them are like this." He held two crossed fingers up in front of his face.

"Who's the girl at the candy counter?" said Cass, trying to sound uninterested.

"Name's Maddy. She's been here for about six months. She's okay, kind of quiet. A little strange. She spends a lot of time reading. Fischer's got eyes for her. You can always tell when she's going to be on, because he saturates himself with after-shave and wears his Italian loafers. He's tried to corner her in the supply closet a couple of times, but she's too smart to go for a jerk like him. I'm surprised she's lasted this long, to tell you the truth."

Someone leaned over the railing of the loges and gave them a loud *shh*. Zeke smiled benignly up at the shadow.

"Better go," he said. "I'll see you later."

He walked back to the other side of the stairs and stationed himself there. Now and then, as the movie went on, Cass could hear the crack of sunflower seeds from the shadows.

The intermission passed without incident, with Jack and Fischer stationed down by the exit doors in the lobby, whispering in each other's ear and watching the crowd at the candy counter.

Midway through the second feature, a western called *Dodge City* which was putting him to sleep, Zeke wandered over again.

"Look alert," he said. "Maddy's finished her cleanup. Anytime now Jack's door will open and he'll come out with the night's takings. He'll walk over to the night deposit at the bank on the corner with Fischer. When they get back he'll head over to the candy counter and clean up what's left of the popcorn in the machine. Then he'll wander up here to see if we're still alive and to catch a bit of the film.

"There goes Maddy now. She tries to time her leaving close to Jack's coming out so that Fischer will be less likely to bother her on the way out."

The girl emerged from behind the counter in her familiar tweed coat and quickly crossed the lobby. Fischer, who had been busy sifting butts from the sand ashtrays, dropped what he was doing and shadowed her to the door, the image of cheerful goodwill, his arm hovering just above her shoulder.

She disappeared through the doors and out into the night. She hadn't been gone five minutes when Jack's door opened and he proceeded to do exactly what Zeke had predicted.

"I tell you the guy's a machine," said Zeke later as Cass and he were doing the cleanup, roving the deserted theater from row to row with plastic garbage bags in tow, scooping up popcorn boxes, candy wrappers, paper cups.

"I don't think he ever leaves the place. I swear he just plugs himself into the light socket when everyone goes and sits there all night at his desk on standby. Look, maybe you should quit this place while you've still got the chance. Working here does strange things to your head after a while. Take Fischer, for instance. Once upon a time he may have been a perfectly ordinary homicidal maniac, and now look at him." They tied up the bags and dragged them down to the fire doors at the front of the theater behind the screen. The lobby lights were off as they descended the stairs on their way to the change room. A band of jaundiced yellow light showed under Jack's door.

Fischer was long gone. Being head usher, he got to leave as soon as the washrooms were cleared and the last of the patrons had left the theater. He had rolled his uniform into a ball and left it lying in the sink for Cass.

Zeke quickly sloughed off his uniform, hung it on a hanger, and tucked it out of sight behind the lockers.

"When are you on again?" he asked as he pulled on his coat.

"Monday."

"Me too. I guess I'll see you then." He disappeared through the door.

Cass fished Fischer's uniform out of the sink and stuffed it along with his own into an empty green garbage bag. It was just after eleven as he left the Palace for the long walk home.

—— 6 ——

THE YOUNG SOLDIER stared silently up at him from the mirror as Cass quietly shed his clothes and pulled on his pajamas. Alison was already fast asleep. He had found her that way when he came in, sunk in the rocker, her books and papers spread out on the rug around her like an enormous, impossible puzzle. She had awakened only enough to ask how things had gone, and to gather the mess into a pile before stumbling off to bed. He could hear the low, steady lilt of her breathing from the next room as he switched off the desk lamp and settled into bed.

Soon he became aware of other sounds, those faint and now-familiar noises from the flat below. They were a far cry from the clamor of street noise that he had been accustomed to, but now that he had grown attuned to them, they were as constant and as comforting.

They came quietly drifting through the heat register on the wall by his bed, like the smoke that spilled lazily from the chimney out back. Small, strangely hollow noises, sounding as though they had traveled vast distances.

Some he recognized, others remained frustratingly out of reach. There was the soft shuffling of footsteps across an uncarpeted floor, the predictable creak in the floorboards at a certain spot on the path between bedroom and kitchen, the complaint of pipes as a tap was turned on, then off, the opening and closing of drawers, the shrill wail of the whistling kettle. And sometimes an odd whirring, beating sound that utterly baffled him.

Occasionally there would be the faintly chilling sound of a voice, barely audible, rising briefly above the texture of sounds, like and yet distinct from them, as if the house itself were speaking.

He lay in the dark now, listening as the footsteps crossed the floor in the room directly below. Seconds later the sound of an old record came crackling through the register. He knew it was a record because he had heard it before. It was one of perhaps a dozen that the old man played repeatedly.

He imagined the room was a bedroom, and tried to picture how it might look. But all he could summon up was a vague sense of darkness, clutter, and dust, images gleaned from the forgotten ornaments on the windowsill, the old wicker buggy on the boot tray. And in the midst of it an old man, moving quietly about like some strange night creature traveling its narrow pathways.

Tonight, for the first time, he had seen a light on inside the flat as he returned home, the dull golden glow of a table lamp in the front room. It had cast the objects on the sill into sharp relief, and despite himself he had paused momentarily on the top step of the porch to peer in wonder through the suddenly transparent web of lace. Like a scene surfacing from the darkness of a stage, he saw the dim outline of furniture, shelves of books, a mantelpiece busy with ornaments, pictures on the walls; and then, at the heart of the room, a strange labyrinth of shadows, and moving within it a lean, stooped figure, no more than a shadow itself.

It was like an image from a dream. And as he lay in bed now, teetering on the brink of sleep, he was half inclined to believe he had imagined it all.

The room was washed with moonlight, making it seem ghostly, just barely real. The sound of the record snaked eerily through the register beside him. He shifted his pillow over against the wall and cocked his ear to catch the words.

Oh the rain comes a pitter patter,
And I'd like to be safe in bed.
Skies are weeping, while the world is
sleeping,
Trouble heaping on our heads . . .

As he lay there on the edge of sleep, the music echoing in his mind, he found himself first humming then, strangely, singing along, the words coming inexplicably to mind.

Helter skelter, I must run for shelter,
Till the clouds roll by.

He stared up at the crack snaking its way through the ceiling, following it from where it began as a tiny trickle of dark just above the bed, watching it widen as it went, till by the window it disappeared down a ragged hole in the chimney flue. It had become a nightly ritual. Following it, he seemed to fall asleep through that hole. And in the morning it was as if he reemerged, traveling that trickle of dark until it stopped above the bed and dropped him back to waking once again.

But it seemed now that he was looking down on it from a great distance, and the crack was like a cleft of darkness snaking through a countryside. Downstairs the music died. He felt himself drifting downward, ever downward, saw the crack yawn open under him, and felt the darkness draw him slowly in.

In the dream he was back at the Palace, standing in the dark at the top of the stairs. But the walkway had grown impossibly narrow and seemed to stretch off endlessly in both directions. And the low walls on either side now loomed up over his head so that he could no longer see the screen. Occasionally he would hear the random crack of gunfire or see an eerie flickering of lights over the wall that told him the picture was still playing.

The uniform was cold and clammy against him. The stench was unbearable and his skin felt as if it were crawling with something. There was a sudden smell of smoke in the air. He looked up and saw it eddying against the lights above the wall, and suddenly he remembered what Zeke had said about the smoke screwing up the projection. He had to find out who it was and tell them to put it out. But the openings to the aisles were gone, and the wall was far too high to see over.

As he walked over to it he felt his feet sink down into the floor with each step as though the carpet had turned to mud. At the base of the wall he jumped, his hands caught hold of the top edge, and he strained to hoist himself up to see over it. But as he pulled himself level with the top of the wall, he watched in horror as it turned soft and slick in his hands and a great lump of it sheared away under his weight. He fell back to the bottom in a heap, dirt raining down on his head, and found himself facing a wall of ragged earth and mud rising above him like the gaping mouth of a grave.

A light flickered on, and huddled against the wall beside him he saw a figure. At first he thought it was Zeke searching for something with his flashlight against the base of the wall. But then he realized that it was someone with a candle, bent over the pages of a book. His face, his hands, his clothes—everything was covered in mud, so that it almost seemed that he might have sprung from the side of the wall where he squatted.

One thing about him, though, stood out from the pallid uniformity of the mud. And that was a ring coiled tightly around his finger and gleaming dully in the candlelight. It

*was a large gold ring shaped like a snake—a snake with its
tail gripped between its teeth.*

*As he stared at it, fascinated, the night was suddenly pierced
by a low, unearthly wail. The candle winked instantly out,
and in the sudden darkness the sound grew steadily louder
and more menacing, until it seemed like some demon swooping down on him. There was a sudden deafening roar, and all
went dark. . . .*

He was suddenly jerked awake. He lay there rigid in the
bed, barely daring to breathe, his every nerve on edge. The
room was hushed with moonlight, the house deathly still. The
dream slid noiselessly out of sight.

Then he heard it, a dull, rhythmic thud that seemed to
come from outside. He slid quietly from the covers and crept
across the cold floor to the window. Looking down into the
yard, he saw that the garage door was open. A light was on
inside. The wind banged the door lightly against a broom that
had been wedged in the doorway.

There was another sound now—the sound of something
being dragged. A shadow emerged from the shelter of the
house and made its way with difficulty toward the garage. In
the light from the door he saw a stooped figure with a cane
dragging a large bundle along the walk behind him. As he
labored the bundle over the threshold and into the garage, he
pulled the broom free and quietly closed the door.

Cass remained at the window for a long time, watching the
uncertain seam of light that outlined the door against the
darkness, wondering what the old man could possibly be up
to out there in the middle of the night.

It was well past one o'clock by the time he finally gave up
the vigil, crept back to bed, and fell into a deep and dreamless
sleep.

Whatever career options Alison may have had open to her, singing was certainly not one of them. Cass sat on the cedar chest in front of the window, trying to piece his pathetic uniform back together and listening to her sing along to the radio as she fixed dinner in the kitchen.

Occasionally he would glance down at the street for signs of Murray's pickup truck. The window was open a crack, and the light breeze blowing against his back brought with it the steady creak of swings from the park and the brisk assault of Mrs. Wharton's broom.

The magnolia tree out front, beautiful in bloom, was now shedding its pale pink petals. The front yard was blanketed with them, and more than a few had blown in the wind into the neighboring yards. Mrs. Wharton seemed to spend the better part of her day now sweeping the intruders from her sidewalk, staring balefully up at the tree, as though warning those that remained of the fate that awaited them should they dare to drift her way. She was busy now with the edge of the broom, working the stubborn petals from the cracks. Cass was dying to see the expression on her face when the battered blue pickup delivered Murray to the door.

First thing that morning he had dropped the two uniforms off at the dry cleaners. The woman had looked at his a little doubtfully as he shook it out of the garbage bag onto the counter, but when he picked them up at noon, even it looked almost respectable, cleaned and pressed and sheathed in plastic. He paid the bill with the last of the money from the wallet, praying that no emergencies would arise between now and next Tuesday when Alison got paid.

He dropped Fischer's uniform off at the Palace, where he was waiting for it, then brought his own back home for major surgery. On the way he decided to take a short side trip down the lane behind the house.

The garage was not difficult to find. The doors were painted the same dull red as the house. Already the weeds were a foot high in front of them, and flourishing. This stood in stark contrast to the other garages that lined the lane, with their louvered metal doors and asphalt ramps. Except for someone busy beneath the hood of a car down near the end of the lane, there was no one around.

There wasn't a hint of a crack or crevice through which he might steal a peek at what was inside the garage. The doors were solid, unmoving. Large nails had been driven into the wood where they met. The nail heads had been painted over the last time the doors had been painted, and that had quite obviously been some time ago. Someone with a can of spray paint had sprayed the word MAGGOTS across the doors.

Between the side of the garage and the old wooden fence that separated the yard from Mrs. Wharton's property there was a narrow crawlspace. It was cluttered with the accumulated garbage of years: old papers, empty pop bottles, sunbleached cigarette packages, and the omnipresent weeds. Halfway down the side of the garage there was a small window covered with a rusty iron grille.

He stood there for what seemed like a long time, debating with himself whether to scale the slack wire fence that barred the entrance to the crawlspace and satisfy his curiosity. But Mrs. Wharton's back door was open and he dared not tempt her omniscience. Besides, even from this vantage point it was clear that the window was coated with years of grime and probably impossible to see through.

Finally, it was the ghostly creak of an automatic garage door sliding open on the other side of the lane that prompted him to leave. The window could wait.

Sewing ranked somewhere near the bottom of his short list

of skills. Still, as he sat slowly mending the torn lining of the uniform, he could feel the needle gradually grow calm between his fingers and see the stitches grow steadily surer.

He had actually asked Alison to do it. She had, of course, laughed uproariously, tears streaming down her cheeks from the mountain of onions she was chopping for the sauce. Sewing did not even make it onto Alison's list. It was down there somewhere with rubbing sticks together to start a fire, and other lost arts. The stuff in the sewing basket just kept accumulating. Periodically they would solve the problem by getting a bigger basket. The stuff now filled a bushel basket that sat in the shadows at the back of her closet.

Once the lining was more or less in one piece and the split in the armpit stitched closed, he turned his attention to the pants. He had purposely left them till last, hoping that by the time he got around to them he would have figured out what to do. He hadn't. Short of putting on a hundred pounds between now and next Monday night, there was no way he was going to fit into those pants.

He considered taking a large tuck in at the waist, but had the sinking feeling that it would just make them look that much more ridiculous. The only solution was to take all the seams in several inches. But where to begin? He bit off a length of the thick black thread he had used on the jacket and was still trying to coax it through the narrow eye of the needle when Alison called from the kitchen.

"Cass, would you mind running up to the corner for me? We need some Parmesan for the spaghetti. Oh, and a loaf of Italian bread. You can get some money from the wallet."

Wrong. But there was no point in bringing up that right now, not with Murray coming over. It would just end up depressing everyone for the rest of the evening.

Then he remembered the pickle jar full of pennies sitting

out with the junk on the sun porch. Alison poked her head around the corner.

"Did you hear me, Cass?"

"Yeah, sorry, Mom. I'm going right now."

She gave him a funny look and went back to work.

There was a square of cardboard where one of the sun-porch windows had been. A couple of days earlier he'd come home from school to discover the window shattered and a rock lying amid shards of glass on the floor. It didn't look much like an accident.

He emptied the jar of coins onto the top of the desk, which was still lying legless on the floor. Apart from half a dozen quarters and a few sad dimes, the rest were pennies. He shook his head and started scooping handfuls of them into his pockets. When he figured he had enough, he hitched up his pants, tightened his belt, and made his way to the bathroom, where he ran the brush glumly through his hair.

The coins chimed miserably in his pockets as he started down the stairs.

7

MAGISTRALE'S FRUIT and Vegetable Market was a small family business that looked as though it had been there for years. There were Mr. Magistrale, his wife, his wife's mother, and the two Magistrale kids, Tony and Maria. Everyone helped out in the operation. Mr. Magistrale worked the small butcher counter at the back of the shop. Tony unloaded boxes, stocked the shelves, and did deliveries in the battered blue van with their name on the side. Mrs. Magistrale usually handled the cash, while her mother sat on a chair at the front of the store and kept an eye on the penny candy. Maria spent her time standing around posing in the mirror mounted above the vegetable counter and talking to her boyfriends on the phone. Occasionally her father would shout "Maria" from the back of the store, and she would hang up and go and spray the vegetables until another boyfriend phoned. Maria was a very popular girl.

Normally Cass avoided the place like the plague. For one thing, the price of everything was always higher than in the stores down on the strip, and it killed him to part with the extra pennies.

The real reason, though, was Maria. She utterly unraveled him. He'd no sooner step through the door and catch a glimpse of her bending over the green peppers and lettuces than his mind would go completely blank, and he'd be left wandering the aisles in a daze, trying to remember what it was he'd come in for.

As he approached the store now, he kept repeating over and over under his breath, "Bread and Parmesan, bread and Parmesan."

Tony Magistrale was out front packing up the stuff on display outside the store, getting ready to close up for the weekend. He was about eighteen and had huge muscles from throwing around boxes half his life. He looked down at Cass as he walked by, as if he might be some bug that had crawled out from under one of the vegetable boxes.

Bread and Parmesan, bread and Parmesan. The bell above the door tinkled as he walked into the store. Maria was sitting on a stool behind the checkout desk doing her nails. He caught a quick scent of her perfume, and his mind emptied like a sieve. He wandered over to the vegetable counter and started picking through the celery, killing time while he rifled his mind for what it was he'd come in for.

He pried a basket from the stack piled on the floor beside the vegetables and started down the aisle, scanning the shelves for clues. Agonizing minutes passed by. Cereal? No. Soup? No. Toilet paper? The bell tinkled again as someone else came in. He found himself in front of the baby food section, staring into the toothless face of the kid on the Pablum box while he wracked his brain.

"Hey, Maria," said a lazy voice from the front of the store.

"Hi, Sid."

"Give me a pack of Golds, will you?"

Cass looked up at the ceiling near the front of the store. A large convex mirror was mounted there to discourage shoplifting. Off to one side of the distorted image he could see the counter, with Maria on one side and someone dressed in black draped over the other. He couldn't see the face, but there was something familiar about the figure.

Then he saw the high-rise handlebars of a bike leaning against the front window. It was the leader of the gang that hung out at the pool. He slunk back against the baby food.

"What are you doing this weekend, Maria?"

"I don't know. Why?"

"Maybe we could go out somewhere, you and me."

"I think maybe I'm busy."

"Next week then. What do you say?"

"I'll have to see."

"Maria." It was Mr. Magistrale bellowing from the back of the store.

"Okay, Papa, okay," she called back. "Look," she said to Sid, "you'd better go now."

"All right. I'll give you a call, okay?"

"Okay."

There was a pronounced shuffle of footsteps, then the little bell tinkled again and Sid was gone.

Cass looked up from the baby food. Mr. Magistrale was standing behind the butcher counter with a long knife in his hand. He was looking at Cass hard, as if he thought he was about to steal something. Beside him, a dead lamb with a startled expression on its face hung upside down from a hook.

He gave Mr. Magistrale a weak little smile, reached up, and dropped a jar of baby food into the basket. Mr. Magistrale turned away and went back to work on the lamb. A few quick cuts, and with a smooth yank he stripped the skin right off it, just as if he were helping Mrs. Magistrale off with her coat.

Suddenly he remembered the Parmesan. On the way to get it he passed the bread bin and remembered that too. He made his way slowly to the front of the store.

Maria was buried in a movie magazine. Her long gold earrings dangled loosely from her ears. He put the basket down on the counter and took out the long stick of bread, the package of Parmesan, the jar of baby food. It was pureed prunes. He raked his hand through his hair.

Maria put down her magazine. Without bothering to look up, she started to ring the stuff up. He died a little as her fingers closed around the jar of pureed prunes. He felt about five years old.

"That's three seventy," she said, snapping open a paper bag with a flick of her wrist, dropping the stuff in.

He wanted to say "Look, Maria, you shouldn't bother with that guy. He's bad news, believe me. There's something creepy about him. Listen, maybe someday when you're not busy we could take a walk together or something."

Instead, he reached into his pocket and came out with a fistful of pennies. He started counting them out on the counter in stacks of ten, setting the dimes and quarters down in front of them in a neat row. He tried to be nonchalant about it, as though this was the way people always paid for their groceries.

Maria kept popping bubbles with her gum all the time he was counting. Her earrings tinkled as she turned her head.

When he was finally finished, she gathered it all up and dropped it noisily into the till.

"Thanks," she said. It sounded as if she didn't mean it.

The toe of his shoe caught in a crack in the linoleum as he was trying to shuffle to the door, and he almost went sailing right through the plate glass window. Maria didn't notice. She was busy with the vegetables again.

"Prunes?" said Alison when she opened the bag.

"Sure. I thought I'd like to try them."

"Baby food?"

"Yeah. Lots of people eat baby food."

She put it down on the table and shrugged her shoulders.

"You know, Cass," she said, "sometimes you confuse me."

"That's all right. Sometimes I confuse myself."

Murray arrived fashionably late. A few more subversive petals had drifted from the magnolia tree onto Mrs. Wharton's walk, but there was no sign of her now. She had retreated to the security of her house, from which she no doubt witnessed the whole thing. Mind you, Murray was hard to miss.

The rusty blue pickup rattled to a halt out front of the house, the door on the driver's side swung open, and Murray coiled out. He was well over six feet tall and as thin as a rake. His long hair was rubber-banded into a ragged tail at the back. He looked a little like a basketball player gone to seed. He walked with a pronounced slouch, as if he were trying to make himself smaller. Normally his taste in clothing tended toward greasy coveralls and black ankle boots, but today he was wearing a white shirt.

The back of the pickup was loaded down with old car radiators and rusty wheel hubs. He reached in among the stuff and came out with a bottle in a brown paper bag.

He loped up the walk, banged the porch door behind him, and took the steps up two at a time. There was a pause outside the door, then a light knock. Alison, who had wandered in from the kitchen, answered it. Murray stood there looking down at her a little sheepishly. A band of rust ran across the front of his white shirt.

"Sorry I'm late," he said as he stepped in and nodded greetings in Cass's direction. "I saw some stuff lying out in front of this service station on the way. I couldn't resist."

When he wasn't busy moving the two of them back and forth across the city, Murray spent his time scavenging for scrap metal that he sold to a junk dealer down by the docks. Nobody could get more excited by junk than Murray. He prided himself on living off what other people threw away. It was like a religion with him. The whole of his apartment was furnished with stuff he'd salvaged from the garbage—*liberated* was the word he used.

Alison forgave him with a brief kiss that she had to reach up with and he had to come down for. They met somewhere in the middle.

"I brought some of that Spanish wine you like," he said, handing her the slightly greasy paper bag. He had noticed the rust mark on his shirt and was busy trying to brush it off as he disappeared with Alison into the kitchen. They talked for a while alone in there, a comforting murmur punctuated by the clatter of china and the chime of silverware being set.

All through dinner Alison talked about her paper. The title was "From Innocence to Experience: The Development of Blake's Thought Between *The Songs of Innocence* and *The Songs of Experience* as Seen in the Shorter Prophecies." It was quite a mouthful. Murray didn't seem to mind. He ate nonstop, pausing only long enough now and then to nod or to ask Cass to pass the garlic bread. What Murray lacked in social skills he more than made up for in appetite. It was a wonder how so much food could fit into someone so skinny. He was well into his third plateful before he showed any signs of slowing at all.

After one watered-down glass of wine, Cass felt the floor do a soft tilt. What Alison was saying was starting to make sense. He switched to tea. It was always interesting to watch Alison when Murray was around. A different side of her surfaced, younger somehow, more carefree, a ghost of the college girl, he supposed, and the days they had spent together then.

Murray was into strange things like auras and astral travel. He sat with a straight face talking for about half an hour about his previous incarnations. Alison, normally the skeptic, sat back with this silly smile on her face, her eyes bright with wine, and let him go.

After the meal, while Alison made coffee, Cass gave Murray the grand tour. He nodded silent approval as they moved from room to room. Finally Cass showed him into his own room. Murray walked through the door and stopped dead. His forehead furrowed in concentration.

He must have stood there for a couple of minutes like that, absorbing the vibrations, typically Murray. Then he slowly opened his eyes.

"What is it?" asked Cass.

"I don't know. Something though. It's gone now." He wandered over to the window and was looking down into the yard.

"Seen much of the guy downstairs?" he asked.

"No. I haven't seen him at all actually. I understand he's really old. He doesn't get out much."

"Mmm," said Murray. "Well, it looks like someone's been out back recently."

He wasted no time in joining Murray at the window. Sure

enough a small section of ground against the garage wall had been turned up since he'd last looked back there. It stood in stark contrast to the wilderness surrounding it. Vagrant branches from the rosebush nearby had been lopped off and lay on the damp soil like withered flowers strewn on a fresh grave. A pair of hedge shears and a spade, abandoned against the garage wall, were already speckled with rust from the recent rain.

The whole scene had an overwhelming aura of defeat about it, as if the task had simply proven too much for the old man. There was something unsettling in the sight of the mud, some memory just out of reach.

"Where did you get this?" said Murray behind him, making him jump.

He turned to find him arched over the bed, studying the picture of the snake.

"Found it. It was in the closet along with some other junk."

"Really?" He lifted it down from its hook. "Do you know what this is?"

"No. A picture of a snake swallowing its tail, I guess."

"It's called an ouroboros. That means 'tail biter' in Greek. It's an ancient alchemical symbol of death and rebirth. The snake has no beginning or end, you see. It devours itself and renews itself endlessly. Death from life, life from death.

"The writing in the center is Greek. It means 'the all is one.' This looks really old. I wouldn't be surprised if it was worth something, you know. It looks like it came from an old book or manuscript of some sort." He returned it carefully to its place on the wall, stood back, studied it.

"It looks at home here," he said.

Later, over coffee in the front room, Murray noticed the uniform draped over the arm of the chair along with the needle and thread. Cass told him about the job at the Palace and his predicament with the uniform.

As it turned out, Murray had been a tailor in a previous incarnation. For the next two hours he sat there cross-legged on the cedar chest, picking out stitches, cutting, measuring, pinning the whole in place. All the while he worked he went on about alchemy. By the time he was finished it was nearly midnight. Alison, always the life of the party, had passed out in the rocker. Murray woke her up and she walked dozily down to the pickup with him. Cass stood at the darkened window watching them say their good-byes, kissing briefly under the streetlamp.

Mrs. Wharton would be scandalized.

—— 8 ——

THE BUS rounded the corner and the park swung into view. Sitting in the safety of the bus, it looked almost magical, like a picture painted from a dream, the green of grass and leaf so luminous that they might still be wet to the touch, the sun couched in the sky like a golden ball in a blue velvet box.

Normally Cass stayed on the bus while it followed the curve of the road around to the stop on the far side of the park, but now he reached up impulsively and pulled the bellcord. The driver, who was almost past the stop, braked hard, and swung over to the curb, then scowled into the mirror while Cass scooped up his stuff and scurried off.

As the bus roared away from the stop, trailing heat and diesel fumes, he glanced over at the newspaper box chained to the pole. The money box had been pried out, like a gold tooth yanked from a dead man's mouth. He had a pretty good idea of who had performed the operation.

Suddenly he felt like a combat soldier dropped behind enemy lines. Where seconds before there had been brilliant sun, now there seemed to be shadows. The wide paved path winding through the park to the tennis courts on the far side now looked like a faint, tenuous trail cut through the wilderness.

He jammed his windbreaker into his bookbag and slung it over his shoulder. As he started down the path, the crazy picture of Judy Garland bouncing down the Yellow Brick Road came into his mind. At any other time it might almost have been funny.

The park was rife with sun worshippers. Summer was finally in the air, and they were out in droves: businessmen sprawled on benches, their jackets draped like sloughed skin over the seats beside them; people scattered over the grass, collars loosened, shoes shed; couples lying lost in each other's arms.

It was completely wasted on him. His entire attention was directed to a point midway along the path, where the wading pool lay.

He could already hear them whooping it up over there, Sid and the boys—a radio cranking out rock, the dull insistent throb of a drumbeat. It wasn't too late, he told himself. If he wanted to, he could still skip off and make his way unseen through the trees that fringed the park.

But something inside him rebelled against the idea, something born no doubt of sun and sweat and the sheer stupidity of spring. It kept him marching right on down the path. After all, what was there to be afraid of, especially with all these people around? Why, for all he knew, the gang wasn't even interested in him, hadn't even the vaguest idea of who he was or where he lived. That rock through the sun-porch window could have been thrown by anyone.

He counted six of them—four buzzing around on bikes, two at the center of the pool. One of two at the center was Sid, the other a tall guy with shades. He was doing drumrolls on the metal lid of the hub in time to the music, while Sid gently bobbed his head like a Kewpie doll on a dashboard.

Sid was the still point at the center of all the action around him, the source of it all and yet somehow supremely above it. He observed it all with a cool, barely concealed boredom. It was just that boredom that sent a chill ripple of ice down Cass's spine as he approached the pool. His legs turned to licorice and the inside of his mouth went dry with dread.

The people near the pool were doing their best to pretend that the gang wasn't really there. Parents sat talking on benches nearby, children rode the metal ponies or scaled the steep rungs of the corkscrew slide, none of them sparing more than the briefest of glances in the direction of the pool, as if the whole thing might simply be a mirage.

Suddenly Cass's eyes fell on a group of younger kids gathered around a picnic table nearby. There was something familiar about them. Then he remembered what it was. These were the kids he'd seen passing the house on their way home from school, the ones who always veered onto the road as they went by.

Now one of them, urged on by the others, peeled slowly away from the table and started walking toward the pool. He stood patiently at the edge, like a subject seeking audience, until Sid finally noticed him there and nodded him over. The kid dodged past the killer bicycles and made his way down to the center of the pool, where he stood face to face with Sid.

The whole scene had a strange aura of ritual to it, and as Cass approached the pool all sense of his own fear instantly faded. He was back up in his window; the watcher was at work.

Right beside the pool there was a water fountain where half a dozen kids were standing in line for a drink. He eased off the path and quietly joined them.

Sid and the younger kid were talking now. The kid said something and Sid nodded, glancing over at the picnic table. They talked for a little longer, and then the kid reached into his pocket and came out with something. In the instant before Sid plucked it from his hand and pocketed it, Cass caught a familiar flash of green. Money. But why should the kid be giving Sid money?

The question had scarcely had a chance to form in his mind before Cass suddenly realized that the line in front of him had dissolved, leaving him standing alone at the edge of the pool, staring. He hurried up to the fountain and leaned in to take a drink. But even as he did he already knew it was too late; they had seen him.

The bowl of the water fountain was full of garbage. A wad of pink gum was glued to the side, the bloated remains of a sandwich clung to the bottom, blocking the drainage holes. A cigarette butt bobbed in the water that had collected around it. The water spilled listlessly from the end of the open spigot down onto the bread. He hovered over it, pretending to drink, hoping that if he just stayed there long enough the gang would magically be gone when he looked up.

The radio died and the drumming with it. An incredible quiet fell over everything. He could hear the soft pop of the balls from the tennis court, the steady creak of the swing, the muffled gurgle of the water escaping beneath the bread.

He could feel the line growing behind him. Finally he glanced up and found Sid, still leaning against the hub at the center of the pool, staring dead at him. His hand rested on the radio. Behind him, the guy with the sunglasses stood with his hands frozen in the middle of a drumroll and a confused expression on his face. The sunglasses made him look like a giant insect.

Cass straightened and started walking slowly away from the

fountain back to the path. He tried to walk casually, as if nothing at all had happened, but the path now felt like a brittle crust underfoot that might give way at any instant and send him plunging down into the darkness. And all the while he was walking he kept feeling those cold eyes on his back, bearing down on him as bloodlessly as a black bicycle on an old man and his buggy.

He didn't feel completely safe until he'd pushed past the lean green fingers of the hedge and heard the gate creak closed behind him.

—— 9 ——

IT WAS less than a week later that he found the bird in the box.

That first taste of summer was just a memory now, one of those little teasers the carnival barker dangles outside the tent. Inside, it was dark and drizzling.

Cass turned up the collar of his jacket as he sprinted down the street from the bus stop on the corner. The park was empty, not a sign of Sid and his gang anywhere. There was nothing but the rain playing on the slick clay courts, spilling down the corkscrew slide, clinging to the painted backs of the pony swings. It had even claimed the wading pool for its own.

He stopped running halfway down the block, winded. The trees provided some shelter. He dashed from one dry oasis of sidewalk to the next.

The house had never looked so good to him. The rain seemed to waken the old paint a little, and the dim light dulled the ragged edges of the place. He hardly even noticed the soggy square of cardboard in the sun-porch window.

He crossed the street, his jacket over his head, and raced up the walk to the shelter of the porch, banging the door behind him on the rain. He peeled off the soaking jacket and raked his dripping hair off his face. It was only then that he noticed the box of groceries sitting on the floor in front of the inside door.

It belonged to Mr. Magnus. Once a week he had a small order delivered from up the street. As he fumbled through his pockets for his keys, Cass let his eyes drift over the contents of the box: a carton of milk, a loaf of brown bread, two small tins of beans, a package of loose tea, a small jar of jam, tobacco, and papers. It was even less than last time. And once again, propped against the box and all but dwarfing it, there stood a large dusty bag of charcoal. It was the second one he'd seen in less than a month. What was the old man doing with the stuff—eating it? There was a slight, steady trickle of smoke spilling from the garage chimney all the time now. The heat was already off in the house, so why on earth would anyone keep a fire going day and night in the garage?

He finally found the key hiding out in a handful of change in his jacket pocket. He fished it out and bent over the box of groceries to slide it into the keyhole. Something stopped him from just picking up his sopping stuff and heading upstairs.

He gave the groceries a long look and then grabbed the top of the charcoal bag and dragged it inside the door. It would save the old guy a few steps anyway. As he pulled it across the carpet to the door of the flat, an image popped into his head. The image of the old man dragging something along behind him in the dark to the door of the garage.

Cass propped the bag against the wall by the door and went back for the box. So that's what it had been. He picked up the box and was heading in with it when he noticed a handbill hanging from the mailbox. He leaned the box against the wall and reached up for it, sliding his hand under the lid of the mailbox to feel for more mail.

He yanked it back with a start. The box of groceries fell with a thud to the floor. His heart was hammering in his chest like someone shut in a locked room.

The lid of the mailbox stood open. There was something in there. He had felt a silken stiffness, a chill curl of claws against his fingers.

He approached it tentatively now, peering through the pattern of holes on the side of the box, then knocking sharply against it with his hand. Nothing seemed to stir. He reached up and slid his hand inside. It came out holding the dead body of a bird by the claws.

It was a starling. He had seen plenty of them over in the park, vying with the pigeons for the garbage. It was cold and hard.

He walked out into the rain with it and lay it at the base of the magnolia, mounding handfuls of the sodden pink petals over it.

He squatted in the grass for a long time, watching the rain pelt down on the petals like small curious fingers feeling for what lay hidden there. As he stood up again he glanced over into the park at the empty pool. He could almost picture Sid, standing there in the rain, smiling at him.

This time he walked back to the house, letting the rain soak him to the skin, letting it wash away the fear that had fallen over him, feeling it begin to uncover something else, something hard and bright beneath that he had hardly known was there before.

The carton of milk had split in the fall, soaking the rest of the stuff in the box, then creeping off through a crack in the floorboards. His bookbag had intercepted the stream. The bottom of the bag was soaking wet. He rescued it, then gathered up the scattered groceries, wiping them off on his jacket and putting them back in the soggy box. Then he headed upstairs for a mop and pail.

When he was finished, the floor looked several shades of gray lighter than it had before. He quietly set the box of groceries down beside the charcoal in front of Mr. Magnum's door.

Upstairs, as he rinsed out the mop, he toyed seriously with the idea of washing his hands of the whole affair. He had simply arrived home, discovered the mess already there, and done the best he could to clean it up. Maybe there wasn't even any need to say anything at all about it to the old man. After all, it was just a carton of milk. The rest of the stuff was fine, more or less. He might not even notice that the milk wasn't there. Maybe he'd figure the box got wet in the rain or something.

That worked for about fifteen minutes. By then he'd put his chemistry notebook under a stack of books to dry and rinsed out the bottom of his bookbag under running water, leaving it draped over the shower head, shedding pale blue tears into the tub.

There was just one flaw in the story he'd worked up: It wasn't true. He hadn't come in and discovered the mess—he'd made it. *He* had broken the carton of milk. And for some reason he lacked the will or whatever it was simply to paper over the flaw and forget about it. The crazy image of a confused old man sorting through his soggy groceries lodged itself in his mind and would not be wished away.

He found himself standing in front of the open fridge, staring at the sparsely populated racks. Their own milk, the last of it until Alison's pay tomorrow, filled barely half the jug.

Beside it sat the remnants of the spaghetti and sauce he'd managed to salvage from Murray's visit—tonight's dinner, along with the tail end of the garlic bread, wrapped in foil on top of the fridge.

He put on the skillet to fry up the spaghetti, dumped the sauce into a pot, and popped the garlic bread into the oven.

At the back of the china cupboard he unearthed the small crystal pitcher he remembered unpacking. It matched the butter dish on the table, and along with it was all that now remained of the set Alison had inherited from her grandmother. He rinsed it out and dried it carefully with the tea towel until the countless facets of the crystal danced with light. Then he filled it nearly to the brim with milk.

It sat there on the counter while the dinner warmed. Now and then he would glance over at it, as if he half expected it to have toddled off and made its way down to the old man's door by itself. But it refused to budge.

Finally, in a moment of madness, he dredged up sufficient courage to scoop it up himself and head for the door. He took the stairs slowly, clutching the handrail, trying to coax the milk into calmness, but watching it toss fretfully back and forth against the sides of the pitcher, threatening to slop over the rim and rain down onto the stairs.

The groceries were gone from Mr. Magnus's door. There was a damp outline on the rug where the box had sat. In the dull yellow of the overhead light the crystal glowed like gold.

He had knocked a second time before he became aware of a slight, nearly noiseless shuffling from the far side of the door. He stood there listening for what seemed an eternity, his heart fluttering in his chest like a bird in a bone cage. Barely an arm's breadth away he knew that Mr. Magnus stood listening too, deciding whether or not to answer the knock.

At last the handle did a slow turn and the door edged open

a crack, just enough for him to sense the dimness of the room beyond and to let the stale smell of smoke and dirt drift eagerly into the hall. A chain hung slack between frame and door, swaying like an empty swing.

"Yes?" said a high, thin voice, like a child's voice gone to rust.

"It's Cass Parry," he said. "From upstairs."

"Yes?" A pale hand hooked around the door. A flash of gold on one finger.

"I was wondering if I could talk to you for a minute. It's about your groceries. You see, I, uh—"

The door closed quietly, cutting the speech short. There was a moment's silence, followed by the muted slide of metal on metal, then the sound of the loose chain bouncing lightly against the door frame.

This time the door opened all the way. And suddenly he found himself face to face with the mysterious Mr. Magnus.

It was something of a shock. He had expected someone taller somehow, more imposing. Yet here in the shadows of the doorway stood a wiry, stooped old man not much bigger than himself. Not the daunting, almost mythic figure imagination might have painted, but just an old man. He was almost disappointed.

Mr. Magnus was wearing a shapeless sweater that seemed far too large for him. It hung slackly from his bony shoulders like something slung haphazardly over the back of a chair. The frayed cuffs almost swallowed up the thin, veined hands, one of which was curled around the worn head of a cane. He glanced up and their eyes met.

"I broke your carton of milk," he said. "I was bringing in the box of groceries, and it fell." He didn't bother to tell him about the bird.

Mr. Magnus just stood there looking at him with those

ancient, unwavering eyes. The silence surrounded him like an aura. Cass had the sudden unnerving feeling that the old man could see straight through him.

"I brought this down for now," he blundered on. "It's not much. I can make up the rest later."

"There's no need for that, young man. I only use the nasty stuff to whiten my tea. The rest just sits in the fridge and spoils anyway." The whisper of a smile crossed his face. For an instant the great gulf of years between them fell away, and Cass found himself staring into the face of the shy young soldier on the mirror. It lasted for only a moment, then time rushed in to reclaim the old man, and the smile was gone.

As he took the jug, their hands touched and something chimed lightly against the crystal. Some milk splashed up over the rim and ran down the side of the pitcher, dripping down onto the rug, making small white explosions in the dust of the boot tray.

Mr. Magnus guided it slowly through the door and set it down on the corner of a paper-strewn table. Cass caught a fleeting glimpse of clutter and chaos beyond. Then the old man straightened and turned back to him.

"Thank you, young man," he said, drawing the door close about him, like the collar on a cloak of shadows.

Cass nodded. "I'm sorry," he said, not really knowing why. But the door closed quietly on the words, and the lock slid home.

PART TWO

Peacock's Tail

*It is found in the country and the village and the
town, in all things created by God, yet it is
despised by all. Rich and poor handle it every
day. It is cast into the street by servant maids.
Children play with it. Yet no one prizes it,
though it is the most beautiful and precious thing
upon the earth.*

*from Gloria Mundi,
an alchemical text*

— 10 —

FISCHER WAS on the make. He was stationed by the candy counter talking with Maddy. His hair stood out from his head like the soft bristles on a baby's brush, and his two-tone Italian loafers shone dully in the lobby light.

He might as well have been talking to himself. Maddy, perched on a stool behind the popcorn machine, was making it more than a little obvious that she was considerably more interested in her paperback book than in Fischer's conversation. The only concession she made to his presence was the occasional glance up over the rim of her glasses and brief bob of her head. It seemed to be more than enough. Fischer had been talking nonstop for the past twenty minutes.

Cass stood in the dark at the top of the stairs, dividing his attention between *Duck Soup* and what was happening downstairs. The movie was running a distant second. Mind you, even the Marx Brothers began to wear a little thin after the third viewing.

Since the Palace was an independent theater, it was entirely in the manager's hands what movies were screened and how long they stayed. According to Zeke, Jack was caught in some sort of time warp. He figured that all the movies that should have been made *had* been made by about 1960, which was likely the last time he had left the theater other than to drop the money in the night deposit at the bank two blocks away.

On a good night there might be about fifty people rattling around in the place. Some were regulars. There was the guy Zeke called the Undertaker, with his chalk-white face and pinstripe suit. He walked as if he had a board up his back and always sat front and center, his handkerchief spread out on the seat under him. There were the two old ladies with wire-rimmed glasses and tight gray perms, who came with their knitting and sat in the first row of the loges delicately rattling their needles in the dark. Then there was the weird guy in the trench coat who looked like he'd walked straight off the screen from one of Jack's gangster pictures. He always sat way up in the corner at the back of the theater by himself. Come cleanup time, you could always tell where he'd been, because there'd be a mound of butts and ashes on the floor under the seat. Zeke figured the guy had a death wish; he was either trying to drive himself crazy on the movies, or kill himself with the cigarettes.

Apart from these, there were the average-looking people who came shuffling up the stairs from the lobby, balancing diet soft drinks and tubs of buttered popcorn, a copy of the program highlights sheet that Jack put together every month tucked under their arm. There were business people out slumming, students in sneakers looking for culture, and men with battered plastic bags looking for a place to sleep.

What kept the Palace from going under completely were the Saturday afternoon matinees. The Palace was the last theater in town to still show double-bill matinees for two dollars. And then the place was packed. On that one day Jack raked in enough money to keep the doors open for the rest of the week.

Zeke was standing in the shadows on the other side of the stairs, cracking sunflower seeds and cackling to himself. Every now and then he'd lope over in a half crouch, arching his eyebrows and flicking his flashlight like a cigar, to try out his Groucho Marx impersonation on Cass.

Maddy had just thrown a couple of scoops of kernels into the popper, getting set for the intermission. Now she was snapping together boxes, lining them up on the ledge under the machine.

Cass didn't know what it was, but he spent a lot of time watching her. She certainly had nothing on Maria Magistrale as far as looks went. She was really very plain: no makeup, nothing. Actually, she seemed to be totally unconcerned with all that stuff. But there was something about her, a sort of quiet self-confidence that enveloped her, that he liked a lot.

He still hadn't worked up the nerve to actually talk to her. These things took time. Right now they were in the nodding and smiling stage. He liked the way she smiled too.

Suddenly Fischer pushed off the counter and started making slow passes over the rug with the carpet sweeper. Five seconds later Jack's door swung open. It was a little scary the way Fischer could always sense when that door was about to open. Jack came out, took a long drink from the water fountain, and went to station himself over by the doors for the intermission. The movie wound down. Fischer put away the carpet sweeper and went over to stand beside him. Jack lit his cigar stump and started talking. They made quite a pair: Jack with his baggy double-breasted suit, and Fischer with his crew cut and two-tone loafers. It was enough to give you nightmares. Zeke said that Fischer had eyes on becoming assistant manager someday. He sure looked the part.

After the intermission Jack disappeared into the office again and Fischer started the cleanup, sifting butts from the sand ashtrays with a sieve from the storage room. Meanwhile, Maddy began closing up the candy counter for the night. She had to tally up the money, record it, and take it to Jack. Then she put the lid on the candy display, locked it, and then locked the leftover soft drink cups in the mirror-fronted cupboard behind the counter where the candy supplies were kept. She cleaned out the popcorn machine, saving whatever was left after the intermission for Jack to eat later that night when they'd gone. Finally she went to the storage cupboard to get a mop and pail to clean up the floor behind the counter, and a rag to wipe down the countertop.

The door closed quietly behind her.

That was Fischer's cue. All the cheap after-shave, the time spent talking at the counter, the two-tone loafers—everything led to this. He had it timed perfectly, so that each night when she went in for the mop he would follow close on her heels to dump the sieve of butts and get the carpet sweeper.

He skittered across the floor now as quick as a cockroach caught in the light. The door of the supply closet closed with a soft *whoosh* on the two of them.

If everything Fischer said was true, which was immediately doubtful, more than one girl had succumbed to his amorous advances while wedged in there between the sink and the carpet sweeper. It could turn your stomach. Zeke said the reason there was such a high turnover in candy-counter attendants was that Fischer ended up frightening them all off. Maddy had already lasted longer than most, but he figured it was just a matter of time. A couple of them had even tried going to Jack about it, not that it did any good. Fischer had Jack wrapped right around his little finger.

Cass stood on the top stair with his eyes glued on the door, counting off the seconds the two of them were alone in there together. Maddy was usually out in little more than a minute, lugging the mop and pail, with Fischer in hot pursuit to help.

He heard the muffled drum of water pouring into the metal pail, then nothing. The seconds ticked by. The door remained closed.

He ventured down one step, then another, straining to catch any sound from the storage room, vowing that if he did he would rush down there in a flash and flatten Fischer. Almost two minutes now. He heard a muffled banging, voices. He went down another step.

"Hey, what's up?" It was Zeke, whispering to him from the top of the stairs.

At that moment the door opened and Maddy burst into the lobby with Fischer right behind her. He made a grab for the bucket she was carrying. She yanked it away and soapy water sloshed over the sides and onto the carpet. Her face was flushed and she looked angry, angrier than Cass had ever seen her. She shot a glance in his direction and he scurried back up the stairs.

"What was that all about?" asked Zeke as he slid back into the shadows.

"I don't know."

"Yeah, well, I do, and if you're smart, you'll stay out of it. You play the hero and you're going to wind up out of a job. Believe me."

"Okay."

"I'm not kidding, Cass. Fischer practically runs this place. You cross him and you'll be doing more than dry cleaning his uniform."

"I said okay." He glanced down at Maddy. She was behind the counter, practically attacking the floor with the mop.

Zeke looked at him and shook his head. "Look," he said, "take my advice—forget it." He headed back to his own side of the stairs.

"Forget what?" Cass called after him, but he didn't answer, or if he did, it was swallowed up by the soundtrack of the film.

Maddy was out the door in ten minutes flat. Fischer was nowhere to be seen. For the next forty-five minutes, Cass stood there with his eyes fixed on the screen, seeing nothing.

They only had to wake up one old guy that night to let him know that the movie was over. Cass watched him gather up his belongings, bundled into half a dozen dingy plastic bags, and shuffle slowly down the stairs and out the door. The image of Mr. Magnus flashed into his mind.

They did the cleanup quickly. Zeke was in a hurry to get home to catch the Late Nite Movie. There was a Bogart movie on, and Zeke was crazy for Bogart. It could be that he was just crazy, period. How anyone could stand in the dark watching movies for four hours, and then go home and watch another one was totally beyond Cass.

Zeke scooted up and down the aisles with a green garbage bag, collecting the big stuff, while Cass followed behind with a broom, sweeping stray candy wrappers and drifts of popcorn out to the edge of the aisle where he would scoop it all up on a final pass through the theater. He was still busy rooting a spill of jelly beans from between the seats of the loges when Zeke said his good-byes and vanished down the stairs.

He discovered the pack of cigarettes in the last row, sitting on the armrest of the seat with the pile of butts beneath it. It was better than half full, with a book of matches tucked inside the sleeve. He had actually thrown them into the bag and started back down the aisle, when for some reason he wasn't ready to analyze he decided to fish them out again. He slid the pack into the pocket of his shirt and dumped the garbage at the fire doors.

Back in the change room, he peeled off the uniform and carefully rolled it up, the way you rolled clothes when you went camping, to keep the wrinkles out. In the small anteroom to the ushers' change room there was a sand ashtray stationed between the two tattered armchairs. He carefully lifted the lid off the ashtray and slid the uniform down inside the hollow base. Someone on another shift had already worn the uniform since he'd had it cleaned, leaving a half-eaten candy bar glued to the inside of one of the pockets. Like Zeke said, it was dog eat dog around here. He went back to the change room, splashed some water on his face, and raked his wet hands through his hair.

It was eleven-fifteen as he crossed the darkened lobby to leave. Jack's door was closed, the light seeping out like melted butter beneath it. It was just too weird to think that he might actually live in there, like Zeke said. But right about now everything was looking a little weird. He pushed open the lobby door, crossed the darkened foyer, and went out to meet the night.

— 11 —

AS ALWAYS, the outer world took him by surprise. It had been raining. Drops of rainwater fell lazily from the edge of the overhang where the marquee lights did their endless dance. The streets were slick, and light played in the puddles on the sidewalk outside the Palace.

As he zipped up his jacket Cass came across the cigarettes. That same curious urge came over him again, and almost before he knew it he was touching the end of a match to one as if he'd done it countless times before.

He flipped up the collar of his coat and left the shelter of the overhang for the street, feeling for all the world like something straight out of one of Jack's forties gangster films. Suddenly the door of the phone booth on the corner across the street creaked open and someone stepped out into the light of a streetlamp.

He stopped dead. It was Maddy. He watched as she walked to the edge of the sidewalk, leaned out, and looked down the street. For a moment he wondered if it might not be better if he just minded his own business and kept right on going, and then he found himself slowly walking in her direction. He was about six feet from her when she turned.

"Oh—hi."

"Hi. Something wrong?"

"No—well, sort of. My father was supposed to pick me up half an hour ago, and there's still no sign of him. I just phoned home. There was no answer."

"He must be on his way, then."

"Yeah, I guess, but with these doctors you never know. Maybe something came up. I'll just wait a few more minutes, and then call a cab."

"Maybe I'll wait with you—if it's all right. This isn't exactly the nicest neighborhood in town, you know."

"You don't have to do that—really. I'm sure he'll be here any minute now."

"It's okay. I don't mind." He took another drag of the cigarette she was looking at, and felt his stomach do a slow roll. The door of the bar across the street fell open. A brief blast of music spilled out onto the street along with a couple laughing hysterically about something. They lurched off down the street, stumbling over shadows, still laughing.

"Your name's Cass, right?" said Maddy as the laughter faded and silence threatened to descend.

"Yeah. And you're Maddy?"

She nodded, then quickly leaned out over the curb and peered down the street again.

"How do you like working at the Palace?" she asked.

"It's okay. Pretty easy job, I guess, getting paid to stand around in the dark. How about you?"

"I don't know. Sometimes I wonder if it's worth the hassle. At least you guys get to watch the movies. Look what I have to look at all night."

"Fischer?"

"Exactly. I swear, someday I'm going to murder that guy."

"Like tonight, you mean?"

"Look, let's not talk about it, okay?"

"Sure." He took another pull on the cigarette. It was something to do. His head was starting to feel like a balloon bobbing around on the end of a string. He leaned it up against the lamppost.

"I didn't know you smoked," she said.

"Oh, sometimes. Off and on."

"Personally I think it's suicidal."

There wasn't much to say to that. They stood together in silence for what seemed an eternity but was likely no more than a minute or two. He took one more halfhearted tug at the cigarette and tossed it into the gutter, where it sizzled out. They watched it drift along a tunnel of rainwater until it disappeared down through the sewer grating.

"You live in the old Magnus house, don't you?" The question seemed to come from out of nowhere. He looked at her, surprised.

"That's right."

"I've seen you when I go by," she explained. "Up in the window."

So much for surreptitiousness.

"But how—?" he blurted out before managing to stop himself.

"How could I see you, you mean?"

"It's just that you always seem to be reading."

She leaned forward a little and pointed to a spot on top of her head.

"Eyes," she said, and smiled that crooked smile of hers. It was a nice smile. He could have watched it for a while, but she yanked it away and her face went serious all of a sudden.

"What do you think of old Maggots?" she said.

"Maggots?" He remembered seeing the name sprayed across the garage door.

"Old man Magnus. The kids call him Maggots."

"I don't know. I don't really know him. Why?" He sensed that she was digging for something, but he didn't know what.

She gave him a strange, searching look.

"Well, you've heard what they say about him, haven't you?"

"What? About his being senile, you mean?"

"No, not that." The silence fell over them like a damp sheet.

"What do you mean, then?" he said, but he wasn't really sure he wanted to know. Something more than the cigarette was tugging at his stomach now. The spell was shattered by the sudden blast of a car horn nearby. They turned to see a small black sports car with one headlight out, pulling up in front of the Palace.

"There's Dad now," said Maddy. "Would you like a lift? Come on, it's the least I can do."

As they approached the car, some sort of foreign model he didn't recognize, the driver's door opened and a tall, thin man in glasses spilled out. He was wiping his hands on a rag.

"Sorry to keep you waiting, love. Bit of car trouble."

"For a change," said Maddy.

"Now, now. No need to get nasty." He looked over at Cass, smiling tentatively. "And who is this young man?"

"Oh, this is Cass, Dad. He's a new usher at the theater. He

lives near us. I told him I thought it would be all right with you to give him a lift home."

"Of course," said her father. He leaned over the hood of the car, extending a long, lean hand. "Basil Harrington. Pleased to meet you, Cass. Okay, everyone hop in now before the old girl throws another conniption."

A large, grease-stained toolbox occupied the passenger seat in the front. Cass squeezed into the back of the small car beside Maddy, who whisked aside a small black leather bag before he sat on it, and put it on the floor under her feet. The car lurched into life and swung around the corner onto the side street by the Palace.

"I got called into the hospital," Dr. Harrington said. "The Patterson baby finally decided to make its appearance. It was already getting late by the time I was done there, and then this dear car decided to act up. I had to take side streets all the way here. I didn't want the police stopping me with just the one light working. I can't understand what the problem could be. I went over the whole electrical system last weekend. Do you know anything about cars, Cass?"

"Sorry."

"That's all right," said Maddy. "Neither does Dad."

"You see what I have to put up with?" said Dr. Harrington, looking at him in the rearview mirror. The car slowed to a halt at a stop sign. "Which way?"

"Straight ahead, Dad," said Maddy. With a jolt the car jerked through the intersection, bouncing the two of them together in the backseat. They traded glances and tried to keep from laughing.

"No comments from the peanut gallery," said Dr. Harrington. "I'll have you know that this car is very sensitive. If you don't want to walk the rest of the way home, you'd be well advised to refrain from ridicule."

"Sorry, Dad."

"That's quite all right. Now, where do you call home, Cass?"

At this, Maddy leaned forward, bracing her arms against the back of the front seat.

"He lives in the old Magnus house," she said in suddenly quite a different tone. Cass watched the quick exchange of glances between them before Maddy settled back in the seat beside him.

A silence fell, the silence that always seemed to follow the mention of Mr. Magnus's name. He stared uneasily out the window, suddenly acutely aware of the touch of Maddy against him, wondering what she had been about to tell him before the car arrived.

Maggots! The car seemed to hiss the word as it crept slowly down the wet street. The streetlamps were like yellow eyes peering from the trees. He thought of the snake staring down from the wall, the teeth about its tail, the rain pelting down on the pink petals where the dead bird lay.

Death from life, life from death.

It was Maddy who spoke first, her words like a pin pricking the silence that had swelled between them.

"Dad knows Mr. Magnus," she said.

"*Knew* would be a better word," said her father.

As the car swung onto Woodlawn Crescent, the dark presence of the park loomed up suddenly on the passenger side, swallowing the feeble beam of the lone headlight. The car slowed to a crawl and eased down the deserted street.

"Back when I was a boy," said Dr. Harrington, "Arthur Magnus used to do odd jobs around the neighborhood—painting, gardening, a little carpentry work. Whatever needed doing. Even then he was what people called 'peculiar.' He kept very much to himself, living in that old house with his mother. His health was never very good. He'd been in the

First War and had been badly wounded at the front, in France I believe. At one point, apparently, it was touch and go whether he'd live at all. Eventually he recovered, but he was never able to work again apart from the odd jobs he did around here. On top of being wounded, he'd been gassed as well, and it did permanent damage to his lungs."

The car pulled to a halt opposite the house. A light was on in the lower window. Dr. Harrington swung sideways in the seat and continued talking.

"My father died when I was a boy. He left us that big old house down there, and not much more. The family was young—I had two younger sisters—and there were a lot of things around the house that my mother was unable to do. So she'd call in Mr. Magnus.

"For a number of years, until I was old enough to do those chores myself, he was a fairly common sight around our house, and I got to know him pretty well. As well as anyone did, at any rate. I guess you could say we became friends, in a funny sort of way. Not that I was ever comfortable with him. There was always a certain measure of, what shall I say, wariness—fear, if you like. He was odd in his ways to begin with, the way solitary people often are. And then there was his leg."

"Leg?" said Cass.

"Yes. He has a wooden leg. You didn't know? They had to amputate his own as a result of his wounds in the war. I remember when he was working in our garden in the hot weather he often found it awkward, and there were times when he'd simply take it off and lay it on the grass beside him while he worked.

"Well, when you're young that sort of thing can make a pretty powerful impression. And the normal response is fear, I suppose. Fear of the strangeness, fear that contact with it might pass it on, like some sort of contagion.

"His voice was odd too—thin, shrill. I suspect now that it might have had something to do with the gassing he got in the war. All in all, he struck rather an odd figure even then. I can remember the stories that used to go around the school about him. Stories I for one knew were complete nonsense, but which I never had the courage to challenge."

Dr. Harrington lapsed into thought, fiddling with the lid of the toolbox on the seat beside him. The rain had started up again, drumming lightly on the roof of the car like restless fingers. Maddy seemed lost in space, staring out the window toward the light in the lower flat.

"What sort of stories?" Cass found himself asking, his voice suddenly sounding to him like a stranger's.

"Oh, the usual, I suppose. Rumors of dark and evil deeds—the sort of thing that has always sprung up around solitary, peculiar people. Over the course of history more than one poor soul has paid for their peculiarities with their life.

"Not that he wasn't strange. He was, and more so after his mother died. He kept more than ever to himself after that. Soon, most of the old people had moved out of the neighborhood or passed away, and the new ones moving in didn't much care to have this odd little man tinkering with their houses. He was getting on then too and not able to do the things he could once.

"In some ways, though, it seems to me that he's always been old. He must be at least ninety now, I'd imagine." He shook his head. "He'll probably outlive us all.

"Well, I guess we'd better push on. It's not getting any earlier, is it? It's been a pleasure meeting you, Cass. I trust I'll be seeing you again sometime." He leaned over, pushed open the passenger door, and pulled the seat forward to let Cass out.

"Good night," said Cass as he scrambled out onto the street.

"And thanks for the lift." He bent down and peered in at the shadowy figure in the backseat.

"Good night, Maddy," he said, realizing it was the first time he'd actually called her by name, and suddenly glad for the shadows.

As he crossed the street to the house, the car started up and drove off slowly down the street. He stood in the rain watching until it turned into a driveway just before the bend in the road; then he hurried into the house.

As he was walking up the dim stairwell to the second floor, he nearly knocked into something sitting on the landing. It was the small crystal pitcher he'd brought the milk down in. A cone of blue paper protruded from it. He took it out, held it to the light, and read in that thin, uncertain script the words: "Thank you. Arthur Magnus."

—— 12 ——

HE WOKE UP the next morning feeling as if Fischer had been emptying the butt sieve in his mouth while he slept. The fact that it was Saturday only slowly dawned on him. He could hear Alison moving around in the kitchen, smell toast, coffee.

He got up and hobbled to the window, his leg asleep. The sun had just crested the housetops on the next street over and was busy burning the dew off the lawns. There wasn't a sign of life yet, except for Mrs. Wharton's underclothes pegged demurely to the line next door, and the soft trickle of smoke from the garage chimney.

The crystal pitcher sat on the dresser, the note beside it. The paper was tissue thin, blue. The small, crabbed handwriting wavered like rippled water. There was a faint trace of scent when he held it to his nose. Lilac, like the old bush recently in bloom at the back of Mrs. Wharton's yard. Something stirred inside: a memory, the ghost of a memory.

Alison called from the kitchen: "Breakfast, Cass." He folded the paper in half and slipped it under the runner out of sight. The memory went with it.

As he splashed water on his face in the bathroom, he thought back to the night before, the conversation in the car. Rumors of dark and evil deeds, the doctor had said. What sort of dark and evil deeds, he wondered. Was that what Maddy had been about to tell him, why she had acted so strange before the car came? He felt her sitting there beside him in the shadows of the backseat.

"Maddy," he whispered to the wet reflection facing him in the mirror, tasting the word on his tongue. He ran the brush through his hair, studied the soft down of mustache forming on his upper lip, tempted now to reach for the razor and shave it off at last.

Alison was sitting hunched over her Blake eating peanut butter on toast when he came into the kitchen. The margins of the page were crammed with cryptic annotations that no one but she could possibly decipher.

"Morning, stranger," she said as she plucked the pencil from behind her ear and added yet another. She began reciting:

> Ah, Sun-flower! weary of time,
> Who countest the steps of the sun,
> Seeking after that sweet golden clime
> Where the traveler's journey is done.

As he shook cereal into his bowl he joined in on the rest:

Where the youth pined away with desire,
And the pale virgin shrouded with snow
Arise from their graves and aspire
Where my sunflower wishes to go.

"Well, well," she said, smiling up at him. "I'm impressed."

"Hey, it's nothing," he said as he emptied the last of the box of cereal into his bowl. "You hear this stuff a few hundred times, it starts to sink in."

Alison slumped back in her seat, clutching her chest.

"Ah," she groaned, "pierced to the quick by the rapier wit of Cass Parry. Imagine how I feel; it's like I've practically been living with this guy for the past three years." She leaned forward across the table, looking conspiratorial. "I'll tell you something, Cass—but don't laugh. Sometimes when I'm working alone in my room I actually start talking to him. No, listen, it gets worse," she whispered. "Sometimes he talks back."

"You're a sick woman. You know that, don't you, Mom?" He dug into his bowl of bran flakes, already adding cereal to his mental shopping list. Talk about sick. Most guys his age had their heads full of hot cars and cool girls, and here he was with backstitching and bran flakes. He must be doing something wrong. It was almost unnatural.

Alison finished up her coffee and started loading her things into the old leather satchel she carried. She had picked it up years before at a church rummage sale. It was covered with ancient and exotic travel stickers from places neither of them had ever been.

"I think I'll take old Billy Blake here for a walk over to the library. They phoned last night to say that a couple of books I'd requested had finally come in. I'll probably just stay for the morning. Maybe a change of scenery will help to shake some of the bats loose from the beams. I've got to get something going on this paper—and quick!"

She tucked her Blake down the side of the satchel. "Okay, old boy, you just have a nice little nap now so that you'll be all rested up for Alison once we get to the library." She went off to gather up the rest of her things.

"Toast's in the oven," she called from the other room.

The toast was in the oven all right. In fact, it looked as if it had been there for quite some time. It was curled up at the corners, and it crumbled all over the plate when he bit into it.

That afternoon he was working his first matinee. The way Zeke went on about the matinees, he felt like he was about to make a short social call on a firing squad or something.

Alison came in, pecked him lightly on the cheek, and wished him luck. He listened to the sound of her footsteps fading on the stairs when she left, the dull thud of the door.

As always, the house seemed to change radically once he was alone. Instantly it felt larger, with the largeness of things remembered from early childhood. Sounds intensified: the glasses chimed like church bells as he set them on the drainboard to dry.

He walked warily from room to room, as if to reclaim them, feeling suddenly like an intruder from another time. The solid old bits of furniture that had been left behind seemed rooted where they stood, while their own sad things seemed to hover in a half light, as if at any moment they might suddenly wink out, and the real rooms emerge. He could almost imagine the sound it might make—a soft pop like a fluorescent tube shattering. He could almost picture what those rooms would look like.

He stood in the doorway of his own room now, unable to enter. The ringed snake staring out at him from above the unmade bed seemed almost to be standing sentry there against him. He could hear Mr. Magnus moving around below: the creak of the floorboard as he passed into the kitchen; the shudder of pipes as the tap was turned on; a cupboard opening, closing; the low murmur of a radio.

And again that strange feeling came over him, the sudden sense that the house was haunted. But this time not simply by that presence puttering about quietly below. No, now for the first time Cass sensed that in some way he too was a ghost.

He escaped to the sun porch, the comfort of confusion, the world seen through windows.

The street was dead as usual. A few doors down a sprinkler fanned listlessly back and forth across a square of green carpeting that was pretending to be a lawn. Before and beyond it was more of the same: carpet, hedge, carpet, hedge, carpet.

And then there was this. The lawn a sea of decaying magnolia blooms and foot-high dandelions gone to seed, the hedge launching off wildly in all directions, like Maria Magistrale's hair on a bad day.

Part of him wanted to exult in that. At least this place wasn't like all the rest. At least it still had some semblance of reality to it. But another part of him blushed right down to the roots at the look of the place. What had Maddy and her father thought, delivering him home to this dive? Didn't he have some sort of responsibility for the place? After all, this was a little different than life above the Bluebird, where you expected the landlord to sweep the garbage from the sidewalk out front, and maybe even wander upstairs with a mop now and then to swab down the hall. And if he didn't, well, it certainly wasn't your problem. You just closed your eyes until you got inside your own place and promptly forgot about it.

Forgetting wasn't working here. Neither was blaming the landlord. Did he actually expect Mr. Magnus to do it? He kept seeing that strange old man standing in the darkened doorway, staring at him.

He did not so much think as act. It all happened in a white heat, his whole body rebelling against being pulled from the window and pushed into action.

He took the stairs down two at a time, pulled the porch door closed behind him, and hurried down the side of the house to the back. He'd never been back there before, and strongly suspected he wasn't supposed to be now. But he turned all that off as he pushed past the protesting gate and entered the small overgrown yard. For an instant an image flashed on his mind: a picture of half a dozen people sitting on wooden deck chairs talking, a thin man with a mustache looking over at him, a woman shielding her eyes against the sun, the sun glinting off the diamond-shaped window in the door of the garage. And then it was gone, and he was making his way up the narrow walk through the dry, groping fingers of the wild grass.

His feet sank in the newly turned soil as he took the rusty shears and rake from against the garage and started back. He kept his eyes fixed on the ground, his feet moving, afraid to look up, afraid that if he did, his resolve would instantly evaporate.

Back out front he attacked the hedge like a madman, lopping off the branches randomly, without pattern or plan. They fell noiselessly into the long grass. He took stabs at that too, shearing the dandelion heads with abandon. He worked feverishly, until his muscles ached and the sweat was streaming down his face, knowing all the while that he was doing battle with far more than the hedge and the lawn.

The green carnage lay everywhere. He raked it up and fed great armfuls of it to the battered tin tub from the side of the house, stamping it down with his feet. Then he went back with a calmer eye and corrected what he had done.

The job was less than perfect. The top of the hedge was all hills and valleys, and the ragged grass he uncovered beneath the blanket of rank magnolia blooms was a jaundiced yellow. Still, it was with a sense of satisfaction that he gathered up the second load and stomped it down into the tub.

It was as he was coaxing the garbage from the base of the bushes with the rake handle that he happened to glance over at the park.

There were three of them there, straddling their bikes in among the trees, watching him. They just stood there, motionless as statues, all the while he worked his way along the bushes dropping the stuff into the small box Mr. Magnus's last load of groceries had come in. He pretended the whole time not to notice them, but as he picked up the box he let his eyes drift in their direction again.

The one in the middle, the tall guy with the wraparound shades, gave him a sick smirk and showed him some teeth. That was supposed to make him wet his pants or something. Yesterday it might have, and tomorrow it might again, but right now he just turned his back on them and made his way up the walk. He put the box by the tub at the side of the house and took the rake and shears to the back. By the time he got back they were gone.

The park looked almost peaceful without them. The shadows under the trees were dappled with sunlight now, and from over in the playground came the rhythmic creak of a solitary rider on the swings. In the empty pool a workman was on hands and knees with a blowtorch and a bucket of tar, patching cracks in the spiderweb of seams that ran through the pool. The spider was nowhere in sight.

What did they want anyway? he wondered. What were they after? Were they simply trying to frighten him, or was there more?

As he started up the porch steps he thought he caught a movement out the corner of his eye. He turned to the window. The figurines sat there, impassive, immobile: the china dog and cat, the crystal unicorn, the stuffed bird on its dusty branch, the wooden monkeys with their steely eyes. But behind them now there was a light ripple of lace as the curtain settled into stillness again.

They were lined up halfway down the block by the time he arrived at the Palace. The box office was still a good twenty minutes from opening, but the noisy crowd of kids was already electric with anticipation. He could practically feel the sparks splashing off the cracked pavement as he walked past.

Jack was standing just inside the foyer doors sucking seriously on his dead cigar, watching the crowd with the wary suspicion of a general observing the enemy. Two large cardboard boxes sat on the ground at his feet. Cass practically had to crawl over them as Jack inched open the door to let him in.

"Afternoon, Mr. Grant."

Jack nodded at him noncommittally. "Here, give me a hand with these, will you, Parry?"

Giving him a hand meant that Jack pointed to where he wanted the boxes put and Cass did his best to drag them there. He'd tried lifting the first one. It felt as if it were bolted to the ground.

Fortunately Jack just wanted them inside the door, next to the ticket box. Both boxes, it turned out, were full of comics—that afternoon's giveaway. Almost every Saturday matinee there was a giveaway along with the price of admission, another of Jack's lures to reel the kids in. Candy bars, baseball cards, samples of one sort or another—whatever Jack had managed to dig up during the week. Today it was comics. It had probably seemed like a good idea at the time.

As he pulled the second box up alongside the first, Cass noticed that the writing on the side of the box was in Spanish. He didn't know what it said, but he knew it was Spanish. He didn't give it another thought as he went and retrieved his uniform from the drum of the sand ashtray and started to dress.

There was a whole different feel to the place. Jack had even lit his cigar. The gut-wrenching smell of it filled the lobby as Cass crossed to the stairs to take up his position.

He stole a quick peek at the candy counter, a little disappointed to see a strange girl behind the counter. She was pale and thin and worried-looking. She didn't even notice him as he passed; her eyes were glued to the lobby door.

Cass scurried upstairs to escape the craziness. There was still no sign of Zeke. Standing up there all alone on the floor, there seemed to be a strange sort of hush to the place. The hush of something holding its breath. It didn't exactly make him feel comfortable.

Somehow with the place empty you noticed the threadbare carpet more, the broken seats, the patches in the limp curtain covering the screen. If there was ever a place born to be in darkness it was the Palace.

Once, way back, it had apparently been one of the showpieces of the city. The only hint of its glory days now were the two gilt statues pedestaled high on the wall to either side of the screen: two young women, turbaned and strategically draped in robes. They looked down on the devastation unperturbed, one eye fixed steadfastly on the screen.

After a few minutes Zeke arrived, looking like he had just run the four-minute mile. He leaned back against the wall and closed his eyes. Downstairs, the candy-counter attendant was lining up box upon box of popcorn on the shelf behind the counter. A couple of minutes earlier Jack had escorted the cashier to the box office out front with her cashbox and rolls of tickets in hand. She would stay in there now for about ten minutes with the curtains drawn while she loaded up the ticket dispenser and the change machine.

At exactly one o'clock there was an ominous rumbling like thunder from out on the street. Zeke bounced off the wall, the front doors flew open, and a mad horde of kids teemed into the theater, scooping up the comics on their way through. Half of them headed for the candy counter, the rest flooded up the stairs to claim the choice seats. Within a matter of minutes the place was crawling with kids, yelling and jostling with one another against the backdrop of the Big Band music Jack piped through the speakers before the show.

By this time some of them had opened their comic books and discovered they were in Spanish. The news spread like brushfire through the theater. Pretty soon it started raining comic books. They flew into the air like a flock of startled birds, then plummeted quickly back into the crowd. Other kids tubed theirs up and made blow guns out of them, shooting soggy wads of newsprint at unsuspecting heads in front of them. A couple of fights broke out.

At last the lights went down, the crowd calmed, and the curtain made its way slowly across the screen in a series of spasmodic lurches that made you wonder if it was really going to make it this time. The screen flickered into life, and the film began.

Today's double bill was *The Wolf Man* and *The Spider*. *The Wolf Man* might have been a really terrifying movie when it first came out fifty or so years ago, but time had not been kind to it. There was more action outside on the street than there was in this movie. The natives began to grow noticeably restless, and it wasn't long before crushed pop cups and Spanish comic books started flying at the screen.

Zeke and Cass headed down the aisles, shining flashlights on delinquent faces, urging feet off the backs of seats, warning the offenders that if they didn't settle down, they'd be kicked out.

Every time they flashed to a shot of the full moon in the film and Lon Chaney looked up and gave it a worried look, wolf howls broke out all over the theater, magnified by comics tubed into megaphones. The noise grew so loud that half the time you couldn't hear the movie. Fischer left his post at the door and drifted halfway up the stairs, listening up into the dark.

A couple of minutes later Jack materialized at the top of the stairs. He took one long look around, shot Cass and Zeke a witting look, then hustled down the aisle to the front of the theater and up onto the stage in front of the screen. For a moment he was nothing more than a squat silhouette dwarfed by the suddenly monstrous figures on the screen, flailing his arms and trying to shout over the soundtrack.

Finally the projectionist caught on. The lights came up and the screen went dark. A chorus of boos and catcalls echoed through the theater. Jack spread his arms for silence, and finally got it. The floor of the stage was littered with crushed pop cups and comics that had been hurled at the screen.

"This is totally unacceptable," Jack said. He waited a few seconds for that to sink in as he ran his gaze over the sea of faces, all innocence now. "There are a few of you out there who are spoiling the movie for the rest who want to see it."

Who was he kidding? One look at the stage should have told him that he had a full-scale riot on his hands. "I'm warning you now that if this continues, if I get one more complaint,

I'll turn off the movie for good and clear the theater. Is that understood?"

He did up the button of his jacket as if he were locking the lid on the candy counter, and made his way slowly down the stairs and up the aisle. Halfway up, he pointed up to the projection booth. The lights went down, and the movie started up again. He didn't bother saying anything to Cass and Zeke as he went by, but as he hit the bottom of the stairs he whipped out his lighter and torched the end of his cigar. He was not happy.

After that the noise level dropped considerably, and there was only the occasional halfhearted wolf call from some stray that had wandered off from the pack. Every fifteen minutes or so Jack would open his door and dangle his head out for a listen, but he didn't actually emerge again until after the intermission, when he went over to refill his bucket with the popcorn gleanings.

The poor girl who had worked the candy counter had left ten minutes earlier, looking thoroughly shell-shocked by the whole experience. She made her way to the door, clutching her purse and glancing nervously over her shoulder. Fischer hadn't even bothered to look up as she was leaving, but she was no sooner out the door than he skittered over to the candy counter and scored a couple of candy bars before snapping shut the padlock that she had forgotten about in her frazzle. Then he ambled over, knocked on Jack's door, and politely handed him the key. That won him a fatherly pat on the shoulder. It was enough to turn your stomach.

The second movie, *The Spider*, won a more enthusiastic response from the crowd. It was a more recent movie, as recent as Jack got, anyway, and it was in color. There was enough gore to keep everyone happy, and there was no more popcorn or candy to throw around.

Finally the film ended, the lights came up, and the whole mass of screaming kids streamed out the doors like dishwater going down the drain. The only ones left to watch the curtain lurch closed were the golden girls. Perched there on their pedestals, they looked down dispassionately at the scene of destruction below.

— 13 —

THE CLEANUP was incredible. The place was like a war zone. There was garbage everywhere: crushed popcorn boxes, comics, candy wrappers, drink containers. As Cass and Zeke prowled the rows picking up the stuff, their feet kept sticking to the concrete floor, slick with spilled drinks. Someone would have to come in and swab down the floor before the seven o'clock show or some people were likely to get permanently glued to it before the end of the night.

When he finally emerged from the theater an hour later, he was surprised to discover the tail end of a sunny Saturday afternoon on the other side of the doors. Four hours in the strange underworld of the Palace, and you began to forget there was a whole other world out there.

He stood for a long moment staring into the display window with its worn poster and glossy stills from *The Spider*, waiting for his eyes to adjust to the light. As he strolled out into the full sunlight, he saw a giant web strung between the drugstore across the street and the service station on the opposite corner, with a couple of desiccated bodies dangling from the strands. He shook his head and it went away.

It was no wonder Zeke was a little weird. Working in that place did strange things to your head. It could have been a lot worse though. That could be Fischer standing up there in the dark with him. How was that for a scary thought?

The thought of Fischer had no sooner crossed his mind than he saw him. He was standing over in the service station parking lot, leaning against his motorbike, his cherry-red helmet gleaming in the sun. Cass thought briefly of waving, then thought better of it. What was Fischer doing there in the first place? He'd gotten out over an hour ago.

The answer lay right around the corner on a narrow strip of grass bordered by a low box hedge that ran along the side of the Palace. Someone was stretched out there, reading a book. The someone was Maddy.

She glanced up as Cass approached, and smiled. "Hi," she said, "I've been waiting for you. I was beginning to think I'd missed you."

"Cleanup," he explained, trying hard to hide his surprise at seeing her there. "It was a zoo in there today."

She nodded sympathetically as she put the book into her bag and scrambled to her feet.

Cass stole a look over his shoulder. Fischer was straddling his bike now, snapping the strap of his helmet closed. The visor hid his face.

Maddy pulled something out of her pocket as she stepped over the hedge.

"Here," she said, handing him the pack of cigarettes. "You dropped these in the car last night. I thought you might be going through withdrawal or something without them."

"Thanks." Over in the lot he could hear the motorcycle kick into life, the engine rev. He knocked one of the cigarettes free and stuck it in his mouth. He pictured Fischer tearing down the street behind them.

"Is there something wrong?" asked Maddy.

"No, nothing." He tapped his pockets for matches.

"They're in the pack."

"Right." For some reason the sound of the engine was growing fainter. When he looked back again, Fischer was gone. He touched the lit match to the end of the cigarette and breathed deeply.

They walked silently down the block, the busy noise of traffic becoming gradually replaced by the light rustle of leaves overhead, the distant clamor of children. He smoked, trying to appear proficient at the art.

"I wanted to thank you again for last night," said Maddy. "I mean waiting with me and all."

"No problem. I enjoyed meeting your father."

"He tends to go on sometimes. I hope he didn't bore you with all that stuff about Mr. Magnus."

"No. He didn't bore me at all." Again he sensed that she was on the verge of saying something, that the small talk was only so much smoke rising from what she really wanted to say.

The moment passed. They walked along in silence for a while, a silence that he already sensed was as much a part of her as it was of him. It curled and wound about them both, spinning delicate bonds between them.

He looked at the houses that lined the street. They were old houses, many of them run-down here, split into separate flats or rooms: half a dozen doorbells mounted on a piece of plywood by the door, battered trash cans huddled by the porch, curtains knotted open to the light. Familiar sights.

But already there were signs of the inevitable takeover. Here and there a building bought out, boarded up; the jarring sight of a sandblasted house with brass hardware wedged between the others, like a rich relative come to stay. Money moving in.

Old faces, wary faces, watched from the shadows of porches

as they passed. They would vanish along with the knotted curtains and battered tin cans in time. Closer to the park they were already a memory.

The cigarette was starting to make him feel sick. He flicked it onto the sidewalk in front of them and crushed it as they passed.

"To tell you the truth," he said, "I don't really smoke. I just found these last night during the cleanup." She didn't say anything, she just sort of looked at him and smiled, as if she'd known all along anyway. Still, it felt good to clear the air. The prospect of having to light up every time he saw her was just too nauseating to handle.

They were nearing the park now. The whole neighborhood had a different feel to it. The green he smelled was more than newly mown grass.

"You're not too thrilled with it—the neighborhood, I mean," said Maddy right out of the blue. He looked at her, she looked back, and for an instant he felt transparent, like that crystal unicorn on Mr. Magnus's windowsill.

"I don't mind it. It's all right."

"You're a pretty lousy liar, you know. Anyone ever tell you that?"

He gave her a look.

"It's your face," she said. "You don't have to say a word. You read like a book."

"Maybe you should stop now then. You might not like the next bit."

"Maybe. But I'm kind of curious about the ending." She just sort of threw the line away. He felt it flutter to the ground like the maple keys that littered the lawns. He kicked it along a little way, not wanting to let it go but afraid to bend and pick it up.

Up ahead on the corner he could see the fruit store. He

thought of Maria, then immediately of Sid draped all over the counter. Again he saw the guys standing in the park this morning, watching him.

The Magistrales' monster dog was out in the dirt yard behind the shop, sharpening its teeth on its chain. It looked up when it heard them coming. Something in its sad excuse for a mind went "Meat!" and it stood up, snarling. Cass smiled at it over the top of the fence as they went by. The dog went into hysterics. It made a mad lunge for the fence and almost broke its stupid neck as the short chain snapped taut and sent it spinning into the dirt. Then it did it all over again. This was not a bright dog.

As they rounded the corner Cass glanced automatically over in the direction of the pool. He could just make it out through the mesh fence that enclosed the tennis courts. There they were, buzzing around on their bikes.

Maddy caught the glance. "What is it?" she asked.

"Those guys at the pool. Who are they, do you know?"

"Yeah, the leader's a kid called Sid Spector. He lives over on the other side of the park somewhere. A real little juvenile delinquent, if you know what I mean. The rest of them I don't know. Just a bunch of bored rich kids looking for trouble. Why? They haven't given you any, have they?"

"Not yet," he said. "But I think they're warming up to it." He told her about the incident in the park last week, the dead bird in the mailbox. Something more than concern came into her eyes.

They stopped in front of the house. Maddy looked at the newly clipped hedge, the lawn, then him. "You?"

He nodded, running his hand across the sharp cut edges of the branches, plucking stray clippings from the hedge. "Look," he said, "there's something happening around here. Something strange. Those guys in the park, the kids on the street.

Whatever it is, this place is right at the center of it, which means that I'm there too, I guess."

He pushed open the gate. "Look, maybe you'd better go now," he said. "They might see you here."

"Wait, Cass." He turned around. "I don't care if they see me. Why don't you walk me home? It's just down the street."

"Okay."

Mrs. Wharton was out dusting her roses. She looked up as they went by and her eyes widened just a little.

"Let me tell you something," said Maddy as soon as they were out of earshot. "When I was a kid I used to be absolutely terrified of that house. I used to walk down the other side of the street rather than have to pass in front of those bushes, because I was convinced that one day Mr. Magnus would creep out from behind them and catch me.

"You know those strange little figurines he has on his windowsill? Well, I used to believe that those were all children he had taken and turned into animals, and I was sure that if he ever did catch me, that's what he would do to me.

"Kids still believe that stuff. And it's not just kids either. Oh, the adults will say things like he's gone senile and can't take care of himself anymore, that he should be put in a home where he can be properly cared for. But what they really mean is that they want rid of him because he's old, because he's odd, because he looks and acts a little strange. But basically because he frightens them, because they're afraid that if they come too close they'll somehow catch it too. In other words, because he's a witch, which is what the kids have been saying all along."

"A witch?"

She nodded. "That's what I was starting to tell you last night."

"But that's crazy."

"Of course it's crazy. People are crazy. Dad says that under the silk dresses and three-piece suits we're all still basically cavemen cowering in the dark. He says that if this were three hundred years ago, they'd have burned that old man at the stake long before now."

They had stopped in front of a house where a familiar black sports car was parked in the drive. Even without the car he might have recognized the house as Maddy's. It was not nearly as prim as its neighbors—the railing comfortably rusty, the flaking turquoise trim completely out of fashion.

"That's where Sid Spector and his gang come in," she said, glancing over at the park. "They feed kids' fears of the old man—and then feed off them. They scare the younger kids half to death with stories of what the old man is up to in his garage and what he'll do to them if he ever catches them. And then they promise they'll protect them from him—for a price. I know; it's not very long ago that I was one of those little kids. It was a different gang then, of course, a different Sid, but it doesn't much matter; they're all the same. They just change the names and faces around a little, that's all."

"Then that's what the money was for," said Cass, half to himself.

She nodded. An old wind chime made from chips of colored glass hung from the roof of the porch, making weird music in the wind.

"Even after I was old enough to know better, I still had a hard time walking past that house. Every time I came near it the little kid in me would start shaking, staring through the branches of the bushes, straining to see whatever might be waiting on the other side.

"Then last winter, a couple of months before you came, something happened that changed all that. Mr. Magnus was on his way back from the corner store one day with his buggy when a kid on a bike ran him down. Everyone said it was an accident, that the kid had skidded on a patch of ice while he was trying to go by. It was no accident, Cass. I saw the whole thing. The kid on the bike was Sid Spector.

"I was just getting off the bus when it happened. There was no one else around. Mr. Magnus was about halfway down the block when Sid appeared from out of nowhere and took a run at him from the top of the hill. He didn't try to slow down, he didn't swerve; he just rammed right into him. The buggy went flying, and Mr. Magnus with it. Sid took off like lightning.

"Mr. Magnus got up and started gathering up the groceries. I could see people standing at their windows watching him, but not one of them came out to help. So I went over. What else could I do? I just couldn't stand to leave him there all alone. He looked so pathetic.

"The buggy was a wreck. The wicker was all bashed in where the bike had hit it, and one of the wheels was broken. I helped him pile all the stuff back into it and then sort of dragged it back to the house with him. We lifted it onto the porch. He hardly looked at me the whole time.

"I could see that he was shaken up. He seemed confused; he kept looking in the buggy, making sure we hadn't left something on the street. The weird thing was that the thing he seemed most concerned about was this little bag of charcoal he'd bought.

"I didn't know what to do. I just stood there with him for a few minutes while he pulled himself together and started searching through his pockets for his keys. He asked me who I was and I told him. He recognized the name right away, and he asked me if I was Basil Harrington's daughter. When I told him yes, he started telling me about how he remembered my dad when he was a little boy and about the things they used to do together. It was like to him it had all happened just yesterday.

"Finally he found his keys. He told me he'd be all right, and he thanked me and asked me to say hello to my father for him. That was it. I left him standing there at his door and I went home.

"That was six months ago, and I haven't seen him since. But every time I walk by now I look for him in the window. That was how I first happened to see you standing up there in the sun porch."

It was his turn to look away. The starlings were swarming over by the pool, fighting over the garbage that Sid and the gang had left in their wake. He could see the bikes disappearing down the path on the far side of the park.

"There's only one thing that still bothers me," said Maddy, her words laced with the strange music that the wind woke in the chimes. "A little more than a month after the day I helped him home I noticed the smoke coming from the garage behind the house. That was obviously what the charcoal he'd been so worried about was for. I'd seen it before, of course, other years. We used to say he was cooking up stray dogs and cats, mixing potions, making spells. But now I started really watching the place. My bedroom window overlooks the lane, and every night when I get ready for bed I look over at the garage. He's always in there, Cass. Every night."

"I know."

"Well, if he's not mixing potions and making spells, then what on earth is he doing in there night after night?"

"I wish I knew."

"Do you really?" Her voice had dropped. She was looking, at him strangely. "Why don't we try and find out, then?"

He just stared at her.

"There's a small window in the side of the garage," she

said. "I know he's in there at night because I can see a light on inside. One night after work, why don't we try to steal a peek through that window?"

"Are you serious?" She was serious all right. "Look, Maddy, I've seen that window too. It's filthy. You'd never see a thing through it."

"Maybe. Maybe not. There's only one way to find out for sure, isn't there?"

She didn't wait for an answer. She turned and headed off up the walk to the house. The bits of broken glass sang in the breeze behind her as she disappeared through the door.

—— 14 ——

LATE SUNDAY NIGHT Cass lugged all the garbage, including the tin tub and the cardboard box of cuttings, out to the sidewalk in front of the hedge for the next day's pickup. When he emerged from the house on Monday morning, he found the tub overturned on the front lawn, the bags split, and half a week's worth of garbage strewn over the grass. Someone was trying to tell him something. It wasn't hard to guess who.

While he was down on hands and knees scooping the disgusting mess back into the tub, the mannequin couple that lived next door came out onto their porch with briefcases in hand and papers tucked dutifully under their arms. As they came down the steps they saw him squatting there on the lawn, surrounded by eggshells and lemon rinds. The brief glimmer of surprise that lit their plaster features settled almost instantly into a dull, studied indifference. They climbed into their car and drove off.

That look stayed with him for the rest of the day. It was not just the neighbors' look. It was the look the houses wore on their smug, sandblasted faces, the look of the kids in the park, the flat, superior expression the entire neighborhood reserved for the house and whoever happened to live in it. It made him sicker than gathering the rotten garbage off the lawn had.

He got home a little after four. He'd wanted to pick up a few things for dinner at Magistrale's, but when he got off the bus he noticed a black bike sprawled on the sidewalk in front of the store. From the opposite side of the street he could see through the plate glass window. Sid Spector was leaning up against the vegetable counter studying Maria's spraying technique and admiring himself in the convex mirror.

Cass imagined himself marching right across the street and into the store, his body swelling to twice its size, sudden muscles straining the seams of his shirt, a thatch of thick hair blooming on his bare chest, like Lon Chaney going through his werewolf changes. He imagined himself bursting into the store and with one wicked blow laying the creep out flat on the lettuces for what he and his buddies had done with the garbage that morning.

He kept imagining it in all its bloody glory while he walked quickly down the opposite side of the street along the edge of the park. The wading pool was deserted, bits of broken glass gleaming in the sun. A couple of kids were abusing the teeter-totters and someone was slowly scaling the rungs of the corkscrew slide. A couple in sweat bands and tennis whites were busy at the tennis court, lobbing the ball back and forth to each other over the net. An old man sat on a bench nearby looking bored. He had a right to.

The little girl on the tricycle was out on patrol. Despite the heat, she was wearing a woolen sweater and matching hat that had "Grandma made me" written all over them. She was parked at the edge of the newly trimmed hedge, obviously wondering what had happened to the jungle that had been there just a couple of days before.

It was surprising, actually, what a change that brief burst of frenzy had made to the house. It looked almost dignified in a down-at-the-heels sort of way, like a proud old lady in a slightly shabby dress. Especially now with the ivy out, the glossy green leaves concealing all the infirmities that winter had revealed.

"Hello," he said to the girl as he picked up the empty tin tub from in front of the bushes. She eyed him narrowly, her face flushed with heat.

"A little hot for a hat today, don't you think?"

She looked briefly down at the heavy sweater, then back up at him. Her eyes opened a crack and she cast a quick backward glance in the direction of her house.

"He's going to eat you, you know," she said.

"Pardon me?"

"He's going to put you in his oven and eat you all up."

"Who?"

She nodded toward the house. "Him."

"Who told you that nonsense?"

She gave him a long, searching look, then whirled the bike around and pedaled off up the street, leaving the question hanging unanswered in the air.

He left the tub in the shade at the side of the house. A small box was waiting just inside the door of the porch when he went in. A quart of milk, a loaf of bread, a small jar of jam, a tub of margarine. Was that what he lived on, bread and jam? With the occasional roasted child thrown in, of course, just for a change.

He glanced back at the sidewalk. The little girl had resumed

her post at the edge of the property. He could just see the top
of her head down to her eyes, which were peering intently
over the hedge in the direction of the porch. She had taken
off her hat.

He picked up the box and let himself into the house. As he
went to set it down on the mat in front of the door, he heard
the dry rasp of a cough, the muffled sound of music through
the door. The image of the snake devouring its tail leaped
into his mind, the thought of tonight.

He's going to eat you, you know.

He set the box down quickly before the door and slipped
upstairs as noiselessly as a ghost.

Blake apparently hadn't had too much use for mundane things
like money. He was far too busy writing poetry and com-
muning with the spirit world for that sort of thing. The only
way his wife, Catherine, could get it into his head that he
should maybe leave off with the spirits for a little while and
make some money was by putting an empty plate in front of
him at dinner. That usually did the trick.

The condition was contagious. Ever since Alison had started
working on the paper in earnest again, Cass swore she hadn't
touched down once. It wasn't until that night that she'd actually noticed that there was anything different about the front
of the house. All through dinner she kept talking about the
pivotal role of *The Book of Thel* in the development of Blake's
idea of a higher innocence beyond the world of experience,
as if he had even the vaguest idea of what she was talking
about. When he came in to kiss her good-bye she was still
sitting at the table, surrounded by dirty dishes, feverishly making notes on a paper napkin.

The bow tie wasn't in the inside pocket of his uniform, where he was sure he'd left it. He went through all the pockets twice in case he'd put it in another by mistake, then went back and felt around in the hollow bottom of the ashtray on the off chance that it might have fallen out.

He had just settled the lid back in place when the door of the anteroom swung open and Fischer breezed in. He had his cherry-red helmet in one hand and his freshly cleaned uniform under plastic in the other. He stopped short, then walked past without a word as Cass stood there, pretending to be studying something very significant in the sand.

As time ticked down and he failed to turn up the tie, it became all too apparent that he was going to have to go and get a new one from Jack. There was something very close to a smirk on Fischer's face as Cass crossed the lobby and rapped twice on the metal-plated door. After what had happened at the matinee on Saturday, Jack was already a little less than thrilled with him. This was going to go over like a lead balloon.

Finally the muffled voice inside called him in. The place smelled like a pizza parlor. Jack was busy eating his dinner. He had a paper napkin tucked into his collar and a half-eaten piece of pizza in his hand. The box was open on the desk in front of him.

"Yeah, what do you want, Parry?" He didn't bother to stop eating while he asked the question.

Cass explained the problem with the tie. Jack gave him a look, took a couple of more pulls from his piece of pizza, and discarded the rest in the boneyard of crusts in the lid of the box. He yanked the napkin off and wiped his face and hands on it.

As he started going through the drawers, he asked Cass if he thought bow ties grew on trees or something. He finally found the box right at the back of the bottom drawer. It was in pretty rough shape. He took the lid off, took out a tie, and rubbed the dust off on his sleeve. He tossed it over to him.

"I should take this out of your pay," he said.

"Yes, sir." The crappy thing was probably worth all of fifty cents. This time he asked him if he thought money grew on trees.

"No, sir." He clipped the tie in place.

"That hair's getting a little long."

He let that one go by. His eyes darted around the room, like a squirrel caught in a cage, settling finally on a spot in the wall just above Jack's head. A slight crack ran from a hole where a picture had once hung. He studied the crack, thinking of the crack in his bedroom ceiling. But as he followed the creeping line across the wall a strange feeling of foreboding suddenly rose up in him, and with it the jagged fragments of a dream he had completely forgotten until now. The uniform felt dank and cold against him. The floor went soft and soggy underfoot. He was only vaguely aware of Jack's voice calling from beyond the welling darkness.

"Parry?" He was looking at him strangely. "You sick or something?"

"No, sir."

"I said you could go now."

"Yes, sir. Thank you, sir." He had to stop his arm from swinging up in a salute as he turned to go.

The movie that night was *Sunset Boulevard.* Jack had given it four stars in the program flyer. At least three of those stars should have been for strangeness.

This was one weird picture. Most of the movie takes place in the mansion of this crazy old silent-film actress. She has shut out the world and surrounded herself with memories of herself in her prime; and every night she sits in the dark and screens the silent films she starred in over and over again.

"We didn't need dialogue. We had faces then."

Completely by chance, a struggling young writer stumbles into this strange, static world. And he is gradually coaxed into staying with her, initially to work on this script of *Salome* she has written, which she believes will be the vehicle for her big comeback. Of course, she falls in love with him. And when he finally tries to break free from her and rejoin the real world, she kills him. In the closing scene the police, accompanied by hordes of reporters and cameramen, come to take her away. But in her madness she believes that it is the film crew come to shoot the climax of her *Salome*.

"I'm ready for my close-up, Mr. De Mille."

The movie was weird enough on its own, but all the way through it Cass kept getting these sudden flashes as one fragment after another from his dream bobbed to the surface of consciousness: the sudden smell of smoke in the air, the sense that the low walls flanking the aisle were suddenly looming up over him, closing in, the crazy feeling that at any moment a light might wink on and he would see someone bent over a book at the base of a muddy wall. And the ring wound around his finger would be a snake swallowing its tail.

Intermission came and went. Maddy and he still hadn't arranged how and where they were going to meet that night, and it was beginning to look like they wouldn't get the chance. Fischer seemed to be spending more time than ever hovering around the candy counter, making a nuisance of himself. Cass took at least half a dozen trips to the can, hoping to get a chance to talk to her on the way back. But when Fischer wasn't right there, he was buzzing around close by.

Maddy started into the cleanup. At one point while she was in behind the popcorn machine filling up the napkin dispenser, she coughed and caught Cass's eye as he stood at his post at the top of the stairs. She wrote something on one of the napkins and slipped it into the dispenser, then tucked a handful in over top of it. She set the dispenser down on the clean countertop beside the machine and continued with her cleanup. Ten minutes later she disappeared out the front door.

His chance came when Jack and Fischer went to walk the money over to the night deposit. He scurried downstairs, scooped a handful of napkins from the dispenser, and fanned through them until he found the one she'd written on. He slipped it into his pocket, replaced the rest, and quickly headed back upstairs. By the light of the flashlight he read:

> *Everything fixed for tonight. Too dangerous to meet here. I'll wait for you in the lane behind the houses. Hurry!*

He flicked out the flashlight and felt the dark wash over him.

The street was empty as he neared the lane. Crates of rotting vegetables were stacked outside the fence of the grocery store for the morning pickup. A dull light from a window upstairs where the Magistrales lived leaked down into the dirt yard behind the store and ran along as far as the small lot beyond it, where the rusted shell of an old car hung in the shadows. Beyond that point the night held sway.

Cass took a deep breath and started down the lane. As he picked his way tentatively along the rutted ground, small pits and potholes swelled into dangerous chasms in the dark. His belly knotted into a ball as he imagined the Magistrales' monster dog skulking in the shadows somewhere. He caught himself glancing repeatedly back at the street like a swimmer in strange water seeking out the shore. He felt for the flashlight in his pocket.

As he drew even with the lot, a shadow detached itself from the rusted remains of the car. For a second it took on the lean, sinister shape of the doberman. His heart stopped—and at that moment it spoke, resolving itself instantly into the familiar figure of Maddy.

"What took you so long?" she said. "I was beginning to wonder if you'd found the note."

"Sorry. Jack collared me on the way out. I got away as quickly as I could."

"I heard him go in about ten minutes ago. We'd better hurry. My dad will be wondering what's keeping me."

They left the dim halo of light behind and crept on into the dark of the lane. Maddy had latched onto the sleeve of his jacket and was practically pulling him along. The lights in most of the houses were out, their occupants asleep. The one in his own room was on, though, like a single eye opened onto the night. He could make out the pattern of the wallpaper through the window, the pink pebbleglass of the overhead light, the dark corner of the dresser. He had the sudden sense that it was someone else's room, not his own at all, and as they crept quietly along the lane he kept looking up at it, as if the real occupant might at any moment appear.

Faint slivers of light outlined the door of the dilapidated garage. The lush weeds before it bristled at the intruders' approach, catching at their legs like silent green sentries. They made their way past them over to the old fence that stood at the entrance to the crawlspace running alongside the garage. With a sharp tug the slack wire fence gave way. Maddy pushed it aside, and turning sideways squeezed through the narrow opening. With one last look back at the street, he turned and followed her.

There was barely enough room between the wall of the garage and Mrs. Wharton's fence to admit his shoulders. It was pitch black, the ground was wet and weedy, and there was a strong smell of leaf mold and the rank odor of decaying lilac from the large bush by the fence.

His heart was hammering crazily in his chest and his breath came quick and curdled with fear. The sharp copper taste of it was on his tongue as he crept along behind the shadow ahead of him.

Halfway along the crawlspace, under the window set in the side of the garage, there was a pale pool of light. Maddy rematerialized as she crawled into it and turned to wait for him. They knelt there with their ears pressed to the wall, listening for a long time before they summoned up enough courage to ease themselves slowly up the side of the wall and attempted to peer through the window.

It was useless; under the wire grating the glass was caked with years of dirt and grime, impossible to penetrate. Short of removing the screen and wiping the glass, there was no way they could see through. They slid back down to the ground, defeated.

It was as they were kneeling in the damp weeds, hearing small noises from inside the garage and barely daring to breathe, let alone discuss what they should do next, that Cass noticed a knothole in one of the boards that ran beneath the window, dimly outlined in the dark. It was only a small hole, and the pencil shaft of light that escaped it was quickly swallowed in the larger light of the window.

Without a word he cautiously eased himself up to it until his face lay in the light. Then he pressed his eye slowly to the hole.

At first he could not quite believe the amazing scene that sprang into view. It felt for one impossible instant as if he were looking not through a hole in a garage wall, but back through a sudden gap in time.

Mr. Magnus was standing near the front of the garage with his back to him, bent over a squat potbellied stove from which a length of stovepipe launched off awkwardly into the ceiling.

He was wearing a tattered dressing gown trimmed with what looked like satin, his thin white hair hanging over the collar. A single bare bulb in the ceiling behind him cast his weedy shadow on the wall. Beside him on the floor stood a bag of charcoal with a ragged gash in its side. Some of the charcoal had spilled onto the dirt floor. Against the wall behind the bag lay the crumpled remains of several others.

Except for the relatively open space around the stove, the rest of the garage was an incredible chaos of junk and clutter. Beyond the dim island of light cast by the bare bulb, the shadows massed and the chaos grew complete.

There were dusty pieces of furniture flung randomly on top of one another, as if the victims of some long-forgotten catastrophe. Here a pile of broken picture frames, there the remnants of half a dozen clocks and radios in varying degrees of disrepair. A workbench littered with lumber stood in the shadows on the wall opposite, the wall above it bristling with pronged and pointed tools made menacing by the dark.

Close by the stove, still in the weak circle of light, rows of rough shelves lined the wall, cluttered with dusty bottles of every size and shape, each one labeled and lidded and housing who knew what within it. They continued onto a round wooden table littered with flasks and beakers, basins and phials, funnels and ladles, and in their midst an ancient set of scales.

All this time the old man had been standing motionless before the stove. Now he moved to one side, plucked a small metal shovel from the table, and scooped a shovelful of charcoal from the bag. In doing so, he revealed a large glass vessel shaped like an enormous egg nestled in an opening on the top of the stove.

Cass gaped in astonishment, for something was moving inside the vessel. Tongues of luminous color lapped against the inner surface of the glass like liquid jewels. Sapphire and emerald, ruby and amethyst, coiling and curling against the glass as if they were alive. It was unlike anything he had ever seen.

He instinctively drew back from the hole and was momentarily shocked to find himself crouched in the narrow crawlspace in the dark, with Maddy by his side.

She gave him a strange look, then maneuvered herself over a little in the cramped space and put her own eye to the hole. He felt her body tense against his, heard the slight gasp as she too took in the sight.

Then, as he was shifting over slightly to give her more room, his knee came down hard on something sharp hidden in the weeds. It bit deeply into his leg, and before he could stop himself he cried out with the pain.

For a brief instant things seemed to stay suspended in time. Then Maddy sprang back from the hole.

"He's heard us," she cried. "Let's get out of here, quick."

And suddenly he was scrambling madly along the crawlspace, bumping off the wall and the fence, panicked, the pain knifing up his leg, and Maddy pushing him desperately on from behind.

Somehow they squeezed back through the narrow opening in the fence at the head of the passageway. But even as they did, a voice burst out behind them.

"You there. What are you doing?"

They launched off in opposite directions without so much as a word passing between them. Maddy disappeared down the lane and over a fence, while Cass raced breathlessly until he had reached the head of the lane and the darkened windows of the Magistrales' store.

He crouched by the crates of rotting vegetables to catch his breath. His leg felt limp. By the light of the streetlamp he saw the deep gash just below the knee, the blood dripping lazily onto the loose lid of one of the crates. He felt suddenly faint, as if he might keel over right there on the sidewalk. Then he clamped the crumpled paper napkin he found in his pocket down on top of it, and breathed deeply until the feeling finally passed.

Alison was sleeping when he got in. He washed the wound off in the bathroom and bandaged it. He was still limp with shock as he peeled off his clothes in the darkened bedroom and crawled beneath the refuge of the covers.

Below, there was silence. His eyes sought out the crack in the shadows of the ceiling, found it, followed it, and felt it slowly draw him deep inside itself to sleep.

—— 15 ——

IT WAS no use; it wasn't there. Cass backed lamely out of the narrow passageway on his wounded knee. Where could it have gone?

He dropped the jagged bottom of the broken pop bottle he'd uncovered lurking in among the weeds onto the ground. It grinned up at him, its victim, with a ring of ragged teeth. He kicked it over and stamped it down into a harmless disc of green glass in the ground.

He glanced up to discover Mrs. Wharton emerging onto her back porch. She had obviously seen him back there and was out investigating. She kept one eye on him while she swept the maple keys from her porch. He swore the woman spent half her time stationed at her window, broom in hand. He left her there sweeping and no doubt wondering what he had been up to, and made his way slowly over to Maddy's house.

The crates were still sitting by the fence at the head of the lane, half a dozen drops of dried blood on a dangling lid the only witness to what had happened the night before. He saw several more drops on his way down the street. How strange to think that short hours earlier he had been limping along here in the dark, his leg bleeding and his heart racing. And now it was past and the same street was bright with sunlight, the park alive with children's laughter, and he was likely the only one who even noticed the dull red spots on the sidewalk or knew what they were.

He had cleaned the cut out again this morning and changed the bandage while Alison slept. The first had nearly soaked through in the night. He should probably have a doctor look at it, but the bleeding had all but stopped now, and he would as soon keep the whole business quiet if he could.

The old wind chime started tinkling as soon as he approached the steps and kept it up all the while he was waiting for someone to answer the bell. When the door finally did open, it was Maddy who stood there. She had the vague, remote look of someone who has just awakened. It didn't help that she wasn't wearing her glasses.

"Oh, hi, Cass," she said, squinting at him. "Come on in." She cleaned her glasses on the tail of the untucked white shirt she was wearing, obviously her father's, and put them on. Her face locked instantly into place.

"I woke you up," he said.

"No, I always look like this. Come on in, will you?" She watched him hobble painfully into the house and closed the door quietly behind him. Her tone abruptly changed.

"Are you all right?" she asked, looking down at the leg.

He nodded. "I cut myself on a piece of broken glass last night. Look, I'm sorry I—"

"Don't be crazy. Come on, I'll put on some tea and we can talk." She headed off down the wide hall in her bare feet and he followed after her.

The house, though large, was comfortably disordered. Stray shoes lay on sections of newspaper strewn down one side of the hall. An old black telephone sat brooding on a basket of clean laundry like a nesting bird. Half a dozen jackets were humped over the newel post at the foot of the stairs.

Opposite the stairs, a door opened off the hall. He caught a glimpse of a large dim room. The walls were lined with shelves of books from floor to ceiling, and an old dark wooden desk stood in the center of the room, piled high with more. An old skull sat among them, looking a little overwhelmed by it all.

Maddy was pouring water into a kettle as he came into the kitchen. She set it on the stove and switched on the gas. Tongues of blue flame leaped up from the burner. A newspaper was spread out on the kitchen table along with a few dirty dishes. His eye lingered on the cup that held the scooped-out shell of an egg.

Maddy whisked the things away and asked him to sit down. He limped over to a chair and sat, his sore leg stretched out straight in front of him, throbbing like crazy now. Maddy set out cups, poured the steaming water into a teapot and sat down opposite him. By the second cup she had started to come around. The puffiness of sleep had all but vanished from her face and her eyes had opened. She ran her finger lightly along the fluted rim of the cup.

"That was close," she said finally.

"Too close. Look, Maddy, I really am sorry."

"Will you stop saying that. It wasn't your fault. It was an accident. And we did manage to get a look inside, at least."

He nodded. The view through the knothole leaped to mind like the fragment of a dream. "What do you think he was up to in there?"

"I don't know. It looked like some sort of an old chemistry lab or something—all those bottles and beakers all over the place."

"And did you see that glass thing on the stove? What on earth was going on inside that thing? It looked alive."

"I don't know. It all happened too fast. I'm not sure what I saw."

Cass poured more tea into his cup, added a splash of milk, and sat there stirring the silence awhile.

"There's a problem," he said at last.

Maddy looked up from her tea. "What?"

"My flashlight. When I went through my stuff this morning, it wasn't there. I must have dropped it last night."

"Oh no."

"I went back just before I came over here," he said. "It's not there."

He watched her finger as it made its slow circuit around the rim of the cup.

"Maybe you didn't drop it in there," she said. "Maybe you lost it somewhere along the way."

"No. I had it when I started down the lane. I can remember feeling for it in my pocket."

"Then maybe it fell out after, when you were running up the lane."

"Maybe. But it's not there now. I looked."

"Well, there's no point in worrying about it, I guess. There's nothing we can do about it now anyway. And even if he did find it, he still won't know who it belongs to unless he got a good look at us, and I don't think he did."

"I hope you're right."

"So do I," she said. "So do I."

Recently the bust of Blake had disappeared from the mantelpiece. Alison had moved it into her room and set it facing her across the typewriter for inspiration. He had his eyes closed, which was probably all for the best; Alison's room was not a pretty sight.

Alison had already left by the time Cass got back in. She had scrawled him a note, which she'd left propped between the salt and pepper penguins on the kitchen table. It was indecipherable as always, but it likely said she was going to the library to catch up on the material that they had managed to get for her over the past week, and that she would be home by four or so to help with dinner. He struggled to make out a familiar word or two among the hieroglyphs, gave up, and left it lying faceup on the table until later.

Alison's bedroom door was open. Her bed, as usual, was all but unmade. She had simply pulled the spread up over the rumpled sheets. Out of sight, out of mind. Her Miss Maid uniform was hanging from the handle of the closet. A couple of pairs of pants, dirty but not quite dirty enough to qualify as laundry yet, were draped over the top of the door. Books sprouting strips of torn typing paper were piled on her dresser and on the floor beside the bed. The Paper, such as it was, lay scattered in numbered sections around the room.

The room smelled of incense and stale tobacco smoke. The Las Vegas Hilton ashtray that Murray had "liberated" from someone's garbage was full. The cup of coffee beside it was growing something green inside it. The typing table was pushed up against the window, which boasted a scenic view of the brickwork on the side of Mrs. Wharton's house, so close you could reach out and touch it. Blake sat on the sill, looking aloof from it all.

Cass managed to muscle the window open a crack to let a little fresh air in. It was something more than passing strange that Alison was actually making her living at the moment cleaning people's houses. If the Miss Maid people ever got a peek at this room, they'd probably pass out on the spot.

He emptied the ashtray into the toilet and dumped the coffee down the kitchen sink. He found a dusty bottle of aspirin languishing in the cupboard behind the huge bottle of fish oil that Alison gagged down every now and then when she was trying to be healthy. He washed down a couple of the aspirin with warm water, and went to lie down on his bed to rest the leg.

The room was bright with sunlight. It felt warm on his face as he lay looking up at the ceiling, the liquid dance of sunlight on the walls.

It felt good to be off the leg. It was a funny thing with pain, the way it sort of wrapped you up in itself. So that somehow all of this, all that had happened over the past day was part of that pain. And he could no more shake it from his mind than he could rid himself of the dull, persistent throb in his leg and the not-unpleasant warmth that was definitely more than the sun on his face.

His mind would not rest. It kept flitting about as restlessly as the sunlight on the ceiling, kept wanting to crawl back up that narrow passageway and peek through that hole in the wall. It kept wanting to take that ring of ragged teeth from the weeds and remove it from the scene, kept wanting to creep down there again in daylight and discover the flashlight right where he had dropped it.

He had almost dozed off, when the sound of a power motor

sputtering into life outside brought him back suddenly. He found himself staring up at the picture of the snake, leaning out from the wall above him.

The longer he stared at it now, the more lifelike the snake appeared, its red and green scales almost iridescent in the sunlight, the teeth gleaming around its tail until it seemed as if it had detached itself completely from the surface of the paper and lay there twitching under the glass, fixing him with its golden eye.

His eye followed the circle that it made, round and round, no beginning, no end, and in his mind he saw Maddy running her finger slowly around the rim of the cup, saw the ring of ragged teeth grinning up at him from the weeds.

Death from life, life from death.

He felt himself starting to drift, the lids of his eyes suddenly leaden, impossible to keep open. Perhaps it was the aspirin making him feel so tired. The dull, steady drone of the mower outside. The sun warm on his face. He thought vaguely that he should get up, get something to eat, but just lay there instead, staring dozily up at the ceiling.

He watched the crack in the ceiling weaving its way toward the corner near the window, gradually widening as it went, so that the gap in the wall near the window was like its head. And as he watched, the part that was its tail shifted and began to edge ever so slowly toward the wall. And the dark head turned, flicked out a lightning tongue, and began to glide to meet it, silently, cautiously, as though it were stalking prey.

The drone of the mower grew louder somehow, more insistent, edged with sudden danger. The direction of the sound had altered, so that now it seemed to fuse with the scene overhead. He felt himself slowly turning, as if he were sliding down the corkscrew slide in the park. His body was one with the bed, but the bed hard against his back now, unyielding, and his mouth as dry as dust.

The drone of the motor grew steadily louder, pushing back the walls of the room, dissolving the ceiling into sky. He watched the snake's mouth slowly widen around the tail, felt the searing pain in his own leg as the teeth took hold. Then the dark enfolded him and he fell asleep.

He was lying flat on his back in a muddy hole. High overhead in an impossibly blue sky a plane was circling, around and around, like a bee buzzing relentlessly around a flower. It's a signal, he thought, a signal of some sort. He could see the markings crystal clear on the wing, hear the dark, somehow sinister sound it made. Off to the left, lower in the sky, he could see an observation balloon. It hung motionless in the air, the tether taut beneath it, anchoring it like an umbilicus to the ground. Reconnaissance. What would it look like from up there, he wondered, in the clear, cool air, with the sky stretching endlessly all around? You could see up over the side of the ridge, no doubt, to farmland and countryside spread out like a dream quilt in the distance. And this, this dead brown strip of mud and slime, was simply a brief disturbance of the dream. The slight unraveling of a seam.

Somewhere nearby there was a moan. It was faint, thin, the sound a child makes in its sleep when nightmares come. He would not let himself look down, look around. Better to lose himself in the slow, endless circuit of the plane overhead, better to fancy himself drifting easily on the wind, up over the ridge and down into that green world on the other side alive with the chatter of birds, the barking of dogs, the contented lowing of cattle. Here no birds sang—there was nothing, nothing but the unbearable stillness of earth itself holding its breath, now and then disrupted by the moans of the dying.

The plane broke off its circling and launched off into the blue. Somewhere a lone gun boomed. He could not feel his legs, could not shift his position. It was as if his body had rooted itself in the muddy soil. He turned his head to one side to assure himself that he could still move that at least. On the far side of the hole his eye fell on a tangled mass of metal that had been the gun placement. Hard by, the mud humped up and made a man shape, then another, curled up like babes in a cot. A helmet lay upturned on the ground beside him—like a bowl set out for supper, he thought. And suddenly his mother was there, smiling tenderly and blowing lightly on a steaming spoon before she brought it to his lips. He opened his mouth slightly—and closed on air. When he opened his eyes she was gone. A puddle of bright red water had taken her place, the sun dancing off its surface like a jewel. Somewhere desperately nearby, that moaning again. But now, stitched in with it, another sound. Someone coming. Perhaps the stretcher bearers moving quietly among the wounded and the dead. Perhaps the enemy, creeping in for the kill. He closed his eyes and lay there motionless, listening as the sound drew ever nearer. . . .

Cass was jerked awake by the sound of someone banging on the door. He stirred, and the dream shattered like delicate crystal, breaking into separate meaningless fragments. *A balloon. A sleeping baby.* His forehead was beaded with sweat and his heart was racing as though he'd just run a mile. He sat up and swung his legs over the side of the bed, rubbing the sleep from his eyes.

He glanced at the clock. Three o'clock. It must be Alison, back from the library.

"Be right there," he called through the door, knocking the sheets back into shape, trying to pull himself together so she wouldn't think he was sick or something. Nurse Alison was the last thing he needed.

The leg actually didn't feel that bad right now, just sort of warm and numb. Likely gangrene setting in, a small voice at the back of his mind muttered cheerfully. He made his way to the door, trying hard not to hobble, shaking the last shards of the dream loose. *A plane. A pool of water. Blue sky. Blood.*

Blood?

He took a deep breath, turned the lock, and pulled open the door, fully expecting to find Alison standing there on the landing rooting through her bag for her key.

Instead, he found himself staring into a blinding beam of light. It hung there for an instant in the air before his eyes, then there was a soft click and it vanished. Standing there on the top step, holding the missing flashlight in his liver-spotted hand, stood Mr. Magnus. They studied each other silently for a few moments that seemed, to Cass, to stretch on forever. Finally Mr. Magnus said in a chill voice,

"I believe this is yours." And he held the flashlight out to him.

Cass couldn't have lied right then if he'd tried. He just reached out and took it from the old man, afraid to meet his eyes. But how did he know it was his?

"I thought so," said Mr. Magnus. "What were you doing back there, you and that other one?"

"Nothing," he said. It was a stupid thing to say.

"Snooping," said the old man. "That's what you were doing. Nosing about in other people's business. Well, I won't have it, do you hear me? I won't have it."

He was shaking with anger, his face going all red and blotchy, his hand clutching the banister to steady himself. He looked like he might have a heart attack or something.

"Look, I'm sorry," said Cass. "We didn't mean any harm. Really. We were just—"

"Save your breath, young man. I know well enough what you were doing. Spying." He had somehow managed to turn himself around on the step without falling down the stairs. "Well, I won't have spies under my roof. Do you hear me?"

It was pretty hard not to hear him. He was practically screaming.

"I want you out, do you understand me? You and your mother. By the end of the month." He started working his way down the stairs sideways, one hand gripping the railing, the other leaning heavily on the cane as he led with his wooden leg.

Cass started down the first step after him. "Wait," he pleaded. "You can't do that."

The old man swung around and fixed him with a piercing glare.

"Oh, can't I?" he said. "We'll see."

It was Monday night. Fischer was on the door, watching him out of the corner of his eye while he pretended to count the stubs. Zeke was upstairs on the floor. Jack's door was closed.

Cass eased his way painfully down the stairs, wincing each time he had to set his full weight down on the leg. He had more than a sneaking suspicion that it had become infected. The skin around the cut had turned a livid red, tender to the touch. He could barely stand the brushing of his pants against it.

It was sheer hell tonight, having to stand up there in the dark, too uncomfortable to get lost in the movie and wanting nothing more in the world than to just lie down on the floor and fall asleep. To top it all off, today happened to be the anniversary of the great silent film director D. W. Griffith's death, and in honor of the occasion Jack had decided to show the full, uncut version of his masterpiece *Intolerance*. Nineteen sixteen had been a long time ago, and the D. W. Griffith's fan club had fallen on hard times. There were about a dozen people in the theater, sitting doggedly through three hours of silence. It was when he caught himself almost nodding off on his feet for the second time that Cass decided to go down to the john and splash some water on his face.

He could feel Fischer's eyes all over him as he limped across the lobby. Maddy was buried in a book and didn't notice him go by.

The washroom was empty, of course. The tile floor was gritty with sand. Obviously some bright kid had done the sand-in-the-hand-dryer number over the weekend. It was a cute trick. You turned the hand-dryer nozzle up, loaded it with handfuls of sand from the ashtray, and turned it on. The sand flew all over the place, and the machine usually broke. It was the sort of thing he could picture Sid and his moron friends doing for a laugh.

He set his flashlight down on the edge of the sink, turned on the tap, and doused his face with water. He ran his wet hands over the back of his neck and through his hair. The towel dispenser had run out. The front end of the loop of cloth had come loose, and hung down the back as far as the floor. It looked like the guys from the service station across the street had dropped by to wipe their hands on it. Very classy.

He hit the knob of the hand dryer with the heel of his hand. It made a wicked grinding noise, gagged up a bit of sand, groaned pitifully, and gave up the ghost.

One of the three toilet stalls had an Out of Order sign taped to it. It smelled like something had crawled in there and died. He pushed open the door of the end stall and went in. He sat down on the seat, unfurled a wad of toilet paper from the roll, and dried his hands and face. Then he eased up the leg of his pants and took a peek. The bandage had come loose again. He dumped it into the toilet, fished a new one from his shirt pocket, and stuck it on. As soon as he flexed his leg, that one would come loose too. He was going to have to get a roll of gauze and another tube of ointment. He'd already gone through everything they had in the house.

He gently eased down the leg of the pants and let out a deep breath. He closed his eyes and let his head droop forward. He would gladly have sat there in that crummy stall with the stale smell of urine rising from the floor, and that dead thing in the toilet two over than head back upstairs to face two more hours of *Intolerance*. But his sixth sense told him that any minute now Fischer would wander in, hoping to find him goofing off so he could have something juicy to whisper in Jack's ear during intermission.

He stood up, slapped himself lightly on the cheek to convince his face that he was still awake, grabbed the flashlight from the edge of the sink, and started for the door. Just the feel of the flashlight in his hand made his stomach sink. He kept wanting to dismiss the whole episode with Mr. Magnus as simply the butt end of a bad dream. But here was the flashlight, cold and hard in his hand, telling him otherwise. How on earth was he ever going to break this to Alison? Another major disruption now would sink the Paper for sure.

He yanked open the door and discovered Fischer halfway across the lobby floor and heading in his direction. When he saw Cass he stopped dead and his face twitched. He took a sharp turn and disappeared into the supply closet, as if that were where he'd been heading all the time.

Maddy had resurfaced from her book for air. She was standing leaning over the counter restocking the candy bars. She caught sight of him and smiled. But as he made his way over to the counter her expression changed.

"You look awful," she said as he stopped in front of the counter.

"Thanks." He glanced over his shoulder at Jack's door. With his luck it would swing open right about now.

"It's your leg, isn't it? It's getting worse."

He nodded, looking down at the floor, slapping the flashlight against the palm of his hand.

"That does it, Cass. You're going to have to get it taken care of, understand?"

A door opened. He snapped to attention and turned to go, but it was just Fischer coming out of the closet with the carpet sweeper.

"I'd better get back up there," he said. "I'll talk to you later."

"Right. Say, that's your flashlight, isn't it? Where'd you finally find it?"

"I didn't," he said. "*He* found it. He knows it was us, Maddy."

Fischer had quickly worked his way toward the counter. Cass could hear the telling squeak of the sweeper directly behind him. He left Maddy standing there with her mouth open, and made his way slowly back up the stairs to his post. Halfway up, he felt the bandage on his leg pop loose.

— 16 —

"AH, YES. That is rather nasty-looking, isn't it?" Maddy's father poked cheerfully around the wound with all the delicacy of a tree surgeon examining a case of root rot. "How did you manage to do this to yourself?"

It was pretty hard to talk when you were trying not to scream.

"Fell on a broken bottle," Cass said breathlessly, tumbling

the words out in a blur. Maddy translated, standing at his side for moral support. It wasn't working. He felt as if he might faint dead away or throw up on the floor of the study at any moment. He didn't imagine either of them would go over too well.

"Broken bottle, eh? Lucky it got you where it did. A little higher up and it could have done some real damage." He gave one more deep poke, lifting Cass about a foot off the chair he was perched on, then turned his attention to the black medical bag on the desk beside them.

He opened it, reached in, and came out with a lethal-looking black leather case. He unzipped it and exposed a set of gleaming instruments nestled in a bed of red velvet. Each one looked worse than the other. Cass felt a despairing whimper start up at the back of his throat. He tried to turn it into a hum. Maddy's hand alighted on his arm.

"I'll have to do a bit of digging, I'm afraid. I think you might still have a little something in there causing the trouble. I could freeze it up for you if you'd like. Hardly necessary though. A big brave fellow like you. It'll be over before you know it. What do you say?"

Put that way, there was hardly a choice. He muttered something inaudible. Maddy translated again.

"Good. Good." The doctor plucked something sharp and pointed from the case. "If the pain bothers you too much, just give a shout and I'll stop."

He swabbed the area down with a cool brown liquid and started in to work.

As the cold steel touched his knee Cass felt every muscle in his body tense. He clamped down hard on his teeth and stared off desperately into the distance, trying to distract himself from the pain of the knife nosing around his leg by thinking of something, anything, else.

The skull grinned up at him from the desk, while against the wall behind it a plastic model of a woman, whose front opened like an icebox to show her insides, stood in the shadows watching the knife work.

His eye fell on a heavy curtain hanging slackly to the side of the front window. It was the brocade in the curtain that captured him—a pattern of large leaves and exotic-looking flowers. He sucked in a sharp breath as a quick stab of pain shot up his leg, and his eye danced feverishly over the pattern, finding here a leaf, there a flower that matched another farther up or over as the pattern repeated itself.

And now it seemed that the large irregular leaves took on other shapes, the pale, curled shapes of sleeping children. Lightning shot up his leg. His hand reached out blindly, seized something, and squeezed for all he was worth.

He lay there motionless, eyes closed, barely daring to breathe.

The sound was very close now, the dull slap of boots laboring through the mud, the light trill of metal on metal. It was not the stretcher bearers, of that much he was sure. This was a solitary figure, moving stealthily through the shell hole. He could sense him pausing again and again to lean down over the dead, could picture cold enemy eyes searching for signs of life, the bloody bayonet eager to do its work.

And then, quite suddenly, he knew that the stalker was standing over him. He could feel the steel eyes boring down on him, could almost see the gleeful smile spread over that chill face. A rough hand suddenly gripped his shoulder, shook him. He opened his eyes and stared up at the muddy figure standing. . . .

"There," said the doctor. All done. You'll be as good as new in a few days."

The curtain fell back into leaves and flowers again. Cass suddenly realized that his hand was clamped tightly around Maddy's wrist. He let it go, afraid to look her in the eye, watching the white streaks on her skin fade and finally vanish.

"This was the problem," said Dr. Harrington, cheerfully brandishing a wedge of dull green glass clutched in a bloody pair of tweezers. He dropped it in the wastebasket by the desk and began cleaning up his instruments.

Cass rolled the leg of his pants down over the clean white bandage wound around his knee.

"Thank you, sir," he said. "Thanks very much." He reached for the pay packet in his pocket. "I could pay you now if you'd like."

"Nonsense." He shook half a dozen pills from a small brown bottle into his palm. "Here, have these. If the pain bothers you, take two of them with water every four hours. Now, off with you both, I've got some work to do."

A light rain was still falling outside, and the murky gray sky made it seem later than it really was. They stood in the shelter of the porch, watching the wind tossle the wet leaves of the trees in the park across the road, listening to the strange random music it coaxed from the wind chime. There was a solitary figure in the park, sitting on the swings in the rain.

"Thanks," said Cass. He had found Maddy waiting on his stairs with a book when he got home from school, waiting to collar him and drag him down to her house despite his protests. "For everything, I mean."

She nodded slightly, still staring out into the rain.

"It was my fault," she said. "All of this: your getting hurt, his telling you you have to leave. If I hadn't taken you down there that night, none of it would have happened."

"You didn't drag me down there. I wanted to see."

"When did he tell you you had to be out by?"

"The end of the month."

"Have you told your mother yet?"

He shook his head. The figure on the swings had gotten up now and was walking slowly in the direction of the pool, trailing smoke. The rain looked more like mist in the distance. He thought of Alison heading home on the bus. Dinner.

"I can't just let this happen," said Maddy. "Not without doing something. I couldn't live with myself if I did."

"Look, Maddy—believe me, it's hopeless. You didn't see him standing there. I thought he was going to have a stroke or something."

"I don't care. I've got to talk to him, that's all there is to it."

"Talk to him? Are you crazy? He won't even answer the door now."

"He'll answer it," she said, and for the first time she was looking straight at him. "He'll answer it."

The figure in the park was propped against the hub of the pool now. He was hardly more than a faint smudge in the mist, but Cass knew well enough who it was. He'd seen that pose too often not to.

Up at the corner the bus stopped, disgorging passengers into the rain. He watched to see if Alison was one of them. She wasn't. "When are you going to do it?"

"I don't know. Soon."

"I'll come with you when you do."

She nodded and made a stab at a smile. "Thanks." There was something between them that hadn't been there before. He wanted to reach out and touch her. Instead, he turned and started down the stairs, flipping up the collar of his coat against the rain. He was halfway down the walk when she called to him.

"Who's Philip?" she said.

He gave her a blank look. "Philip?"

"Yes. When Dad was working on your leg you said something at one point. It sounded like Philip."

"I don't know any Philip," he said. "Maybe it's just a sound I make when I'm trying not to scream."

"Very funny."

All the way up the street the ghostly music of the wind chime was in his ears. He had the uneasy sense of being watched. More than once his eye wandered to the park, and the empty pool.

Just given the law of averages, Jack was occasionally bound to hit a good one. That Friday night he screened *Casablanca*. It was a 1943 black-and-white picture with Humphrey Bogart and Ingrid Bergman. Jack had given it four stars in the flyer he'd done up with this month's listings. "One of Bogart's best," he'd written. "Bergman is stunning. A classic."

A lot of people must have been reading Jack's flyer, because the place was fairly full even for a Friday. Even old Jack himself was out of the office, stationed unobtrusively over by the candy counter with a tub of hot buttered, watching the money roll in the door.

Cass kept trying to convince himself that Jack wasn't really such a bad guy once you got over how weird he was. But then he'd remember how crazy he was for Fischer. Anyone who couldn't see just what a creep Fischer was didn't have a whole lot going for him.

It was becoming more than a little obvious that Fischer was out for blood. He was doing his level best to see that Cass either got fired or quit, and it wasn't hard to guess why. The reason was standing behind the candy counter trying not to get flustered with the crowd milling impatiently around her and Jack standing there calmly feeding his face.

Fischer was convinced that Cass had come along and snatched his next conquest right out from under him, and after he'd invested all that money in after-shave and spent all that time leaning on the carpet sweeper softening her up for the kill. And to add insult to injury, the kid who'd done it didn't even wear two-tone Italian loafers or ride a flashy motorcycle.

The movie started. Maybe it was just that tonight he was ready for the magic, ready to stand there quietly and let it take him where it would, ready to simply get lost in it for a little while. Whatever the reason, Cass was captivated right from the opening scene.

He was no longer standing at his post at the top of the stairs in the Palace Theater, the all-pervasive smell of popcorn in his nose, the irritating squeak of the carpet sweeper fanning back and forth across the lobby rug in his ears. No, now he was in Rick's Place in Casablanca, and the year was 1941.

Bogart played Rick, the owner of the bar: tough, cynical, yet at the same time tender. Cass studied his every move, watching him weave majestically through the smoky little café in his white dinner jacket like a king in his castle. He loved the way he delivered his lines in a half mumble, the way his mouth twisted to one side when he smiled. But all his charm faded to insignificance the instant Ingrid Bergman came on-screen.

It was love at first glance. He felt her reach out, take his heart, and twist it in her hand like a tear-stained tissue. He loved her eyes, her nose, her beautiful full mouth. He loved the way her face lit up when she smiled, the delicate accent to her English when she spoke.

"Play it once, Sam, for old times' sake. Play it, Sam. Play 'As Time Goes By.'"

He was vaguely aware of the cleanup going on downstairs, vaguely aware of the by-now-familiar noises of Maddy closing up the candy counter for the night. He glanced down once and saw her fitting the lid over the display, locking the padlock in place. Then she disappeared into Jack's office with the cashbox containing the evening's takings, and his attention went immediately back to the movie. The Bergman and Bogart characters had been lovers once, it seemed, and then she had run off just before they were to have been married. And now they had met again in Casablanca, purely by chance. Only now she was married to another man. After that the plot got a little thick, and Cass found himself completely lost.

It didn't matter, though; he was happy just to watch the two of them together up there, fighting their way through pain and bitterness and finding they were still very much in love.

"If you knew how much I loved you, how much I still love you. . . . I can't fight it anymore. I ran away from you once; I can't do it again."

Her eyes were glazed with tears. She had come to Rick's apartment with a gun, with the idea of taking the letters of transit she knew he had in order that she and her husband could escape from Casablanca and the German intelligence. Now the gun dropped to her side, they embraced, their lips met.

Cass was standing there in the dark on the verge of tears himself, the tight knot in his throat butting up against his bow tie, when suddenly someone tapped him on the shoulder.

He turned and saw Maddy standing in the shadows beside him.

"Hi," she whispered. "Hope I didn't startle you."

"No. It's all right." He kept his eyes fixed on the floor between them, not wanting her to see that his eyes were full of tears.

"It's good, isn't it? The movie, I mean."

He nodded at the floor. "Not bad," he said.

"Are you all right?"

"Yeah, fine." A lone tear trickled in the shadows down his cheek.

"Look, I've got to run. Jack and Fischer will be back any minute, and Dad's probably waiting outside for me. How's tomorrow morning?"

"You mean—"

"Yeah."

He looked her full in the face. "What time?"

"Around ten. I'll come over."

He nodded. She looked at him closely.

"You sure you're all right?"

He nodded again, and with a quick good-bye she turned and hurried down the stairs. As soon as she was out the door, he wiped his eyes dry on his sleeve. On the other side of the stairs he saw Zeke ease back into the shadows shaking his head.

Cass turned his attention back to the screen. The knot in his throat now was more than movie.

They were standing in the shadows again, this time outside Mr. Magnus's door. Maddy knocked a second time, lightly, as if she weren't really too sure that she wanted to knock at all.

Outside, it was a bright summer morning. If you strained your ears you could even hear the sound of the swings in the park. But all that stopped abruptly at the door, as though even the daylight were afraid to enter here.

Instead, the dim light of the ceiling bulb cast its yellow pall silently over all: the boots on the boot tray, the battered wicker buggy, and now the two of them, rendering them suddenly unreal, devoid of life, like pictures carefully preserved in an old album. Even though they stood outside the door, already they were somehow claimed by the shadow world of the one who lived beyond it.

Cass remembered the first time he had knocked on this door, the pitcher of milk quaking in his hand. He thought of the last time he had seen Mr. Magnus, the terrible anger on his face. Suddenly he felt as if they were standing in front of a door to the underworld.

Maddy knocked again, harder this time, as if to shatter the unease in the air. She was trying to act nonchalant, but he knew her well enough to realize that just below the cool exterior she was every bit as apprehensive as he was.

"Are you sure about this?" he whispered.

"Have you got any other suggestions?"

Suddenly the sullen rumble of the radio they had heard snaking from the flat stopped. Out of the silence came the sound of a floorboard creaking, the dull tap of a cane. Footsteps neared the door. Silence.

"Who's there?" came the thin, brittle voice.

Maddy nodded to Cass.

"It's me, Mr. Magnus," he said. "Cass Parry, from upstairs."

"Go away."

"Could I talk to you for just a minute?"

"I've said all I intend to say to you, young man. Now go."

There was a sharp rap against the inside of the door that made them both jump. Cass gave Maddy his I-told-you-so look as they listened to the retreating tap of the cane.

"Mr. Magnus," cried Maddy suddenly. "Wait. Don't go."

The footsteps stopped.

"Who are you?" said the voice, faint, already falling back into the silence.

"Maddy Harrington," she said. "Basil Harrington's daughter. I helped you home with your buggy. Remember?"

The footsteps approached again.

"What do you want?" he said finally. Something had changed in the tone. Cass was reminded again of a child's voice turned to rust.

"Just to talk," said Maddy.

"Then talk, young lady. I'm listening."

"Couldn't we come in for a minute? It's very important."

There was a long hesitation, and finally a fumbling with the lock and a light rattle as the chain came free. The door edged open. A weedy hand rested on the jamb. Light fell on the ancient face, yellowing it like a piece of crumpled parchment.

"Very well, then," said the old man. "Come in. But mind you close the door behind you."

PART THREE

Redwork

*The problems of three little people don't amount
to a hill of beans in this crazy world.*

*Humphrey Bogart as Rick
in* Casablanca

— 17 —

THE FIRST THING that struck him was the darkness. It was like going underground. What little light there was had managed to creep past the thick lace curtains that covered the front window. But even the dimness could not disguise the incredible scene of chaos spread before them.

"Come into the kitchen," said Mr. Magnus as he hobbled off ahead of them, negotiating a narrow path cut through the confusion.

It looked like someone had reached in and stirred the place with a stick. There was twice as much furniture as there should have been, all of it arranged apparently at random around the room. An old couch against one wall was completely blocked off by two large rocking chairs that had been set in front of it. A large, elaborately carved wardrobe with a mirrored front stood abandoned in the center of the room. Pushed up against the fireplace there was an old rolltop desk piled high with papers.

The piles continued onto the floor. Bundles of old magazines tied with string, piles of newspapers yellow with age, stacks of boxes everywhere. Some of the piles even had ornaments clustered on top of them, as though they had simply become one with the furniture of the room.

Maddy just stood there open-mouthed. Finally Cass nudged her and they started off along the path toward the kitchen, where the old man had now disappeared.

The dining room was in disarray as well, but nothing like the front room had been. Here there was a large old table set with six massive chairs and flanked by a matching buffet full of fine old china white as bone, and crystal quietly arranged in ordered rows. It was obvious that no one had eaten here in years. The tabletop was buried under mounds of books and clutter, and the seats of the chairs were occupied by boxes. Against the wall by the kitchen door there was an old console radio, the dial face glowing green in the dimness. He noted the heat register on the wall beside it.

Everywhere there was a smell. He had caught traces of it before in the hall, but here it was all-pervading. It was the acrid smell of smoke and dirt and things shut in too long. It seemed to reach out and enfold them and draw them into itself the deeper they went into the house.

Mr. Magnus was muttering to himself in the kitchen. As Cass came even with the radio, the floor gave a familiar creak. How strange it was, he thought, to be making that creak himself after having heard it so often upstairs. But then, everything seemed laced with strangeness now.

The plan of the rooms exactly matched that of the upstairs flat, but beyond that shared pattern, how vastly different their lives were. He wondered what lay beyond those closed doors here, which upstairs would have opened onto his and Alison's rooms.

It was Maddy who entered the kitchen first. She stopped dead just inside the door, and Cass, who had been following close on her heels, ran headlong into her.

Sitting in the middle of the kitchen floor was a round wooden table, and on that table stood a huge pagoda-shaped bird cage. The table beneath the cage was shrouded with sheets of newspaper peppered with droppings, feathers, the scattered hulls of seeds. The mess carried over onto the floor around the table, also spread with paper.

Just inside the door of the cage, completely oblivious to the confusion, a large rainbow parakeet stood preening itself on a perch, like an emperor enthroned in the midst of chaos. As they entered the room, the bird left off its preening and sidled along the perch farther into the cage, craning its neck to study them with a single eye.

Mr. Magnus stood in front of the sink, pouring water into a small copper kettle. The tap shuddered as he twisted it off. "Come in," he said. "Sit down. Don't mind Petrus. He's a little wary of strangers." The bird gave an assenting squawk and retreated behind its mirror at the back of the cage.

The kitchen was something straight out of a museum, the sink low and shallow, the cupboards deep and fronted with glass doors. The appliances were ancient: the fridge low and squat with the round motor mounted on top, the stove raised off the floor on metal legs, yellow enamel with black trim, the thermostat mounted on the oven door.

Maddy pulled a chair up to the table and sat down amid the seed hulls and stray feathers that covered all but one bare corner of the table, obviously the spot where Mr. Magnus sat.

As he sat down beside her, Cass watched as Mr. Magnus settled the kettle on one of the burners, then fiddled impatiently with first one and then another of the knobs before the flame finally leaped up and the old kettle began to sputter.

The counter was piled with dishes, chipped, dingy-looking dishes waiting to be washed. Nothing at all like the dishes in the dining room. In among the dishes there was an open packet of loose tea, the tail end of a loaf of bread, a small jar of strawberry jam, empty, with a spoon standing in it—all of them items Cass remembered from the weekly delivery of groceries. A dull brown teapot with a broken spout sat beside the jam. Mr. Magnus emptied it into the sink, where still more dishes sat half submerged in tea-colored water. He ran water into the pot to rinse it out.

Cass was looking at the tile floor, filthy, some of the tiles near the sink curled up at the corners like the dried rinds of fruit, when Mr. Magnus turned around, looked hard at him, and shuffled over to the chair on the side of the table opposite to where they were sitting.

Maddy was busy making kissy noises at the cage, trying to coax the bird out from behind its mirror. It wanted nothing to do with the idea. Mr. Magnus watched quietly for a minute, then reached into his pocket and pulled out a package of loose tobacco and papers. He was wearing a threadbare gray jacket over a tired old shirt that had once been white.

Cass noticed a tarnished silver medal pinned to the lapel. He couldn't quite make out what it was.

"So you were the other one, then," said the old man to Maddy. "With him, that night."

Maddy stiffened with surprise, then slowly nodded, still staring into the cage.

"That doesn't sound like Basil's daughter," he said. The cigarette papers must have been those that had gotten wet in the accident. Mr. Magnus was struggling to separate a paper that had stuck to the one following it.

"You wouldn't have caught that boy snooping about in the dark like a thief." He was beginning to get excited again. The blotches started to show on his face, and his hands shook as he tried to tap the tobacco from the packet into the paper trough in his hand, sending a shower of the dry brown shreds spilling to the dirty floor.

"I've a good mind to tell your father," he muttered as he set the tobacco down on the edge of the table. He evened out the thin line of tobacco in the paper, carefully wound it closed, licked the gummed edge slowly, and finally sealed it shut. He pinched the loose shreds from the ends and tucked the cigarette into the corner of his mouth.

He tapped his pockets for matches, found a pack in his coat pocket, lit one, and touched it to the end of the cigarette.

Inhaling deeply, he shook the match out and dropped it into the already full ashtray perched on the edge of the table. He breathed the smoke stream out his nose as he picked stray shreds of tobacco from the tip of his tongue.

The cigarette seemed to calm him. The blotchy patches slowly started to fade. He turned his attention to the bird, running a horny fingernail lightly along the bars of the cage. The silence fell over them like a musty old blanket. For a while it seemed as if he'd almost forgotten about them, as though they had simply become one with the furniture, the way the junk in the front room had. The bird had ventured out from behind the refuge of the mirror, and pecked playfully at the lean finger thrust between the bars. Occasionally, as he smoked, the old man would glance over at them through the cage.

Cass couldn't help but feel that somehow they were being tested. Plunged headlong into this strange world, with its long-drawn-out silences, its dirt and clutter and confusion, the old man was seeing how they would react. And no doubt expecting they would run, as everyone else did.

The kettle started shuddering madly on the burner, finally bursting into a shrill, familiar shriek, steam spewing from its spout. Mr. Magnus limped over to get it, hooking his cane over the edge of the counter while he prepared the pot of tea. He carried it and three cups from the drainboard back to the table and arranged them on the narrow clearing in front of him.

"I suppose you drink tea," he said. "Don't do much talking, do you, considering that's why you're here? I get more conversation from that bird."

He took another long drag from the cigarette, perched it on the edge of the ashtray, and peeked into the pot. Then he poured the dark strong tea, laced with leaves, into the three dingy cups, passing the better two to them, keeping the one with the large chip out of the lip for himself.

"I've no milk," he said. "You'll have to drink it dark." He cupped his pale, thin hands like delicate petals around the tea and sipped loudly, staring at them over the rim all the while.

And then Cass saw it. He had noticed the gold ring on the old man's finger when he first started rolling the cigarette, but now for the first time he saw it as it sat nestled in the laced, lean fingers. A loop of coiled gold in the shape of a snake. A snake swallowing its tail.

Something in his look must have caught Mr. Magnus's attention, because he was suddenly aware of those old eyes settling on him. He took a quick sip of tea, staring desperately down into the cup, watching the leaves whirl back to the bottom, feeling the bitter tea burn down the back of his throat. The ouroboros. But why? What did it mean? For the first time in a week he was aware of his leg. It was suddenly throbbing, throbbing as painfully as it had that first night, as if cold spiked jaws had clamped suddenly around it.

Finally Maddy spoke, breaking the spell of strangeness that had fallen over the room, shifting the old man's attention to her.

"It was my idea," she said. "We wouldn't have been there that night if it weren't for me."

Mr. Magnus took one last tug on the cigarette and crushed it out in the ashtray.

"I expected as much," he said.

"So it's me you should blame, you see. Not Cass. You can't send them away on account of me. Please don't." Her voice was strained, as if she were fighting back tears.

"If you're thinking of crying, you can leave this instant. There'll be none of that in this house, do you hear me? I'm too old for that nonsense, far too old."

"I wasn't going to cry."

"Well, mind that you don't. You should be ashamed of yourself, the two of you. Ashamed. Mucking about like that in the dead of night. Especially you. Young women were different in my day, I'll tell you.

"And never mind your faces, they won't frighten me."

He reached for his tobacco and papers and began the slow ritual of rolling another cigarette. This time, though, Cass noted a slight tremor of the hand as the old man guided the match to the end of the cigarette. He drew deeply on the cigarette and waved out the match. Smoke momentarily enshrouded his head.

"And what were you after, I'd like to know. A glimpse of the witch at work, is that what it was? Or was it worse mischief you were up to? You're no different than the rest of them, either of you."

"That's not fair."

"Don't talk to me about fair, young lady. I've a good mind to turn the both of you into toads, or whatever it is they say I do."

"You're no more a witch than we are. We know that; both of us know that. And I'm not frightened of you, if that's what you'd like me to be. We were just curious, that's all. Just curious. And if that's such a terrible crime, then I guess you'd better just go ahead and do whatever it is you're going to do. But if you think we're just like the others, you're wrong. You don't know how wrong."

Mr. Magnus didn't say a word. He just got up, dumped his teacup into the dull brown water in the sink, and made his way out of the room. The floor creaked as he passed the radio; a door opened and closed again. In a minute music came on in the small back bedroom.

They waited for a while, watching the bird, listening to the muted strains of the music. And when it grew obvious that he wasn't coming back, they rinsed their tea things in the sink, left them dripping on the drainboard, and made their way quietly out of the flat.

—— 18 ——

IN 1953 3-D movies had been all the rage. The movie moguls had come out with them in an attempt to lure people away from their television sets. TV was new then, and it was taking a big bite out of the theater box offices. 3-D was their way of biting back.

The way 3-D worked was that in the filming stage the movie was shot from two slightly different angles of vision, and in the theater when the film was shown, two projectors would superimpose those two different images onto the screen at the same time through colored filters. The people in the audience had to wear special polarized glasses to correct the image for the eye. If everything worked the way it was supposed to, the effect was to lift the images right off the screen and into the theater.

The problem was it often didn't. There were difficulties in projecting with the precision demanded, and people complained of headaches and eyestrain from the glasses. On top of that the whole process was just too expensive to produce. By 1954 3-D had all but died.

Somebody had forgotten to tell Jack. From somewhere in the basement vaults he had managed to unearth a mint copy of the 1953 3-D film *House of Wax* along with a dusty box of cardboard 3-D glasses. Now he was standing down at the door beside Fischer, handing each patron that came through a set of the cardboard glasses and letting them know he'd like them back at the end if they didn't mind.

He'd even brought in an extra projectionist for the night to give the regular guy a hand. You could always tell when Jack was excited; he'd throw away the dead cigar he'd been walking around with for God knows how long and plug in a new one. He had a new one in now, unlit of course, and was chewing the end to goo for all he was worth.

Cass stood up on the floor beside Zeke, watching him. It was kind of sad really. It was Friday night and most of the people coming through the door were teenagers out for a laugh. They really couldn't have cared less for Jack and his crazy old films; they were out for a kick. Jack didn't seem to notice. He had his suit jacket done up and his iridescent blue tie on. He was handing out those old glasses just as if it were opening night, 1953.

Some of the people wandering around in the lobby or straggling up the stairs had already put the glasses on. One of the lenses was green and the other red. They looked pretty weird.

Beside him, Zeke was sniffing. "Hey, do you smell something?" he said.

"No, I don't smell a thing." He was lying. He smelled it loud and clear. Butts and ashes, the latest action in Fischer's continuing war of attrition. He looked down at him stationed at the door beside Jack, smiling benignly as he took the tickets from the people coming in and did his one-handed tearing trick before handing them the stub. It was enough to make you throw up.

Cass had arrived twenty minutes early today, as usual, so that he could fetch his uniform from his hiding spot and put it on in peace. When he lifted the lid off the sand ashtray, he discovered a giant mound of butts and ashes dumped on top of the rolled-up uniform. He'd managed to remove most of the dirt with wads of wet toilet paper, but the smell was there to stay. It didn't take much imagination to figure that Fischer had found his hiding place. And it wasn't hard to guess what had happened to his bow tie the week before.

"I've got it," said Zeke.

"What?"

"That smell. I figured out what it is. It smells like the butt can."

"Yeah."

Jack padded across the lobby floor and reached inside the office door to ring the two-minute-warning bell. The crowd in the lobby started drifting in the direction of the stairs. A couple of them scurried over to the candy counter to stock up before the show began. He watched Maddy reach into the popcorn machine with a jumbo bucket and scoop it full, pump two squirts of the glop they called butter over the top of it, and fill two large cups with cola and ice. She snapped the lids on, pointed to the box of straws over by the napkins, and took the bill the guy held out to her. And then she just stood there, holding the money in midair and staring toward the door.

He followed her gaze, and his heart stopped. Standing just inside the door were four figures, laughing heartily among themselves as Fischer tore their tickets and Jack scraped the bottom of the box for four pairs of glasses.

It was Sid Spector with Maria Magistrale on his arm. And trailing behind them were two of the other gang members, the one with the chalk white face and the tall one who always wore shades. He was slipping the shades off now and putting on the 3-D glasses. The other guy followed suit, and the four of them made their way over to the candy counter.

Sid was dressed to kill. He wore a leather vest over a black turtleneck. His shoes put Fischer's to shame. Maria looked as if she were about to melt into him. She had on her spiderweb stockings and a short leather skirt that her father wouldn't have liked at all. Her hair looked like she'd just stuck her finger in a socket. She had her chandelier earrings on, the ones that chimed when she turned her head.

The other two hadn't bothered to dress up. They just shadowed along behind them with their green and red glasses, trying to look unobtrusive, like a couple of secret service types out guarding the royal couple.

"Hey," said Zeke out of the side of his mouth. "Check out the gorilla in the army fatigues down there. How would you like to run into that in a dark alley?"

The lights dimmed and they made their way to their respective posts on either side of the stairs. The curtain lurched away from the screen, there was that moment of expectant darkness, and the screen filled with light and sound. There was a general rustling through the theater as people fumbled for their 3-D glasses and put them on. Zeke had managed to get hold of a couple of pairs on his way in and had given one of them to Cass. He took them from his pocket now, folded the arms back along the scored edge, and slipped them on. The screen, which had been a blur of reds and greens, leaped instantly into life, and the credits rolled by.

He couldn't keep his mind on the screen though. He was waiting for the footsteps on the stairs. They came soon enough.

He could hear them shuffling up together, talking too loud, Maria laughing self-consciously. Out of the corner of his eye he could make out the four of them as they came to the top of the stairs and stood transfixed, staring down at the screen.

"Far out," said one of them.

He kept his eyes fixed on the screen, praying they would go to Zeke's side, trying to fuse himself flat with the wall.

They turned and started walking toward him. He peeled himself off the wall and flicked on the flashlight, pointing it down at the carpet at their feet. There was no way in the world they would be able to recognize him, he tried to tell himself. Not in the dark, not with those glasses on. He could barely see a foot in front of himself.

"Smoking or nonsmoking?" he asked.

"Smoking," said a voice he immediately recognized as Sid's.

"This way." He turned and led them up to the loges, making his way up the stairs on instinct more than sight, keeping his bearings by the dull glow of the lights mounted intermittently on the sides of the aisle seats.

He lit their way to the last row and fanned the light against the seats as they filed past. Maria and Sid sat in the center, with the two goons like bookends on either side of them. He flicked off the flashlight and took the stairs down two at a time. With any luck at all that would be the last he'd see of them tonight. He slumped against the wall and let the relief wash over him.

Downstairs he could hear Maddy popping up a fresh batch of popcorn. He could just see the top of her head as she perched on the stool reading behind the machine. She had moved it there to be out of Fischer's line of sight. She said she didn't like the way he'd been looking at her lately.

It had been nearly a week now since their visit to Mr. Magnus, and in all that time there had been barely a peep from his flat. All of the familiar noises Cass had come to expect from below had suddenly stopped. He was beginning to get worried. Perhaps their visit had so upset the old man that he really had had a stroke or something. The night before he'd spent nearly an hour on hands and knees with his ear pressed to the bedroom register, listening in vain for signs of life. The only thing that calmed his fears was the trickle of smoke that continued to spill from the garage.

The roses had begun to bloom. Tomorrow would be the last day of the month, and he still hadn't managed to mention a word of all this to Alison. She had already tucked the rent money into a blue airmail envelope to be slid under the old man's door sometime over the weekend. Despite eating, sleeping, and breathing Blake for the past few months, she was still lucid enough to sense that something was on his mind. However, she was convinced it was love.

Earlier in the week he'd made the mistake of introducing her to Maddy. Of course, he'd already told her about the girl down the street who also worked at the Palace. But on Monday evening he'd asked Maddy to drop by and pick him up on the way to work. He wanted to tell her about the picture of the ouroboros that hung on the wall of his room and how it had reappeared as a ring in one of those dreams he'd been having, and now again on the old man's hand.

When she arrived at the door, in a moment of madness he'd called Alison down to meet her. He'd paid for it ever since. Now everything he did, from brushing his hair to spending long stretches of time closeted in his room, was put down to romance. Alison could be so incredibly immature at times.

The 3-D glasses were giving him a headache. His mind wasn't really on the movie anyway, but every time he'd look away something would leap off the screen to draw him back in. Chairs appeared to fly out into the audience, a barker batted a paddle ball that seemed to bounce out into the crowd, smoke from a fire onscreen billowed into the theater. It could all be a little unnerving if you weren't in the mood.

There were a lot of offscreen sound effects as well to enhance the 3-D effect. Blood-chilling screams sounded from the speakers at the back of the theater. As a character rushed from the screen, fading footsteps echoed from the speakers at the side. All of this, of course, elicited the expected "oohs" and "ahs." But as time went on, an increasingly more vocal response came from the upper reaches of the loges.

He did his best to ignore it at first: the voices rising above the soundtrack, the random catcalls, the loud laughter that came at entirely the wrong times. But he knew well enough where they were coming from, and it wasn't long before someone finally came down to complain.

Zeke wandered over. "We'd better go up there and shut those guys up before someone goes down to Jack."

"It's my side," said Cass. "I'll go."

A loud solitary laugh erupted from somewhere up in the dark.

"We'd better both go," said Zeke.

They walked solemnly up the stairs side by side, the twin beams of their flashlights snaking up the carpeted stairs.

Sid and the rest were stretched out in the back row where he had left them. The seats all around them were empty. The tall guy on the end had his big feet draped all over the back of the seat in front of him. Sid had his arm wrapped around Maria's shoulder. With their 3-D glasses on they looked like a band of aliens.

As they came closer Cass saw Sid quickly tuck something out of sight under his jacket.

When they were about two rows away, the guy on the aisle leaned toward Sid and said with mock fear, "Oh-oh, Sid. We're in trouble now."

The guy on the far end thought that was real funny. He gagged on his pop. Sid turned to Maria and whispered something into her chandeliers. She giggled. Cass had heard that giggle before, when she'd been on the phone with one of her friends while he was in the store. Back then he'd even thought it was sort of sexy, like her spiderweb stockings and her dangly earrings. But hearing it now and seeing her sitting there with those stupid glasses on and Sid draped all over, he thought it was the most nauseating sound he had ever heard.

"What can we do for you boys?" said Sid.

Cass, still hoping not to be recognized, stood on the step below Zeke and waited for him to say something. When it became clear that he wasn't going to talk, Cass finally broke the silence.

"People are complaining about the noise up here," he said. "If you don't keep it down, we're going to have to report you to the manager."

"Noise?" said Sid, acting very surprised. "Did anyone here hear any noise?" They shrugged their shoulders and shook their heads.

"Sorry," he said, leaning forward in his seat. "No noise here, buddy." He took off his cardboard glasses and looked Cass straight in the face. "You must have the wrong number. Anything else you have to say?"

"Yes," said Cass, not really believing the words that were coming out of his mouth. "You could tell your friend here to take his feet off the seat."

The big guy didn't like that. The smile dropped off his face like a cardboard cutout and he uncurled himself from the seat and stood up.

That was enough for Zeke. "Come on," he said, tugging at Cass's sleeve as he turned and took off down the stairs.

Cass didn't budge. The big guy moved toward him, a little unsteadily it seemed. He balled his hand into a fist and twisted it into the palm of his other hand.

"What did you say, buddy?" he whispered. His breath was laced with alcohol. They'd been spiking their drinks. That was what he'd seen Sid sliding into his pocket—a bottle.

"Sit down, Benny," said Sid softly, as if he were talking to a two-year-old. Benny turned and stumbled back to his seat. He reached for his Coke.

"You're the kid that lives over top of old man Maggots," said Sid. "Right?"

Cass just kept looking at him, at Maria sitting there studying her nails in the dark.

"Benny said you worked here. I didn't believe him. I mean, this place is a dump, man." He slapped the back of the seat in front of him for emphasis. It was pretty clear he'd been into the bottle.

"Sit down," he said, gesturing to a seat in the vacant row in front of him. "We have to have a little talk, you and me."

Cass shook his head. "I can't. I'm working."

"Listen, kid, do us both a big favor. Sit down for a minute."

Cass glanced over at the one called Benny. He was crushing pieces of popcorn to flat wafers between his fingers and flicking them into the air.

Cass sat down. He could smell Maria's musky perfume behind him woven in with the liquor. He could smell the cologne he'd splashed on for no real reason before leaving home, and the ashy stench of the uniform.

Sid leaned over the back of the seat beside him.

"What's your name, kid?"

Cass studied the backs of the heads a few rows down, all of them choosing to ignore what might be happening behind them. "Cass," he said. His hands felt clammy against the barrel of the flashlight.

"Well, Cass, I've got a bit of friendly advice for you. You're on dangerous ground, living there with that old witch doctor. That place has a bad reputation, you know what I mean?"

He shook his head.

"Well, I'll tell you, then. Some people think that old man

Maggots is into magic. Black magic, you understand. A few years ago a kid wandered by there one night and—" He reached over and ran the nail of one finger along Cass's throat. Cass could feel his rank breath against the back of his neck. He squirmed.

"You don't believe me, is that it? Well, let me tell you something, Casper, you'd better believe it. For your own good. Don't mess around with that old guy, understand? People might get the wrong impression. They might think you're in with him. It could be hazardous to your health."

There was a quick tug on the back of his hair, and Sid bounced off the back of the seat and was gone. He heard a high, delicate chime as he settled back in beside Maria.

Cass didn't bother to look back. He just got up and made his way back down the darkened stairs to his post. He felt vaguely sick to his stomach. Zeke was waiting there for him.

"You all right? I was just about to go down and get Jack."

"I'm fine. Don't worry about it."

"Look, I'm sorry I left, but you shouldn't have talked to that guy like that. I thought he was going to murder us both."

"It's okay. Forget it, all right?"

"Yeah, sure. Forget it."

Zeke wandered slowly back to his side. Cass knew that he must have felt bad about having left him up there alone with those guys, but somehow he couldn't bring himself to bother about it right now. He had other things on his mind—like Sid's all-too-clear warning to stay away from Mr. Magnus. But he knew as well as Sid did that it wasn't because of anything that Mr. Magnus might do to him. No, it was because of what Sid and his friends would do to him if he didn't.

He should have been petrified, but for some strange reason he just didn't care anymore. Sure, he'd been afraid up there alone with those guys, but even that fear had been different, as though it were someone else's fear that he was just watching.

Suddenly he thought of strange old Mr. Magnus sitting in that bombed-out kitchen rolling cigarettes. He remembered the look in those ancient eyes when the old man caught him staring at the ring and looked right up at him with that clear, piercing glance that seemed to see straight through him. That was the way he'd felt up there looking at Sid, as if he could see right through him. And somehow nothing that Sid could do to him could really touch him. Some part of him was safe from Sid and everyone else, just like some part of Mr. Magnus existed whole and untouched beneath all the clutter and confusion and the strangeness of age.

He spent the last half hour pacing back and forth along the walkway between the aisle and the loges, waiting for the film to end, hoping that Maddy would be outside waiting for him. As soon as the lights came up he was down getting the broom and the garbage bags. By the time he got back, the place had all but emptied and Sid and the boys had gone.

He took the loges, Zeke the orchestra. He worked quickly, gathering up the garbage, putting whatever glasses he found on the floor into his pocket for Jack. Up in the back row he found an empty pint bottle of bourbon pushed down into one of the paper cups.

Downstairs, he shed the uniform quickly and rolled it into a ball to take to the cleaners. He dropped the glasses in the bin by the door on his way out.

It was warm outside and the sky was studded with stars. Maddy wasn't in front of the theater. She wasn't in the phone booth across the street. She wasn't waiting on the narrow strip of grass around the corner. He stopped to zip up his jacket and tuck the uniform up under his arm. Then he walked slowly home alone.

—— 19 ——

ALISON was typing up a storm in her bedroom, and had been since first thing this morning when she'd awakened him with it. A couple of hours earlier Cass had ventured into the bedroom with a cup of coffee and a slice of toast. He'd found her sitting at the typewriter in a trance, a pencil wedged between her teeth, the floor around her adrift with papers, like the pale pink petals that had blanketed the grass around the base of the magnolia. She was staring at the blank sheet of paper in the typewriter as if all the wisdom in the world were written there. Disturbing her had been like suddenly jarring her through two centuries. She gave him a strange, bewildered look, followed by a stranger smile when she saw the toast and coffee. Even her thank-you had sounded strange, like a snatch of tape played on a machine at the wrong speed. He set the stuff down on the edge of the typing table and made a quick exit.

Shortly afterward the typing had started up again. First a few tentative taps like a light fall of rain spattering the sidewalk, then a sudden torrent as the heavens opened and the words teemed down. Now and then the noise would settle briefly into silence, only to start up the same way again.

Either Alison had made a real breakthrough on the paper or else she had totally flipped. He remembered the story she told about this guy who had stayed up three days straight cramming for a big college exam. He went in, wrote for three

hours nonstop, and came out convinced it was the best thing
he'd ever done. A week later they called him in and showed
him his exam. Across the top of the first page he'd written
his name. Below it, filling the rest of that page and the fifteen
pages that followed, he'd written his name again. And again.
And again.

Occasionally, as the morning wore on, Cass became aware
of other sounds wound in with the muted staccato of the
typewriter. Sounds from the flat below: the creak of the floorboards, the shiver of pipes, the low drone of the radio. And
as he sat in the front room listening while he leafed yet again
through yesterday's paper, it suddenly seemed to him that the
floor beneath his feet was made of glass.

He could see the dark, cluttered room directly below, the
dusty ornaments and figurines forgotten on the mantelpiece,
the buffet in the far room full of delicate, unused china, like
a display case in a museum, the green dial of the radio glowing
in the dimness. And hovering right above that room, their
own, as empty as that one was full. The half-dozen boxes of
books still unpacked because there was no place to put them,
the two wooden deck chairs looking lost and out of place, the
impressionist posters thumbtacked to the wall and seeming
every bit as sad as the dogeared posters that hung in the display
window in front of the Palace.

In one sense he was relieved to be hearing Mr. Magnus
moving around again, back to the normal routine that their
visit seemed to have disrupted for a time. But then his eye
would wander to the pale blue envelope propped against the
mantel mirror, the rent money he should have already taken
down, and a sudden dread would wash over him. He found
himself listening for the labored sound of footsteps on the
stairs, waiting for the sharp rap of the cane against the door.

Before that happened he would have to say something to Alison.

Lunch was canned tomato soup with crackers—a gourmet delight. Alison floated in with a handful of typewritten pages and a wild look in her eyes. She had a habit of doing strange things to her hair while she was waiting for inspiration. This time she had somehow managed to scoop it up onto the top of her head and braid it. The stubby little braid stuck straight up from her skull, topped by a little tuft of hair that fanned down like a fountain.

"I see you've had a good morning," he said.

"Pardon, love?"

"I said, it looks like you've had a good morning's work."

"Yes, very good actually. Things are finally starting to fall into place, I hope." She shifted her attention back to the sheets, reading closely while she proceeded to crumble cracker after cracker into the soup. By the time she finally got around to eating it, most of the liquid had been absorbed and she was left spooning up lumpfuls of pink paste. It was too disgusting for words.

Finally he couldn't stand it anymore. He went and got the soup off the stove and ladled a little more of it into Alison's bowl.

"Thanks, Cass."

"Sure."

She read on quite happily for a while, reaching by instinct for the crackers, spooning up the soup like an automaton. There was no point at all in trying to talk to her when she was in this state. The trouble was, it was beginning to look as if she might be locked in this state permanently.

Suddenly she glanced up from the page, a glazed look in her eyes, staring through him rather than at him.

"Something wrong?" he said.

"Umm? No, just thinking. You know, the more I read it, the more it seems to me that *The Book of Thel* occupies a profoundly important place in the development of Blake's thought. You see, Blake believed that the only way of attaining the realm of higher innocence was to pass through the world of experience, to endure what on the surface looked like death in order to gain a higher life. The great tragedy of Thel is that out of fear she is unable to bring herself to act, to go down into the grave of experience, knowing, as Blake says, "tis given thee to enter / And to return; fear nothing.' As a result, Thel becomes the symbol for all who fail out of fear to bring the life within them, whatever form that life may take, to fruition, and instead flee back like Thel to the unborn world."

It was the most she had said in more than a week. It was a shame he didn't have a clue to what she was talking about. Reciting her name over a few dozen times would have been more enlightening. There was no point in telling her that, though. It would just start her off explaining it all for the next half hour, and he wouldn't be any the wiser at the end of it anyway. He nodded and smiled.

That seemed to satisfy her. She took another cracker and crumbled it into her soup. There was not enough liquid left to absorb it. It just lay there in crumbs on top of the paste.

He started cleaning up the plates, all hopes of saying anything to her about Mr. Magnus now completely quashed. His mind moved to other matters.

"Did you remember to phone Murray? He's called a couple of times now, you know."

Since this last surge of work had started, Alison had gone strictly incommunicado. All of her calls now came through Cass. So far, that had amounted to the two calls from Murray, making sure she was still firmly anchored to the earth, and one from the Miss Maid people, wondering if she was any better and would she be back on Monday. She had taken the past few days off with a severe case of deadline fever. Less than one month left now, and counting.

"Maybe I'll give Murray a call now." She went away, dialed, muttered into the phone for a few minutes and came back into the kitchen undoing the braid.

"Lord," she said, "I just caught a look at myself in the mirror. Do I look a sight. Murray's going to drop by in a bit. He said he was beginning to forget what I looked like. He suggested we drive down to the boardwalk and take a break from Billy Blake for a couple of hours. He offered to put together a little picnic lunch for the three of us, if you'd like to come."

"Thanks, but I think I'll stick here. There's some things I have to do."

"All right. Suit yourself. Look, I'm going to try to pull myself together. Listen for the horn, will you, love?"

Ten minutes later Murray was leaning on the horn outside the house. Mrs. Wharton was out watering her garden, looking like she might turn the hose on him if he honked just once more. He had pulled the tarp up over whatever rusted remains lay in the back of the pickup. Cass hurried Alison along, finally wrenching her from her room and pushing her bodily out the door. He watched from the window as she climbed into the pickup, waved up at him, and disappeared down the street. Mrs. Wharton watched too.

Over in the park the wading pool had been filled for the first time. A dozen kids were splashing around in the sun, while an attendant sat on a chair at the edge of the pool watching them. Sid and the gang had set up court in the summer palace, a picnic table over by the utility shed. Five bikes lay scattered on the grass around it now. The gang was playing wall ball against the side of the shed. The strike zone had been chalked onto the wall. There was a pitcher, a batter, and two outfielders. None of them was Sid. Benny was at bat. The strike zone was somewhere down below his knees, and the bat looked about the size of a matchstick in his hand. He was still wearing his 3-D glasses.

They were playing with a tennis ball. Benny looked over half a dozen pitches he didn't like, then lay back and let loose on one. He absolutely murdered the ball. It sailed in a high arc over the fielders' heads and bounced over under the trees near the tennis courts.

As it came to a stop, Cass suddenly became aware of someone else, sitting perched on the back of a bench in the shadows of the trees. It was Sid, and he was staring straight up at him. He must have been sitting there all the while, Cass realized, watching Alison leave with Murray, watching everything.

A chill ran down his spine and he backed away from the window as Sid leaped off the table and went to retrieve the ball. When he checked again a few minutes later, the bunch of them were over by the shed, the game apparently over. Sid was sitting up on the picnic table with a couple of the boys, while a bunch of younger kids sat in thrall on the ground around him.

Suddenly the house felt full of eyes. Twice he went back to the window to look down at the empty bench tucked under the trees to assure himself there was no one there. It wasn't until he had retreated to his room with the door closed that the house seemed finally to settle into stillness again. Still, there was a strange chill in the air now that no amount of reasoning would relieve. He went searching through his dresser for a sweater. The only thing he could find was a threadbare old thing that Alison had passed on to him. It was all stretched out of shape and half the buttons were missing, but he took it out anyway.

As he was closing the dresser drawer his eye fell on a corner of blue paper peeking out from under the runner. It was the note Mr. Magnus had tucked inside the crystal pitcher. He had forgotten about it. He unfolded it now and again read the brief thank-you. His eyes lingered on the cramped letters, as though they might be coaxed to say something more than they simply did. He touched the paper to his nose and was stirred again by that faint, half-familiar scent of lilac.

He set the paper down and pulled the sweater on, watching his reflection in the mirror as his fingers fed the buttons through the holes. It was an old mirror and in spots the silvering had worn off behind, so that here and there the reflection failed and there was a sudden glimpse of darkness through the glass.

The shy young soldier peered up at him from the picture tucked into the frame at mirror's edge. How often had that boy stood before this very mirror, he wondered. What secrets lay buried in the pits that pocked the mirror's surface?

The doorbell rang. It had a strange, empty sound as it echoed through the flat. His first thought was that it was Mr. Magnus. But why would he ring the bell and not simply come up the stairs? Then the picture of Sid sitting on the picnic table flashed into his mind. They had waited, waited until they were sure he was home alone.

He made his way cautiously to the front door of the flat, crouching at the window to peer down onto the empty street. He had almost convinced himself that whoever it was had given up and gone away, when two sharp chimes almost stopped his heart.

He opened the door and crept quietly down the first few stairs, until he was able to squat down and peer through the rungs of the railing at the window in the downstairs door.

Through the thin film of curtain that covered the glass he saw a familiar profile. He ran the rest of the way down.

"Hi," said Maddy as he opened the door, "I was beginning to think there was no one home." She had a book tucked under her arm.

"Hi." He couldn't help glancing over her shoulder in the direction of the park.

"It's okay. They've gone," she said. "I waited till they left before I came over. Can I come in for a minute? I've got something to show you."

"Yeah, sure." The hall was dark once he'd closed the door. They couldn't talk here. Memories of Mr. Magnus hung heavily in the air. He would have to invite her up, he realized, seized with sudden panic.

"Would you like to come up?" he heard himself saying.

"If it's all right. Is your mom in?"

"No, she had to go out for a while." He started up the stairs ahead of her, painfully aware of the ratty slippers he was wearing, of the worn old sweater that was too big by far. "I'm afraid the place is a bit of a mess," he said over his shoulder.

"That's all right. I like messes."

Suddenly he was seeing the house for the first time again, all its infirmities glaring at him: the chipped linoleum on the stairs, the ancient wallpaper, the hardwood that wanted cleaning, their own few pitiful things scattered about and looking like the poor relations of the pieces that had been left behind. He couldn't remember the last time he'd invited a friend into his house, save for a disastrous birthday party he'd had once in one of the string of storetop apartments they'd inhabited before moving here.

He felt utterly naked standing there in the front room with her, as if every secret part of him had suddenly been yanked out into the light for her to see. He scooped up the scattered sections of yesterday's paper from the floor and dropped them on the table, then noticed the bald spot in the rug that they had hid and wished he hadn't.

Maddy's eyes drifted over the room, but not critically like Mrs. Wharton's had, more just taking things in. They settled on one of the posters in the other room.

"That's by Blake, isn't it?"

He was impressed. "That's right. It's one of his illustrations to *The Book of Job*. Alison's crazy about Blake. She's doing a thesis on him now."

She went over and studied the poster: the figure of Job gazing skyward, the white-bearded God hovering above him encircled by a stream of angels. The face of God and Job seemed to be the same face.

"'The Lord Speaks to Job out of the Whirlwind,'" she read from the fine print at the bottom of the poster. "Very nice."

She had set her book down on the sideboard. She paused as she picked it up. "This is like the furniture downstairs," she said.

"Yeah. It was here when we moved in, along with some other things." His eye fell on the envelope again. "Would you like some tea?"

"All right."

Once they were in the kitchen he felt immediately more at ease. It was the one room in the house that seemed wholly theirs. The rest had other, earlier allegiances. Sitting at the table while the water boiled, Maddy seemed to relax as well. She played with the salt and pepper penguins and looked around.

"I wanted to wait for you last night, but there was something I had to do. What did they want?"

"You mean Sid and them?"

"Yes. I figured it was more than mere coincidence, them

showing up at the Palace. And then I saw Sid planted right across from your place this morning. What's up?"

"Nothing much. Just a friendly little warning not to mess around with Mr. Magnus, or else. They didn't go into details." He took down two of the better cups and brought the tea over to the table.

"You sound pretty casual about it. They're serious, you know. Having you around is the last thing they want. Taking in the old man's groceries, cleaning up his yard, living here and having nothing bad happen to you—it might make the little kids they make their money from think twice about the old man really being a witch. They can't have that; it's bad for business."

"Look, Maddy, for all I know we could be kicked out of here today. I don't think Mr. Magnus wants us to mess around with him either.

"You still haven't heard anything then?"

"No, not a thing."

"I shouldn't have lost my temper with him."

"Let's not start in on that again, okay?"

She nodded and sipped at the tea. The silence settled over them. He found himself watching her full red lips resting against the rim of the cup and quickly pulled his eyes away, letting them rest instead on the tooled binding of the book she'd brought. He tried to make out the worn words on the spine. Her cup came down lightly on the table in front of it.

"Can you show me the ouroboros?" she said. "Do you mind?"

"No, I don't mind. It's in my room, on the wall."

He led her in and lifted it down for her to look at. She walked over to the window and studied it silently for a minute in the light.

"Amazing," she said, more than half to herself. She glanced

down into the lane. "I went back there last night," she said. "After I left the Palace."

"Where? To the garage? Are you crazy or something?"

"Probably, but I wanted to make sure he was all right after you said you hadn't heard a thing from him all week. And I figured if he'd be anywhere, he'd be there. Besides, I wanted to see something."

"You could have asked me to come with you."

"No, I couldn't. I had do this myself."

"And?"

"He was there all right, hard at work. But this time I got a good look." She handed him back the picture, and he returned it to its hook on the wall. It hung there watching them steadily with its single eye.

"After you told me about finding the picture," said Maddy when they returned to the kitchen, "and what your mother's friend had said about its having been an alchemical symbol, something clicked. I remembered having seen a book about alchemy in Dad's study. It took me a while to unearth it, but here it is." She picked up the book she had brought with her and started leafing through it.

"What this is is a history of alchemy and of famous alchemists, along with a selection of old texts. A lot of it's pretty hard going. In order to keep their secrets from the outside world, alchemists described their experiments in complicated codes and in strange symbols. The ouroboros was one of the symbols.

"From what I can piece together, the aim of the alchemists was to prepare something they called the philosophers' stone. They believed this stone possessed magical powers: the power to change base metals into gold, but more than that, the power to cure evil, heal disease, even to grant immortality.

"It wasn't until the past couple of nights at work that I

really had a chance to sit down with this. It's still pretty much a muddle to me, I have to admit, and I was just about ready to give up on it last night, when I saw this, and it stopped me dead."

She held the pages of the book splayed open between them on the table. He found himself looking down at a reproduction of what seemed to be an old woodcut of a workshop of some sort. There were all sorts of strangely shaped bottles and odd implements scattered over the tabletops and on the floor. In the midst of this a cloaked figure was bent over a small furnace, while a boy on the ground at his feet worked a small bellows. What almost immediately caught Cass's attention, however, was what sat on top of the furnace—an egg-shaped vessel exactly like that they had seen through the hole. He looked quickly at Maddy, then back at the picture.

"Yes," she said. "It's the same. That's why I had to go back again last night, just to be sure."

Underneath the picture he read the words "A Seventeenth-Century Alchemical Laboratory (after the engraving by Maier, Frankfort, 1678)."

"You see, Cass, it all fits together: the ouroboros you found, the ring, the mysterious goings-on in the garage, and now this. I know it sounds completely crazy, but maybe it's alchemy that he's up to out there."

She took her hand from the book. Instantly it fanned itself through its final pages and lay there suddenly still between them, its back cover opened onto brightly marbled endpapers. As he looked, for a moment the marbling seemed to slowly curl, like smoke rising lazily from a chimney, like the lithe body of a snake coiling upon itself, like the delicate living tongues of light he had seen swirling against the inner side of the glass. Suddenly Maddy spoke, breaking the spell.

"Did you leave the stove on?" she said, sniffing.

He went to check. "No, everything's off. Why?"

"I don't know. I thought I smelled something for a moment there. Gas or something."

He sniffed the air and shrugged. "Maybe the pilot light's gone out." He flicked one of the knobs on the stove. Instantly a burner leaped into light. "No, it seems to be okay."

"Don't worry about it," said Maddy. "It's probably just my imagination."

The phone rang and he went to get it. It was Alison, saying that Murray would be dropping by for dinner, and asking him to take the fish from the freezer to thaw. He could hear the sound of traffic in the background. She must have been calling from a phone booth. He was tempted to tell her everything right then and there, but the moment slipped away and he was saying good-bye and listening to the click on the end of the line.

By the time he got off, Maddy had wandered into the front room and was looking out the window.

"It's so strange. The park out there, the kids playing in the pool. It's like it's all happening in another world. I feel like we've stepped inside a dream." She turned to him. "I think I'd better be going. I'm supposed to be doing some shopping. Dad will be wondering what's happened to me. I'll leave the book with you. If you get the chance, maybe you can look through it. And if you hear anything from Mr. Magnus, anything at all, let me know."

"Hang on, I'll walk you down." He swept the envelope from the sideboard and followed her out the door. He'd just slide it quietly under Mr. Magnus's door, and pray.

He noticed the smell of gas as soon as they were on the stairs. It got stronger as they came down onto the landing.

"There," said Maddy. "Do you smell it now?"

"I sure do." He leaned down to slide the envelope under

Mr. Magnus's door and got a sudden sickening whiff of the gas creeping stealthily along the floor.

"It's coming from inside there."

"Oh my God! I'll bet he's fallen asleep or something and left it on."

They started banging on the door, their alarm only increasing as the knocks went unanswered. The sharp, deadly odor of the gas quietly filled the hall. He felt it silently ease inside him, twisting his belly into a nauseous ball, pouring its sweet poison over his panic. The lion's head knocker looked on unperturbed.

Maddy tried the door. It opened an inch, then banged up against the chain.

"We've got to get in there," she cried. "We'll have to shoulder it open. If we both hit it at the same time, the chain should give."

They took a few steps back, then ran together at the door. There was an instant of resistance, the sound of wood groaning under their weight, then a sudden splintering and the clatter of metal as the door burst open.

Here the gas held sway. It rose to meet them like a beast disturbed at its prey. Mr. Magnus lay slumped in the old padded armchair in the corner of the room.

"Open the window," shouted Maddy through the sweater she had pulled up over her nose. She ran over to the old man and tried to rouse him.

The window was locked. Cass finally found the catch and threw it open, knocking several of the dusty figurines onto the floor.

Maddy was still shaking the limp figure, shouting the old man's name as Cass ran past on his way to the kitchen. Here the gas hissed menacingly like a snake. He felt it coil itself swiftly around him as he came into the room, squeezing the breath from his lungs. He lunged for the stove, fumbling frantically with the unfamiliar knobs until suddenly the hissing stopped.

He flung open the back door. For a long while he stood there, leaning against the door frame, breathing greedy gulps of the pure cool air. Finally from the depths of the house he heard the sound of coughing, a dry, rasping cough he recognized at once, and Maddy called out to him.

It was as he turned back into the kitchen that he saw the bird lying motionless on the bottom of the cage.

The smell had almost cleared from the place. Mr. Magnus sat in the old chair, still racked by the occasional fit of coughing, but otherwise none the worse for wear. The pagoda cage sat on the stool in front of him, its door open. The bird lay on his lap.

Despite their protests, the old man had adamantly refused to let them have Maddy's father take a look at him. He wanted nothing to do with doctors, thank you very much. He'd seen worse than this in his day, and if only they would stop fussing over him he would be fine.

He seemed much more concerned about the bird. He sat there talking to it like a child and softly stroking its rainbow feathers with his horny finger, occasionally glancing up to watch as Maddy struggled to reattach the lock to the front door with a screwdriver they had unearthed from one of the kitchen drawers.

The wind lightly rustled the old lace in the front window. Patches of sunlight danced on the worn carpet below, like kittens frisking about in some forbidden room. Cass bent down and picked up the ornaments that had fallen from the sill when he opened the window. All were unharmed but one, the crystal unicorn, whose horn had broken in the fall. He picked the pieces up together and laid them side by side on the sill, hoping the old man wouldn't notice. The view of the park from the window struck him strange; it was like a tinted picture from an old book, somehow not the same park he saw from the upstairs window at all.

"It's cold," complained Mr. Magnus from the shadows of the room. "Shut that window, young man. And bring that broken thing to me."

The window only closed reluctantly, as if unwilling once open to shut out the sudden rush of world again. The curtain settled into stillness; the sunlight leaped nimbly back up to the sill beside the broken unicorn and was still. The room shivered softly once, and shrank into itself again. He picked up the broken bits and carried them across the room to the old man. The bird was stirring in his lap.

"There," said Maddy with a final twist of the screwdriver. "That should do it. We can fix this broken piece here later with a little glue and a clamp."

She went over and set the screwdriver down on the arm of the old man's chair. He looked up briefly from the bird. His eyes were full of distance.

"How is he?" she asked, bending to stroke the bird.

"Alive," he said, "which is a damn sight better than we'd both be if it hadn't been for you two." He seemed more than a little sheepish now as he sat fiddling with the screwdriver and shifting awkwardly in his chair, like a small boy whose foolishness had been found out.

"May I?" said Maddy, cupping her hands about the bird. He nodded, and she picked it up, cradling it to her breast, softly stroking its head.

"Have you something to wrap him in?" she asked. "We should keep him warm."

Cass remembered the clean handkerchief in his pocket, pulled it out, and helped her swaddle the warm, feathered thing in it. A light brush of claws brought the image of the dead bird in the mailbox flashing back into his mind. And for the first time since they'd burst through the door, he saw the chaos that surrounded them: the confusion of furniture, the piles of magazines and papers, the narrow path that had widened inexplicably in their panic. And in the midst of it all, mirrored in the dusty depths of the wardrobe that stood in the center of the room, an old man sitting in a tattered chair, leaning on a cane, like a king on a moldering throne, his kingdom gone to ruin around him.

That night his sleep was troubled with dreams.

He was back in the crawlspace with Maddy. But the weeds and garbage were gone now, and in their place was mud—thick, glutinous mud. He was inching forward through it on his belly, crawling and crawling until he could crawl no more and in desperation latched on to Maddy's boot and let her drag him along behind her.

The passageway stretched off endlessly ahead of them, and where the odor of decaying lilac had been there was now the deadly stench of the gas, snaking silently through the mud, inescapable. He kept swallowing great, searing gulps of it, wretching and coughing uncontrollably, and all the while clinging desperately to the muddy boot. . . .

Cass woke up racked with coughing, slick with sweat. He sat up, hanging his legs over the edge of the bed, until the spasms finally stopped and the nightmare faded. It was then, in the sudden silence, that he heard the faint, chill echo of his own cough from the room below.

—— 20 ——

OVER THE COURSE of the next couple of weeks Cass and
Maddy took to dropping in on Mr. Magnus from time to time.
Officially they were there to see how the bird was faring.
Maddy always brought along a little something for him: a box
of bird treat, a bottle of vitamins from the pet shop on the
strip, to be added sparingly to his water, a new bell for the
cage. In fact, though, they were there as much to check up
on the old man. Both man and bird seemed all but mended,
though the one still coughed too much and the other still
spent too much time on the bottom of the cage.

They would sit uncomfortably together in the kitchen,
watching the bird while Mr. Magnus ritually rolled cigarette
after cigarette and sipped from an old, cold pot of tea. Words
were few and failing between them, as though the silence that
sat with them had laid its old lips on theirs and sucked them
dry of speech. For where could one begin? With the weather?
But here there was no weather. These few sad rooms were
the old man's world. His horizons all were walls.

The house no longer had its own shape. The shape it had
now was his. It had settled around him like a second skin.
Even the shadows seemed webbed with nerve endings, so that
the merest glance was enough to spark his notice. Cass found
he had constantly to stop himself from staring, for the old
man would invariably look up and those searching eyes settle
instantly where his just had.

But there was so much that one had to pretend not to see:
the incredible clutter that threatened to overtake the entire
flat save for those few narrow paths that the old man moved
on; the acrid odor of dirt and neglect that pervaded the place

and worked its way into your pores, so that you carried it with you long after you had left; his odd ways, born of living for so long in an absence of mirrors.

He would sit there silently, smoking, watching, while Cass and Maddy babbled on nervously about work or whatever happened into their heads, until ultimately the babble ran dry and the three of them would be left in silence, staring warily through the bars of the cage at the bird and one another.

Perhaps it was because of the picture of the young soldier tucked in his mirror, perhaps because for four months now he had shared the house in silence with the old man and come to know the pattern of his ways. Whatever the reason, despite the great gulf of time that divided them, Cass increasingly felt a strange affinity between himself and this odd creature.

Beneath the silent, forbidding exterior that seemed bent on driving them off, he began to sense a guarded softness and fragility. Beneath the brusqueness of his manner there was a nervousness that reminded him of his own unease when Maddy had first visited upstairs. Surely Mr. Magnus was aware of the state of the house, and perhaps having them there brought that all the more acutely to his mind. So that the defiant pride that smoldered in those eyes was born, in part at least, of embarrassment, and a stubborn defense of the squalor that surrounded him.

Though nothing was ever said, by the beginning of the second week it had become apparent that Mr. Magnus was not about to kick Cass and Alison out of the upper flat. Already, beneath the silences and scowls that had seemed at first designed to scare them off, they began to catch hints of a reluctant delight in having them there. He could not commit himself to it wholly. The long years of living alone had made him wary of emotions, and they had withered with neglect like the poor plants ranged on the kitchen sill, so that now the slightest trace of a smile on that ancient face was tantamount to ecstasy.

It was Maddy who more often than not coaxed those rare smiles to the surface at first. She spoke to him in a direct, often irreverent manner that seemed to strike a chord in the old man. Under her onslaughts the guardedness began by slow degrees to melt away, like the last ice on a pond in spring. He began to speak in more than the brief, barely audible bursts he had used before. And as the words came, the darkness and clutter of the house seemed to recede and a new and unexpected world emerged.

The door of the cage was open, as always. And as always Petrus had retired to the far side of the highest perch, as far away from it as possible. There he passed the time batting his bell with his beak and talking to his bird friend in the mirror, bent upon doing his best to ignore the two intruders in his kingdom. Now and then he would peek furtively from behind the mirror to see if they were still there, then quickly retreat to the refuge of his reflection in the glass.

Earlier, Maddy had wedged a celery stick between the bars of the cage by way of a peace offering. Now she was easing her hand into the cage, trying to coax Petrus to step onto her finger. Petrus wanted none of it. He took one look at the thin, bony thing inching toward him and flew in a flurry to the ceiling of the cage, where he hung upside down from the bars.

"Come on, Petrus, I'm not going to hurt you. Who do you think brought you that nice stick of celery, and put that bird treat in your cup and that nice clean paper on the bottom of your cage?"

Petrus looked skeptically over his shoulder at her and hid his head behind the celery. A white stream came splattering down onto the clean bottom of the cage.

Actually the only thing they had managed to accomplish in the two weeks they had been coming was to clean the cage. It still sat smack in the middle of the kitchen table like an emperor's palace, but gone now were the drifts of yellowed newspaper spattered with droppings and feathers. They had cleaned out the long-neglected bottom of the cage as well and lined it with fresh paper. Maddy had bought a new box of birdseed at the corner. All in vain; Petrus still wanted no part of her finger.

She yanked her hand out and banged the door of the cage closed. Mr. Magnus let out a mischievous little cackle, took one last drag of a cigarette sucked down so low that there was barely a stub of it left, and butted it in the ashtray. His pale, almost transparent hands with their intricate vinework of veins were stained a dark yellow from nicotine on the first two fingers.

"You shouldn't smoke so much," said Maddy, flicking her hair back behind her ear.

"Oh, and why is that, dear girl?" He picked a shred of tobacco from the tip of his tongue.

"Because it's bad for you, that's why. It'll ruin your health."

"Well, I must say I'm touched that people are suddenly so concerned about my health. But to tell you the truth, my dear, my health is the least of my worries. It's my head that bothers me."

He said everything in such a deadpan way that it was always hard to tell when to take him seriously.

"Do you know how long I've been smoking these wicked things?" He knocked the ashtray lightly with the back of his hand. "Since I was fifteen. Back in the war. That's more than seventy-five years ago now. So if they intend to ruin my health, they'd better start soon before something else has a go."

He leaned forward, braced his hands on his knees, and pushed himself slowly to his feet. Unhooking the cane from the back of the chair, he made his way slowly over to the sink. But then, everything was slow about him: the way he moved, the way he talked. He was so old, so very old. It was almost frightening that one could live to be so old.

"Teatime," he said as he ran water into the old kettle. It seemed that it was perpetually either teatime or cigarette time.

"Would you two young people care to join me? Or will that ruin your health as well?"

Maddy made a face at his back as he made his way to the stove. He did not so much walk as lurch along, his artificial leg swinging out in an awkward arc from his side with each step and coming down with a dull, dead thud on the floor. It was as if his every movement demanded a conscious act of will to be executed. Cass watched as he went through the now-familiar ritual with the knobs on the stove, setting the kettle down, and vainly twisting one knob after another until the flame finally danced up under it.

There was a sudden glint of gold on the frail hand as the ringed finger caught the light. And for one impossible instant the scene was overlaid with the image of an aging alchemist tending his sacred fire, trying desperately to coax magic from the mud. Could the old man actually believe such things were possible?

"Now, let me see," he said, glancing uncertainly up at the glass doors on the cupboards over the sink. "I suppose you'd like something sweet to go with your tea. There are some cookies here somewhere."

"None for me, thanks."

"Or me," added Maddy immediately.

They had already encountered the cookie tin on a previous visit, though Mr. Magnus seemed to have forgotten. It was a very old cookie tin, full of very old cookies. The painted lid displayed a portrait of a solemn-looking woman wearing a rather dusty crown. The woman was dusty too, and no doubt long dead. She had a slightly sour expression on her face, as though she might have tasted one of the cookies in her tin.

The cookies had been shortbreads once. Now their mummified remains lay permanently in state on pallets of corrugated red cardboard. Even with the tea it had been impossible to choke one of the rancid things down.

Mr. Magnus was not about to abandon the search, however. He opened first one cupboard, then another, straining to straighten his bowed back to see up to the higher shelves. It was obvious that those shelves were used hardly ever, if at all. They were packed with stacks of dishes, antique tins and boxes, canisters with pale flowers stenciled on their faded sides, a motley group of green and brown liquor bottles looking lonely, and on the topmost shelf the inevitable jars of dried beans standing like sentries in a solemn row.

Mr. Magnus stared up at the shelves like someone surveying a wilderness.

"They're here somewhere," he said, impatience sliding quickly into irritation now.

The lower shelves were almost bare. Here, in no apparent order, he kept the things he dealt with daily: a box of birdseed, another of oatmeal, small tins of pork and beans tucked among the random dishes. At the far end of the shelf Cass spotted the missing tin of cookies under a pile of plates.

By now Mr. Magnus had dragged over the metal stepstool, prepared to climb it in search of the cookies, when Cass pointed them out to him, adding again that they really weren't hungry right now.

The kettle boiled. Mr. Magnus emptied the old pot into the sink, rinsed the pot with a bit of boiling water, then spooned in the tea. He filled it to the brim with boiling water and shut the lid on the steam. He sorted through the cups on the counter until he found three that were reasonably clean. Everything was done slowly, methodically, as if it were some magical rite demanding utmost care in its execution.

The container of milk, which he set on the table between them when he brought the tea, looked as if it had been sitting on the counter since the last time they had visited. Cass took one look at the thick yellow ring that had formed around the inner side of the jug and decided to take his tea black.

The tea was strong and bitter, as always. Mr. Magnus drank it with his body hunched about the steaming cup as if about some vital fire. He had the habit of nodding to himself from time to time, as if he were responding to some ongoing inner dialogue. He sat there now, sipping and nodding, seeming at best only intermittently aware of them. It was no wonder people thought him strange. He was strange.

The thought drew a look, one of those piercing looks he carried in his arsenal, a look that seemed to say he had caught the thought, that the inside of Cass's mind was as clear to him as the rows of dusty dishes through the glassed cupboard doors.

"You think I'm a crazy old bugger, don't you?"

"No," he lied.

"It's no use contradicting me, young man. I see you sitting there thinking. I may be a little hard of hearing, but I can still hear you thinking plain enough. You're thinking, this old Magnus fellow's a crazy bugger. Well, maybe you're right." He leaned forward in his chair and whispered conspiratorially, as though he might be overheard.

"I'll tell you a little secret," he said. "I sometimes forget things." He studied their reactions, as if he'd just made some momentous revelation, then he sat back in his chair and his hands fell to his lap.

It was very strange, but when he was speaking you almost

forgot his extreme age for the moment. His voice, though oddly pitched and rusty from disuse, was still strong and sure. It was in the spaces between speech, like now, when the hands on his lap seemed to take on a life of their own and the distance opened in his eyes, that you most profoundly felt his age.

"It's a funny business, this growing old. A very funny business, let me tell you. I can't make head or tail of it, to tell you the truth. This old brain is full of gaps and gullies. Things keep slipping down the cracks. One minute there's something on my mind, and the next minute it's gone and there's something else there instead.

"It's no use worrying about it, I tell myself. You're old, that's what you are. *Old.* You're supposed to forget things. Let them go. That's what I try to do now—let them go. Just sit here as though I were a little boy again sitting in the dark watching the picture show. Oh, how I used to love the pictures. Valentino, Fairbanks, Chaplin—I can see them all still, up there on the screen, making magic in the silence.

"It's like that, you see. I can sit that way for hours. just sit. I was never one for sitting when I was young. Oh, no, but now I'll sit, and it's as if I go on a little vacation. I'll go places in my mind that I'd forgotten I'd ever been to, see people I haven't seen in years, talk to them, just like I'm talking to you now. Bah, I *am* a crazy old bugger, and that's the truth."

He ran a horny fingernail along the bars of the cage, sending Petrus into a startled flurry, and started to roll himself another cigarette. This time Maddy didn't say anything.

"I'll tell you something," he said. "Inside this sad old bag of a body here that can barely hobble from one end of this place to the other, there's a young boy no older than you, who could run all day with never a thought of it. That boy's been there all the while, you see, biding his time, waiting, watching. And now that this body has slowed me down so much that it's all I can do just to drag myself from my bed in the morning, now that young boy has suddenly sprung up inside me again."

He sealed the cigarette shut, struck a match against the underside of the table, and lit it. Smoke momentarily enshrouded his head.

"It all comes back so clearly," he said. "That's the strangeness of it. If only you knew how clearly it all comes back. It's as though it were sometime yesterday, those many years ago that I was a boy. As though I lay down for a little nap then, and woke up now. And all the time between, no more than this."

And he waved his hand absently through the smoke.

—— 21 ——

THINGS were deteriorating badly at the Palace. Since Fischer had emptied the butt can on his uniform, Cass had had no choice but to bring the uniform home with him every night, which was more than a slight pain in the neck. He had quit going in early as well. For one thing, there was no longer any uniform to retrieve; for another, Fischer had started getting there early himself.

The first time he'd done it he'd practically scared the life out of Cass. Cass had been there in the change room getting himself ready and quietly singing to himself. "You must remember this, a kiss is still a kiss—" when suddenly the door to one of the stalls swung open. There was Fischer, sitting on one of the cans with his feet tucked up, just watching him. That was the last time he had gone in early.

It wasn't really that he was frightened of Fischer, not in

any ordinary sort of way, at least. When it came to that, he realized that Fischer was little more than a mouth with a motorcycle. But there was this strangeness about him that was more than a little unnerving. You were never quite sure exactly what he might do if one of the hairline cracks in his head widened a little and the weirdness took over for a while. Fischer was the perfect image of the quiet neighbor who suddenly ups and murders a few people because he doesn't like the way they're looking at him or something.

So for the past couple of weeks Cass had taken to rushing in at the last possible moment with his uniform flying out behind him, making a mad dash to get changed before he was due up on the floor. Of course, Fischer had not failed to take advantage of the opportunity, and more than once he had made sure to time a quick visit to Jack so that the manager would be sure to catch sight of Cass tearing out of the change room to get up on the floor in time.

It was becoming increasingly apparent that Jack's initially positive attitude toward him was rapidly eroding. The last time he'd collected his pay he discovered that he'd been docked twice for lateness. On top of that, Jack had made another crack about his hair and warned him that if he didn't shape up soon he was going to be out of a job. It was as if he were being told that the opportunity of a lifetime was about to slip through his fingers or something. His initial impulse had been to tell Jack where he could stick his job, but that would have been stupid.

For one thing, the sad fact of the matter was that he really did need the job. With Alison calling in sick an average of once a week now, finances were tighter than ever, and the job with the Miss Maid people seemed to be dangling from a rather frayed thread.

For another thing, there was Maddy. Fischer was doing his

utmost to make life just as miserable as he possibly could for her right now. He spent all his time hovering around the candy counter leering at her and pocketing stuff whenever she happened to turn her back. More than once Cass had been on the brink of going downstairs and popping the jerk right in the nose. But he knew that was exactly what Fischer was hoping would happen. It was only a question of time before it did, but now was definitely not the time.

For some reason he didn't entirely understand, Maddy's father had decided he could trust his daughter with him on the short walk home after work. So now on the nights they worked together Maddy would steal upstairs and take a seat in the back row of the orchestra after she had finished her cleanup, while Jack and Fischer were off dropping the money in the night deposit. She would watch the end of the movie and then sit there reading while Zeke and he did a quick cleanup. Zeke did a fairly good job of pretending he didn't really see her, in the interests of hanging on to his job. Twice in the past week Cass had discovered a mass of junk in the upper reaches of the loges when there had been no one sitting up there. It wasn't hard to guess that Fischer had taken to coming in early and systematically scattering around the garbage they had collected the night before, just to make life miserable. Yes, it was definitely just a matter of time.

It was usually still pretty lively on the street by the time they got out. Summer had brought everyone out of their houses. For the past few days the first heat wave of the season had covered the city like a damp rag. Part of the reason why the place had almost been full tonight, despite the fact that it was the third weekend in a row that Jack had screened *Casablanca*, was no doubt because of the Palace's air-conditioning system.

Maddy and he had long stretches of dialogue in the film

down by heart. And as they walked along the dark and muggy street now they traded lines back and forth and laughed like fools. Not that it was really that funny, but it was strange and somehow magical to be walking along in the heat, still wrapped in the spell that always lingered for a while after a film. And the queer way it made him feel to be with her could be answered only by laughter, because once the laughter stopped there would be something else there, something that neither of them, he was sure, had planned on being there at all.

It was well after eleven, but the street was far from empty. Windows had been thrown open in hopes of charming a stray breeze inside. Music spilled out onto the street, coloring the dark. Ghostly presences lurked on unlit porches, betrayed here and there by the bright end of a cigarette flaring, the clink of glasses, the muted murmur of conversation. They must have thought the two of them were completely crazy, laughing along together in the dark.

As they neared the park, the open windows gave way to air conditioners purring contentedly to one another like cats perched on window ledges. Here the porch lights were on, the porches deserted, the doors sealed shut to keep in the cold. Inside, the chill blue light of televisions flickered in downstairs windows.

The spell between them broke. For the first time Cass was aware of the sound of their separate footsteps echoing off the sidewalk. The uniform slung over his shoulder on a hanger smelled of smoke. The hanger wire bit into his shoulder. He shifted it to the other hand.

Maddy was digging through her shoulder bag for something. She came out with the book. After briefly lending it to him, she'd been hanging on to it herself for the past couple of weeks, her head buried in its pages half the time she was working at the Palace. On their walks home afterward she'd share with him whatever it was she happened to be reading about that night.

He'd learned about the shadowy beginnings of alchemy back in ancient Egypt, its gradual spread through the Arab world, and the final flourishing of the art in Europe four or five hundred years before, until the birth of modern chemistry brought its dreams abruptly to an end. She'd shared with him some of the stories of supposed transmutations, and the greed and obsession that surrounded the doomed efforts of those who were in it only for the promise of gold. "Puffers" they were called by the true alchemists, who claimed that the real aim of their work lay in the quest for spiritual as well as material perfection, and that the two went hand in hand.

The more Maddy read about this stuff, the surer she was that old Mr. Magnus was really some sort of an alchemist. Cass himself was not so sure. Magic was not quite up his alley.

"Tonight I was reading about the *prima materia*, the raw material that went into the fashioning of the philosopher's stone," she said as she walked along with the book in her hand. "Interested?"

"Sure." She didn't seem completely convinced by that, but she went on anyway.

"You see, the whole success of the alchemists' work centered on the raw material they started with, and yet the alchemical texts are nowhere more obscure than in identifying what exactly that raw material might be. The only thing they are clear about is that whatever this substance is, it lies all around us, ignored. People handle it every day, and yet throw it away as something of no value.

"Alchemists would spend years and years putting every substance they could think of to the test, perhaps testing the same one hundreds of times over, hoping that it would somehow yield the Stone. Mercury was very popular as a possibility, as was sulphur, and more than one poor soul ended up accidentally poisoning himself on the fumes or blowing himself up.

"They were also convinced that celestial influences had to be just right for the Work to succeed. The project had to be begun in the spring under the sign of Aries and had to be brought to completion on a specific date near the end of the summer, when the sun and moon converged in the sign of Leo."

She was looking up into the night sky now, searching.

"There," she said, pointing. "You see that bright star there? That's part of the constellation of Leo. It's hard to see with all these lights around, but if you look closely you can make out a pattern of stars around it. That one there, over to the left, is the tip of the lion's tail. Those faint ones there make up the body and the head."

He pretended to see, nodding seriously as he followed the angle of her arm up into the confusion of stars overhead, almost breaking his neck in the process as he stumbled off the sidewalk at the corner of their street.

"Stop goofing around, Cass," she snapped.

"Goofing around? I almost kill myself, and you say I'm goofing around."

She turned on him. "You think all this is crazy, don't you?"

"No, not really."

"Oh, that's very convincing."

"Knock it off, Maddy, will you? It's late."

They kicked down the street silently for a little way, nearing the house. A dim light shone in the lower window. Maddy's eyes were fixed sullenly on the ground as she shuffled along beside him. He wasn't in the mood.

"Okay," he said, "maybe I'm not so sure about all this." It was the heat talking now, the fatigue. "Maybe I can't quite convince myself that this old guy is about to make some magic stone. So maybe he is doing alchemy. Okay, all right, no argument—a sad old man who thinks he can make magic. But suddenly you seem to believe he can do it or something. That's crazy. I mean, I'm no Einstein, but even I know that it's crazy."

"Fine, okay, it's crazy. There was something I wanted you to see in the book here, but that's fine. I understand. Forget it." She sloughed off her shoulder bag and started jamming the book back in.

He tried to stop her; his hand closed on her bare arm, sending a warm rush through him. "Wait, Maddy. Don't. I'm sorry. I'm just tired, that's all. I'd like to take a look at it. Really."

He reached for the book. For a long moment he stood looking at her, the book like a bridge between them, their separate lives flowing back and forth between it. And suddenly he had the crazy feeling he was going to kiss her.

He leaned forward and briefly touched his lips to hers. Bergman and Bogart. She looked at him curiously for a minute, then let go of the book.

"I marked the page," she said.

He nodded, and before he knew it she had said good-night and he was watching her run down the street to her house.

The room was washed in moonlight. He undressed quickly, quietly, glad to be free of his clothes in the heat. The flat was stifling, barely a breath of air. He could hear the dull whir of the fan in Alison's bedroom, hear the sound of her tossing and turning, trying to get comfortable.

The book was lying on his bed, a paper napkin marking the place Maddy wanted him to read. By bringing it into the room he had somehow brought her with it. He closed his eyes and instantly he was standing on the street with her again, feeling the warmth of her arm in his hand, the fullness of that long moment before he had kissed her. And now the close heat of the room momentarily took flesh, and he leaned forward and kissed the darkness lightly on the lips.

Silent eyes had caught him in the act. He caught sight of himself in the mirror, feeling suddenly ridiculous, standing there in his underwear kissing the shadows. The solemn young soldier studied him from his post at the mirror's edge, unmoved by the display, his sad eyes staring in their strange, penetrating way.

The ouroboros leaned down from the wall to look as he lay down on the bed and opened the book. The margin was penciled beside a passage on the page she'd marked. He began to read:

While the material was confined in the vessel it was closely watched. If the heat was kept constant and all was going well, there were a number of changes in color that were to occur and a fixed order in which they were to appear if success were to be achieved. The alchemists thought of these changes as the death and rebirth of the substance, for they believed that it was only through the death of the old substance that the new and more perfect matter could appear.

The first color, then, was black as the substance in the vessel underwent the process of death and decay. This stage was known as Raven's Head, and was said to end with the appearance of a starry glow on the surface of the substance, which the alchemists likened to the morning star that heralded the dawn.

During the second stage the heat was gradually increased over a period of weeks. This was a critical moment in the progress of the Work, and if one was on the right path a number of luminous colors were said to appear, encircling the substance. This was called the Peacock's Tail.

Cass looked up suddenly from the book. For an instant he felt himself crouched in the crawlspace again, peering through the hole at the vessel on the stove, the colors curling magically against the glass.

The end of the second stage was signaled by the appearance of a dazzling whiteness in the substance. Once this was achieved, the substance was considered strong enough to endure the final and most dangerous phase of the operation, the stage known as Redwork.

He lay there for a long time looking at the page, looking through it. It was nearly one by the time he turned out the light and went to open the window in hopes of luring in a little air while he slept. His mind was all awhirl with Maddy and alchemy, with furnaces and fires and kisses under streetlamps, and strange dreams of magical stones.

Outside, the night reigned, and the world that seemed so solid and sure in the light had suddenly turned loose and liquid. The murky shapes of trees and houses merged with the night sky. Dreams woke in the darkness and whispered from their beds. And for a moment the rigid pattern of lawns and lane fell away and he could almost feel himself cast back to a time when magic moved upon the earth.

He yanked the window wide and felt the night air ease into the room. He lay down on the bed, listened awhile to the whispering outside, and finally fell asleep.

—— 22 ——

"I READ THIS story once," said Maddy, "about these two brothers who lived alone in an old brownstone in Brooklyn. They'd been living there for years and years, and they were both very old. One of them was blind and partly paralyzed, and the other took care of him. He fed him nothing but buns and oranges, because for some strange reason he was convinced that they would restore his brother's sight—I'm not making this up. And he used to play to him all day long on the piano. He'd been a concert pianist when he was young.

"Anyway, the pianist never threw any of the papers away, just in case his brother might want to read them when he got his sight back, you see. He just kept piling them in the halls and in the basement along with all the other stuff he saved. Of course, the halls eventually became choked up with papers, and pretty soon there were just these narrow passages running like tunnels between the rooms. The pianist built booby traps in the passages to catch the robbers he was convinced were about to break into his house.

"Then one day the police got a call from a neighbor who suspected there was something wrong at the old place. The papers were piling up on the porch and no one had taken in the mail in nearly a month. The police failed to rouse anyone inside, so they decided to break in the front door. But they couldn't get in because of the papers. Finally they had the fire department put a ladder up to the second floor, and when they got in they discovered the blind brother sitting in his wheel-chair, dead of starvation. But there was no sign of the other brother. In the end, they made a hole in the roof and another in the basement and they just started taking things out both ends. Eventually they found the other brother, dead too, caught in a booby trap right outside his brother's door. But in the process of finding him they'd taken out one hundred and twenty tons of garbage and fourteen pianos."

Large portions of Mr. Magnus's place had simply lapsed back into wilderness. He had his appointed paths, which he traveled daily in fulfilling his limited tasks. What lay upon those paths and was close at hand formed part of his world. What lay beyond them or had for some reason become mislaid was simply forgotten. As for the confusion, it was as if he really didn't see it. His thoughts were occupied elsewhere, and in some strange way, the more cluttered and confining his quarters became, the freer he seemed to be inwardly.

After two weeks of sitting in the kitchen staring at the bird, Maddy breezed through the back door one afternoon carrying the old metal toolbox Cass remembered from her father's car. She didn't say so much as a word about it; she just set it down on the edge of the table and started in playing with Petrus. The bird was becoming accustomed to her hand in his cage, and just the last visit he had even gone so far as to put one foot tentatively on her finger, like a swimmer testing the water with a toe.

Mr. Magnus sat there sullenly with his false leg slung out straight in front of him and a disconcerting glimpse of wood showing below his pant cuff. He rolled himself another cigarette and smoked it down, eyeing the toolbox suspiciously all the while. It wasn't until he leaned forward to butt it out in the ashtray that he made a curt nod in the direction of the box.

"What's that for?" he said.

"Oh," said Maddy, all innocence, "I thought we might work on fixing up that front door frame."

He grunted. So far, except on the day of the accident, they had never strayed beyond the kitchen. And except for a quick walk through the clutter to bring in his groceries and mail or to wind the mantel clock, Cass had the feeling that Mr. Magnus rarely dared the front room himself. A thick layer of dust and neglect lay over everything, and bird droppings were liberally scattered about the room, as if it were Petrus's private preserve.

The bird put one foot on Maddy's finger as she nudged the perch, slowly did the splits as she edged it away, then with a quick jump found himself suddenly with both claws curled around her finger. He glanced nervously about as she eased her hand slowly out of the cage. She had no sooner gotten him through the door than the bird took to the air with a flurry and flew off into the wilds of the flat. It was the first time since the accident that he had left the cage.

Mr. Magnus had still not responded to Maddy's suggestion. He had allowed them this far into his life, this one small corner at the rear of his flat. And though he was more or less comfortable with that now, he was not likely to let them further in, it seemed.

But a few silent minutes after Petrus had flown off, he pushed himself out of his chair and reached for his cane.

"Better check on that bird," he said as he shuffled toward the door. "Come along, you two. And bring that box, young lady."

Cass carried in the teapot and cups and set them on the footstool in front of the old flowered armchair where Mr. Magnus had settled. Petrus flew contentedly from one room to another now, perching atop stray pieces of furniture, settling on the rabbit ears of an old TV pushed facefirst against the wall, as happy as if he had been set loose in the forest. The whir of his wings filled the air, that strange sound Cass had heard so often through the heat register in his room and been unable to place. He was tempted to duck for cover now whenever it came near.

Maddy carefully glued the broken pieces of frame she had put aside before, and Cass fitted them back like the pieces of a puzzle and held them in place. Now and then as they worked, Mr. Magnus would leave off watching them, lean forward and peer tentatively into one of the boxes spread around the floor at his feet, poke furtively among its contents, then slump back in the chair. He fiddled again for a while with the broken unicorn on the shelf by the chair, as if he more than half believed that the severed pieces might magically mend themselves if he simply held them the right way.

Meanwhile, Cass and Maddy talked between themselves as they worked. It was as she was struggling to tighten a large C clamp in place against the mended frame that she came out with the story of the weird brothers in Brooklyn.

Mr. Magnus, who until that time had appeared oblivious to their talk, looked up from the unicorn.

"A little cautionary tale, I take it," he said. "Like those nursery stories they used to force-feed children when I was young."

Maddy smiled as she screwed the clamp snug. Nothing more was said, but from that point on they spent their visits in the front room at his request, gradually chipping away at the accumulated junk.

As it turned out, most of the furniture and boxes had come from upstairs, where Mr. Magnus had lived while his mother was alive. After she had died and the stairs became too much for him, he had come back downstairs to live. But somehow he had found it impossible to throw her stuff out. So when he decided finally to rent out the upstairs as a separate flat in order to bring in some much-needed money, the renovator had simply emptied everything from the upstairs rooms and dumped it in the downstairs living room. Mr. Magnus had meant to go through it, sorting out the worthless from the worthwhile, but he had quickly come to realize how overwhelming a task it was. That had been several years earlier. Now he had simply learned to live with it. It had become part of the landscape.

This helped to explain the strange contrast in the rooms. The delicate order around the fringes of the place were his mother's: the ornaments on the mantelpiece, the crystal in the cupboards. The confusion at the heart of it was his own. He was like a permanent squatter in a shrine.

The first few meetings in the front room were painful for all. Mr. Magnus hovered over them constantly, apparently convinced that removing just one stack of the crumbling newspapers he had kept for some unfathomable reason or crushing one pile of the empty boxes he insisted on saving would somehow threaten the order of the universe. He insisted on opening each bundle and going through it piece by piece in case there might be something important in it. It was a rare occasion when he didn't discover something momentous buried in the pages of any given paper, and he would put it aside with promises to go through it and clip the article when they were gone.

In no time at all an enormous pile of papers had accumulated beside his chair. And all they had to show after a week's worth of work was a slim bundle of thirty-year-old classifieds and a few flattened boxes. Gradually though, grudgingly, he began to see the futility of the exercise. They were simply picking up the junk piece by piece and shifting it all five feet over, in front of the chair. In no time at all the chair would disappear completely behind the piles.

All this time Maddy had managed to hold her tongue, but every time she and Mr. Magnus traded glances, Cass could see the story of the weird brothers pass silently between them.

Eventually he grew more or less resigned to throwing out the newspapers unseen, along with the egg cartons and empty chocolate boxes that covered the couch. From that point on there were never less than two green garbage bags of junk waiting for the garbage men on collection days. The paths through the place grew gradually wider, the room brighter, and one day Cass realized with a jolt that he could actually see large parts of the pattern in the old Persian carpet that covered the floor.

Now Mr. Magnus contented himself with sitting in his chair, sifting through the bundles of old magazines that had surfaced once the first load of papers had been removed. These he did insist on seeing, and soon the old stuffed chair was surrounded by neat piles of them. There were stacks of *Life*, *The Saturday Evening Post*, *Chatelaine*, and a few other glossy-style magazines that he called "slicks," along with an incredible collection of what he called "pulps," printed on newsprint, with lurid covers that had Maddy arching her eyebrows, and titles like *Black Mask*, *Startling Stories*, and *Weird Tales*.

He pored over them patiently with the large magnifying glass he used for reading, discovering lost gold. Sometimes he would softly chuckle to himself or point out something that had caught his eye or read them a few clichéd lines from one of the old stories. Now and then he would glance up at them while they worked, but now not nearly with the same suspicion he had followed them with at first. For the most part he was content to sit in the big chair and watch, smoking cigarettes and sipping endless cups of tea.

Sometimes he would nod off in the midst of his reading. His head would slump slowly forward onto his chest and the magnifying glass would fall from his hand with a soft thud to the floor. These little interludes would rarely last more than a few minutes, and then he would just open his eyes, look on the ground for the glass, and begin again as if he had simply paused for an instant to rub his eyes.

After one such episode he realized he didn't have his glasses and began feeling around for them. He found them on the footstool, put them on, and settled back in the chair, looking over at them.

"No need to stare," he said. "I was sleeping. You do that when you're old, you know. I was dreaming about my mother. I dream about her a good deal these days, always the way she was when I was young, not when she was old and potty like me."

"You're not potty," said Maddy.

He ignored her. "Sometimes I can go for the better part of a day, dragging the remnants of these dreams around with me. It gets harder and harder to tell where the waking ends and the dreaming begins."

He took a sip of his tea and reached into his pocket for his tobacco. He was wearing one of the old summer suits they had uncovered on the couch under the egg cartons and empty boxes. There had been two of them, along with a neat pile of stiff-collared white shirts. Mr. Magnus had no idea where they had come from or how long they had been lying there, although he admitted they looked faintly familiar. Maddy had hung the suits on hangers and hooked the hangers from the door frame leading to the bathroom and the two rooms with permanently closed doors beyond. They had hung there for a week or more. Mr. Magnus was supposed to put them away, but somehow he just never got around to it, and pretty soon he simply got used to having to brush by them on his way to the bathroom.

But today they were gone and he was wearing one of them along with a clean white shirt. It was the first time they had seen him in anything but the formless brown pants and threadbare jacket he always wore. He felt through the unfamiliar pockets for the tobacco, finally turned it up, and began to roll himself a cigarette.

For a moment, as he sat there in his new suit going through the ritual, it seemed to Cass that all traces of the shuffling old man had suddenly vanished. It was as if some door had secretly opened inside him for a time and some near-forgotten ghost of himself had dashed out to fill the lean frame to overflowing. The cast dropped from his eyes, the uncertain hands grew steady and strong. He licked the paper and sealed it shut.

"What was I talking about?" he said as he lit a match and touched it to the end of the cigarette.

"Your mother," said Cass, remembering the pictures in the cardboard box in his closet: the group gathered in the yard, the woman shielding her eyes against the sun, the young man sitting beside her, smoking, smiling; words scrawled across the bottom of the soldier's picture—"For Mother—much love, Arthur."

Mr. Magnus stopped, the match still lit in his hand, and looked at him. Again for a long moment that uncanny feeling passed between them. Then he waved the match out and dropped it in the ashtray.

"Yes," he said, "my mother. I was going to tell you what happened to me after you left last time. I was sitting here, reading one of these fool magazines, and I fell asleep. When I woke up I had no idea what time it was. I was completely confused, and to top it off I couldn't find my glasses, which only made it that much worse. They weren't on the table or the footstool and I hadn't a clue where I might have set them down. So I got up and went looking for them. I was still more than half asleep.

"Well, I was walking over there." He made a vague sweep with his hand toward the bathroom. "And I bumped into those bloody suits hanging there and knocked them down. It nearly scared the life out of me, I'll tell you. Well, I was bending to pick them up, you see, and suddenly I heard my mother's voice calling to me through the door of her room. There," he said, turning to Maddy. "Now tell me I'm not potty.

"Yet the funny thing was that at the time it didn't surprise me in the least to hear her voice. She sounded exactly as she had sounded when I was a child, and she called me by the name she called me then. 'Artie,' she said. 'Is everything all right?'

"I felt like a little boy again. The door handle had the same awkward feel in my hand, and the smell that met me as I went into the room was the painfully familiar smell of the lilac powder she used to use. The room was dim, of course. By then I had gathered that it must be evening, and yet I didn't turn on the light. I knew somehow that I dare not.

"She was sitting at her mirror, letting down her hair. She wore her hair in a braid always, caught up into a bun at the back. Beautiful hair, auburn, very thick. As she unpinned it she dropped the pins with a little 'ping' into the porcelain dish on the dressing table. Without my glasses I could only half see her in the uncertain light.

"'Is everything all right?' she said again. 'I heard something fall.'

"'Yes, Mother,' I said. 'Everything is fine.'

"I walked toward her. She was separating the braid now with her fingers, and when she was done she picked up her brush and began to comb out her hair. I stood and watched, just watched, as I had so often back then, listening to the swish and crackle of the brush, seeing the bright sparks of static dancing off the hair in the dim room, and feeling an aching longing the like of which I have not felt in years.

"'You've lost your glasses,' she said quite calmly, glancing up at me in the mirror. "'You look older without them.'"

"'Yes,' I said, and the word echoed in my mind like something shouted down a tunnel. She gave a quick toss of her head and her hair fell loose down her back. Then she held out the brush to me. It was part of a nightly ritual we performed. She would hand it to me, and I would finish the brushing out for her while she sat and talked.

"I stood there, afraid that stirring would break the spell, and she looked at me in the mirror with her head cocked to one side as if to say, 'What's the matter, dear? Is there something wrong?' So I slowly crossed the room to her, reached out, and took the brush from her hand.

"In that instant she was gone. And there I was, alone in the room in front of my mother's mirror, staring at a mad old man holding a brush in his hand.

"I finally found the glasses. I'd left them lying in the kitchen. But since then there's not a time I walk by her door that I don't stop and listen a bit, hoping that I'll hear her there, that she'll call out to me again."

He stopped speaking, and for a long while he was far away, lost in thought. The house was so still that Cass could hear the muffled sound of children playing in the park through the closed window. It sent a ripple of strangeness through him, for it seemed that it was something happening far off in another world entirely.

Removing the newspapers simply served to uncover more junk buried beneath, like small treasures tucked away under tissue paper for safekeeping. Dusty boxes full of musty-smelling books that had been stored in the attic for countless years before the renovations had disturbed them. Old novels neither of them had ever heard of, ancient schoolbooks, books of poetry with brittle flowers pressed between their brittle pages. Letters kept in candy boxes, wound with ribbon, still smelling faintly of scent, the envelopes gone yellow with age, all of them postmarked fifty years past. Boxes of photographs, some secure in albums, others come loose and lying curled and brown like drifts of dry leaves. Heavy boxes of dusty, mismatched dishes, their patterns chipped and faded. A set of tarnished silverware lying sadly in state in its velvet-lined box. Boxes of broken ornaments wrapped in tissue and laid to rest: a pale dancer in pirouette lacking both arms, a woman in formal dress, her head tucked in tissue at her feet. Old 78-rpm records housed in cumbersome album books, each thick disc tucked in a separate sleeve.

They would lug each box over in front of the flowered chair and set it on the footstool to be opened. Mr. Magnus would peek in, sift hesitantly through the contents, perhaps leafing briefly through a photo album or fanning through some half-forgotten book, sending bits of leaf and flower drifting to the floor. But his interest was at best halfhearted, and he seemed happiest when the box was closed once again on the memories it contained.

Maddy labeled each one with large letters on the side and set them against the wall under the window: LETTERS, ORNAMENTS, BOOKS, in bold block letters.

"Memories," muttered Mr. Magnus as yet another box was added to the pile. "Too bloody many memories." He swept the bird from his shoulder, where it was in the habit of sitting, and reached for his cigarette.

"I can feel them perched here like this bird, their sharp

claws fixed in my shoulder, babbling in my ear. I can feel them crowding round me, trying to crush me as flat and dead as those dreadful flowers. Well, I won't have it," he shouted at the boxes. "Do you hear me in there? I won't have it." His face had gone all blotchy again.

At that moment the old clock on the mantel began to chime the hour. He looked up at it, then at them, then labored himself out of the chair and went shuffling off to the kitchen. There was a light slap of the screen door behind him as he left the house, heading for the garage.

This had by now become a familiar routine. For on each day they visited, at exactly four o'clock, he would rise from his chair and go shuffling off for ten or fifteen minutes. And when he got back, his hands would be dirty with charcoal and a certain magic would smolder in his eyes.

"He's gone off to check the fire," Maddy said when he had gone. And as always, they were sorely tempted to give their freedom a little reign and perhaps peek into one of the two rooms that remained closed to them. But again, as always, they did not.

They had just managed to drag the large wardrobe that had been sitting in the middle of the living room floor into the dining room and had pushed it up against the wall beside the radio, where it seemed quite at home. Twenty minutes had gone by and Mr. Magnus still had not returned.

Maddy turned her attention to the large old box that sat alone now in the middle of the living room floor. It was too awkward to lift, and therefore had been left until last. Unlike the others, this was a wooden box, a sort of glorified packing crate, the lid hinged with wire. Another twist of wire secured the hasp. Maddy managed to unwind it and work it free.

As she lifted the lid Cass felt a chill race down his spine. Lying there on top of the box was an old brown coat with tarnished brass buttons running down the front. It was the uniform jacket that the young soldier was wearing in the photo on the mirror. He knew it instantly, as if it were his own. He walked over to the box. Maddy was still standing over it, seemingly afraid to touch it, sensing the spell that lay over the contents of the box. He had the sudden sense that they had just entered some corner of Mr. Magnus as secret as the work he was engaged in in the garage, as hidden as the rooms that remained closed.

There was a powerful smell of mothballs and mildew in the air now. He bent down and picked up the jacket. Half a dozen mothballs rained down onto the rug. He noticed the large irregular stain running down one side of the uniform, the ragged gash in the wool. For an instant it felt as if he were squeezed back in the crawlspace again, the pain knifing up his leg as he knelt down on the jagged ring of glass.

Suddenly the stain felt warm and wet in his hand. The room flickered before his eyes, like a candle about to wink out, and the floor went sickeningly soft underfoot. He jumped, and let the jacket fall in a harmless heap to the floor. Something tumbled from the pocket and lay among the mothballs on the rug.

Maddy looked at him a long time before she stooped and picked it up. It was a small object wrapped in a bloodstained piece of cloth. The unwrapping revealed a blackened bit of metal, ragged around the edges, curled up like the dried rind of an orange.

"What *is* it?" she whispered.

"I don't know." But even as he said it he knew suddenly exactly what it was.

"Feel it," she said. "It's heavy." And she handed it to him.

It was no sooner in his hand than the wave of panic washed over him again. But this time there was nothing he could do.

His feet felt fused to the floor and he watched in horror as one by one the objects on the walls winked out, and the walls advanced upon him, crumbling into mud as they came. The air was thick with lightning and thunder, and the bright copper taste of terror was on his tongue.

He looked down desperately at Maddy, saw the sudden shock register in her eyes, then felt a thin arm reach down over his shoulder and pluck the piece of metal from his hand.

He crumpled to the floor as if a cord that held him up had been cut.

— 23 —

WHEN THE ROOM snapped back into shape again, Mr. Magnus was standing over him with the blackened bit of metal in his hand.

"Get him some water," he said to Maddy. He looked down at the open box, the uniform jacket lying in a heap on the floor.

"I'm sorry," said Cass. "I—"

"Don't bother apologizing, young man. I know well enough what happened." He lowered himself slowly into his chair and set the piece of metal on his lap.

"Ghosts," he said. "I could hear them come howling out of that box from all the way out there." He shifted his wooden leg over in front of him. Maddy came back with a teacup full of water. She sat down on the floor beside Cass and handed it to him, her face full of concern.

"Are you all right?" she asked.

"Yes, I'm all right. Just a bit of a faint or something." He sipped the warm water, avoiding Maddy's eyes, watching Mr. Magnus fiddle with the twisted scrap of metal.

"Ghosts," muttered the old man again, his eyes roving around the room, plumbing the shadows as if for signs. He reached for his tobacco, his fingers stained with soot, and began the slow ritual of rolling himself a cigarette. Petrus looked on from his perch on the mantelpiece.

"Do either of you know what this is?" said Mr. Magnus finally, nodding down at the lump of metal in his lap. Maddy shook her head.

"It's a piece of pig iron," said the old man as he moistened the paper and sealed it shut. "A bit of shrapnel from a mortar shell. Back in what they like to call the Great War the shells were full of scrap iron like this, you see. And when they exploded—well, you can imagine for yourself the terrible damage they'd do." He lit the cigarette, started to cough, and looked deliberately at Maddy, who looked away.

"This bit here ended the war for me. The doctors took it from my hip. Lucky to be alive, they said. Lucky, indeed. There were others not so lucky."

He picked up the jagged piece of iron and studied it against the light. The silence, *his* silence, washed over them.

"It's so long ago," he said. "So very very long ago. I was fifteen, no older than you are now, when I was sent to the Front. I lied about my age. I wasn't the only one, mind you. No, the trenches were full of boys—none of them nearly old enough to vote, but all of them more than old enough to die. And die they did, by the thousands, like sheep sent to the slaughter.

"What fools we were. We couldn't wait to get over there. Couldn't wait. Our only fear was that it might end before we got there, that we'd miss all the fun. We had no idea what was in store. It was all just a glorious adventure, you see. The stuff we'd seen in schoolbooks—men marching proudly into battle, colors flying, swords bared. And barely a whisper of blood. Barely a whisper."

There were a few minutes of smoky silence. Cass sat on the floor, fingering the buttons of the old uniform, feeling more like running than he had ever felt in his life. A crack of darkness was quietly widening under him.

"It's as if it happened yesterday. Yet years and years and years have gone by. Years when I wouldn't spare it so much as a thought, absolutely refused to, you see. It already had enough of me. It took this body and bent it like a piece of pipe cleaner. I wasn't about to let it take my mind too. It did others, you know. Lived their whole lives through as though the bloody mess had never ended. They couldn't stand to let it end somehow, couldn't stand the waste.

"But suddenly it's all come back, come back with a terrible clarity. There's barely a night goes by now that I don't dream of it. I lay there and suddenly it's as if I'm back there again, with the snap of the guns overhead and that awful moaning of the shells in the air. And I can feel the mud thick between my toes, and the lice moving over my skin."

He leaned forward and crushed out the cigarette in the ashtray. His eyes were full of distance, and the silence of the room swelled around them. Cass and Maddy knew enough by now to say nothing, for to prod him would make him immediately suspicious and apt to stop.

"Trenches they called them. Ditches was what they were. Hundreds of miles of them stretching across the countryside in a double line. Us here, the enemy there, with barely a hundred yards between us in places. And over everything this terrible silence, a silence that could be shattered in an instant by a sudden shelling or the quick snap of a sniper's gun. That silence stays with me still.

"Most of it was waiting, just waiting there in the mud for

something to happen—waiting for death to happen. It drove some men mad. Shell shock, they called it. It was nothing of the kind. Exhaustion was what it was. Sheer exhaustion at having to live day in and day out in that awful mud, mud so thick it would rip the soles right off your shoes, eating nothing but tinned beef and hardtack with plum jam. Unable to sleep because of the cold, because of the mud, because of the bloody lice. Lice so bad you couldn't stand it. Once a day we'd strip off our shirts and run a lighter along the seams to kill off as many as we could. It didn't help, nothing helped.

"And if you did manage to doze off, there were the rats. Huge rats, rats the size of cats, foraging on the great heaps of garbage that grew alongside the trenches. Thousands upon thousands of them, everywhere, squealing incessantly, nipping your legs up to the knees while you slept, dropping down over the edge of the parapet in the dark."

Mr. Magnus looked down and saw Cass and Maddy staring up at him open-mouthed.

"Bah," he said. "Enough of this nonsense." He banged the lump of shrapnel down on the shelf beside the chair. "It's done, over and done." He took a long, loud sip of tea, then sat there fidgeting with the ring on his finger, twisting it like a talisman that might lay to rest the ghosts they had raised and charm the silence back again. But the silence that fell was not the same silence, and the ghosts would not be stilled.

"How were you wounded?" Cass found himself saying as he stared down at the dark stain on the side of the uniform. And when Mr. Magnus pretended not to hear, the question came again.

"And what's this?" said Mr. Magnus. "Let's humor the old man? Well, you needn't bother, my boy."

"Nobody's humoring anyone," said Cass. "I want to know. I *have* to know."

He looked up, and for one alarming moment he was staring

into the wide, frightened eyes of the boy in the photo, sitting there with that old body wrapped about him like a blanket, peering out through the eyeholes back at him. Then it was gone, and the old man was reaching for his tobacco again. He didn't say a word all the time he was rolling the cigarette, but his fingers trembled at the task and the dry tobacco rained down onto his lap.

"We knew the big attack was coming," he said as he lit the cigarette. "It was just a matter of when. We'd been training for it for months, poring over maps, learning every inch of the no-man's-land that lay between ourselves and the enemy, each of us drilled repeatedly on the task assigned to him in the attack.

"Still, when word finally came down that it was 'over the top' next morning at first light, I found myself suddenly gripped with absolute terror, terror such as I've never felt before or since. I'd never been in an actual attack before. Oh, there were the occasional trench raids under cover of darkness, the odd skirmish meant to keep the enemy off guard. But this was different. This was staring death straight in the face.

"There was no sleep that night. We were wedged in there like sardines, shoulder to shoulder, standing knee-deep in mud in full battle kit, without the slightest hope of rest. I thought that night would never end.

"Standing beside me in the trench was a fellow I'd become friends with. He was much older than I and he'd taken me under his wing in the months I'd been there, shown me the ropes, the little things one needed to know just to keep one's sanity amid all that madness. In any event, we'd become friends.

"He had some sort of an accent. I don't know what it was, something European, maybe even German. He was from somewhere out west, I think, though he was always very vague about exactly where. He was rather a queer fellow in many ways, and the others kept their distance from him. It might have had something to do with the accent, but there was more to it than that. He was a very solitary sort, and whenever he had a free moment, his head was always buried in a book. It was always the same book, a small old book he carried around with him in his pack, wrapped up in a piece of oilskin.

"Well, something about this fellow piqued my curiosity. It might have been the book, might have been the mystery that surrounded him. He struck me as an almost magical figure, a creature from another place and time who had magically appeared from the mud. I was more than a little mad even then, you see.

"I hung about him and eventually he took notice of me, and by and by, as I say, we became friends. It's hard for me to describe how close men grew under the conditions we lived in. It was only friendship that allowed you to rise above the horror that surrounded you, that enabled you to escape from it for a time.

"I knew this man for less than a year of this ridiculously long life I've lived and yet I can say quite truthfully that I have never in all these long years since then known anyone as intimately as I came to know that man in those few horrifying months we lived together in hell.

"But I'm wandering in the story. I'm allowed to do that, you know. When you're as old as I am you're expected to wander a little.

"I was talking about the last night, the night before my life was to be changed forever. Some men were speaking in whispers among themselves, others were deathly silent, their minds on what lay ahead. Philip was beside me."

"Philip?" said Maddy. She looked suddenly at Cass. "Yes, that was my friend's name—Philip. Philip Von something or other. It doesn't matter. He spent the first part of the night hunched over a candle end, busy with his book, writing brief letters back home, as were many others, just in case. Anyway, he must have sensed how terrified I was, because he suddenly left off with what he was doing, pinched out the candle, and came up with me there in the dark.

"It was a brilliantly clear night. The sky was alive with stars, and now and then it would briefly light up like day as an enemy flare went up over no-man's-land. Philip read the sky the way other people read books. He could pick out all the constellations, whatever planets were visible, and tell you everything you ever wanted to know about them. He believed that the position of the planets and the constellations influenced us somehow. That was another reason why people thought he was a little crazy. He had a whole host of odd notions about things that struck one strange.

"Well, on this night I was ready for whatever strangeness he could offer, and he was much more talkative than usual. Perhaps it was the effect of the fear on him, I don't know. It doesn't matter. In any event, he talked the whole of that long, horrifying night through with me. And in the process he told me of things the like of which I had never dreamed before. Strange, secret things. It seemed utterly fantastic to me. I wasn't sure, between the fear and the fatigue at having been awake for so long, that I was even hearing him right. But he seemed very concerned that I hear him out, so hear him out I did. And all the while the rats were scurrying about our feet and the lice were moving on our skin, and we were standing there up to our boot tops in mud waiting for dawn.

"At first light there was a stirring in the line and the rum jar came along. It was Jamaican rum, very strong. Everyone took a good long swallow. A few minutes later the order to "fix bayonets" came down, and all along the line you could hear the rattle of the loose rings locking into place. It was a terrible, desolate sound. The morning was cold and the mud was dusted with frost, but already the rum was doing its work and the chill was off us. I could hear the faint drone of a plane overhead, and I remember wondering if it was one of ours or one of theirs. And suddenly all hell broke loose.

"The big guns started thundering all at once. It was a noise impossible to describe, like nothing I've heard before or since, and we were ordered over the top. Men started scrambling one after another up the ladders. I was absolutely paralyzed with fear, but somehow I made it up. And then it was just running, running madly through the mud and the shell holes with the artillery raining a thick curtain of shell cover just in front of us as we advanced up the ridge. We'd been drilled over and over on our individual objectives, warned time and again not to get ahead of the guns as we advanced. But all of that went out of my mind and a great swelling panic took its place as I saw the whole world suddenly become a screaming, churning bedlam. I had no idea where I was or what I was supposed to be doing. I could hear the sharp jackhammer stutter of the enemy machine guns and I could see the men in front falling just like wheat before the scythe. Someone screamed out beside me and lurched forward, landing face first in the bottom of a shell hole, unmoving. I stopped, just gaping at the dead man, utterly unable to go on.

"It was Philip who turned and saw me there and came back for me. That was the first time that day he was to save my life. He pulled me along by the sleeve until we reached the large crater that was our objective. The others were already there and the machine gun had been set up and was already doing its work. I unwound the ammunition strips I was carrying and collapsed against the side of the hole.

"Gradually the raging of the battle around us died down as the troops dug in, having broken through the forward lines of the enemy defenses. But there was still far too much fire-power from their rear lines for the reserve troops to move forward. We found ourselves out in the middle of nowhere under heavy fire, with nowhere to go. We kept firing away, but we were firing at ghosts really. And all the while the shells kept coming over and hitting very close by.

"Then suddenly, out of all that tumult, I could hear the low moan of a large shell coming. The sound it made was different somehow from that of any other shell I had ever heard. It was as if it were alive, and immediately I knew it was going to hit us. I flung myself down on the ground against the side of the crater facefirst. There was a sudden horrific roar, and then there was nothing.

"When I came around again it was daylight. I had no idea how long I'd been lying there. The first thing I saw was the cloud of yellow gas creeping over the edge of the shell hole. An enemy plane was circling high in the sky overhead. I thought I must be the only one left. There wasn't a sign of life from the others, what was left of them. And so I lay there with the blood flowing out of me, the gas flowing in like fire, and knowing in a distant sort of way that I was dying. And my only fear was that the enemy might find me first.

"Suddenly I sensed someone moving around in the hole. He came nearer and nearer until I felt him bending over me. Then I heard my name, and I opened my eyes, and Philip was standing there before me absolutely covered in mud from head to toe. I thought at first I must be dreaming, for I was sure he was dead, you see, dead, along with all the others. But there he was.

"'Can you move?' he said. 'We have to get you back.' I told him yes, I could move, but it was desperation really. I just didn't want him to leave me lying there with the life going out of me and the enemy all around.

"The only way to get back to safety was to crawl, he said, so that the snipers wouldn't pick us off. He took the front and I followed. We hadn't gone more than a few yards before I realized it was useless, I would never make it. 'Hang on to my foot,' he said to me. And I did and in that way he dragged me all the way back, choking on the gas, clutching his boots with both hands. It felt like forever until we finally reached our lines. But then we were there, and he pushed something into my hand and lowered me down over the edge of the trench.

"The rest is vague. I suppose they saw right quick what sort of shape I was in and I was taken to the dressing station, then away by ambulance, and finally by boat to a hospital in England, and me fading in and out all the while.

"The leg was beyond saving. They had patched me up as best they could, took that lump there from my hip, dug bits of shrapnel from my back, changed the dressings daily on my stump. It was as they were first tending to me that the nurse on duty discovered my hands clenched into fists. I'd kept them closed tight with the pain all that time. She eventually had to pry them open, and when she did she discovered along with the stinking mud from the battlefield this ring." He raised the ringed hand. "His ring."

"That was the last I saw of Philip. Later they sent me that book of his along with a brief note saying that they'd found it among his things with a note willing it to me should anything happen to him. They found him along with all the others in our section in that shell hole out in the middle of no-man's-land, dead. And so, you see, I owe my life to a ghost."

He looked down at them briefly, then got up and wandered off to the kitchen with his cup. A few seconds later the screen door banged shut with a shudder behind him.

Cass folded the uniform jacket and returned it carefully to the box. He gathered up the mothballs that had fallen to the floor and tucked them along with the bloodied bit of cloth the piece of shrapnel had come wrapped in into the pocket of the jacket. He had not the slightest desire to rummage through the rest of the box, to pull out the old helmet whose round dome rose above the bundle of letters and other belongings hidden beneath. They had already raised quite enough ghosts, and to coax them back into the box now would be as futile as coaxing Petrus back into his cage. He could hear them moving about the room, but the sound they made was not the rapid whir of wings. It was the dreadful howl of shells, the moans of dying men.

He no longer felt faint, but an overwhelming sense of strangeness surrounded him as he quietly returned the things to the box, closed the lid, and secured the wire in the hasp. He felt like someone moving in his sleep, someone who was more than merely he.

Once the box was closed the room began to settle into its accustomed shape, the tide of memory retreated, and the objects of the room emerged wet, as though reborn. Maddy was perched on the edge of the couch, staring at him. He was almost surprised to discover her in the room with him.

"We should go," she said.

"Yes." Go where, he wondered. Wasn't this home?

She retrieved their coats from the kitchen, took him from where he was standing in the middle of the room, and guided him to the door. She closed the door quickly behind them, as quickly as he had closed the lid on the box. For a few minutes they stood there in silence at the foot of the stairs.

"Are you going to tell me?" she said finally.

"Tell you what?"

"What happened in there with you and him. I was watching

you, Cass. You knew, didn't you? Somehow you knew the whole story already. Just like you knew Philip's name."

He nodded slowly, hardly able to admit it to himself.

"But how could you have? How?"

The question followed him around for the rest of the day. Even Alison noticed he was acting strangely. He told her it was nothing, just a headache. He spent the better part of the evening in his room, lying on the bed, staring at the portrait of the soldier on the mirror.

Something had happened. Somehow their separate lives had become linked, even as far as their dreams. It was as if his coming to this house had completed something—like the teeth of the snake coming down on its tail.

He was no longer who he had been. The boy watching invisibly from windows was gone, gone forever. Another now stood in his place. It had happened slowly, steadily, like the smoke drifting from the chimney, the music rising through the register. Yet somehow he had sensed it from the very start: that odd feeling of familiarity he'd had on that first day sitting with Alison on the bench in the snow; the sense of rightness he'd felt when he first entered this room; the magic of the moment when he'd first looked into the face of the shy young soldier. In some strange way, in coming here he had come home.

It was late now. He was standing in front of the dresser pulling on his pajamas, studying his reflection in the mirror. And suddenly it seemed that up through the flaws that riddled the mirror's surface like shell holes, another image crept quietly over the glass. So that now the hands that fed the buttons through the holes were frail, the skin sere and thin, the delicate webwork of veins spun just below the surface.

He slowly raised his head until his eyes met those of the

figure in the glass—not a stranger's eyes, but his own, staring in wonder from an ancient face. It lasted but a moment, and then it was gone, and there was only his own pale reflection peering back at him.

Suddenly he recalled what Mr. Magnus had said about the boy who lived inside him still. And for the first time Cass realized that this old man lived inside him in the same way, and that in meeting Mr. Magnus he had not simply met some sad old man struggling to make magic, but some secret part of himself he had not even dreamed was there. They were but different moments in the one cycle.

No beginning, no end.

He lay for a long time in bed that night, looking up at the ceiling, at the same time feeling himself squatting in a muddy ditch staring up into the night sky.

Things had blurred, the boundaries had faded. He no longer knew where he ended and Mr. Magnus began.

— 24 —

ONCE ALL THE BOXES had been identified and labeled, there arose the troublesome question of what on earth to do with them all. They couldn't very well leave them stacked in precarious piles against the walls of the room as they were now. Much of the stuff was really only good for the garbage, but to convince Mr. Magnus of that was nothing short of impossible. Finally, with the exception of two large boxes full of jars and bottles that were destined for the garage, they decided that the rest should be banished to the basement.

"If it's still there," said Mr. Magnus, for it seemed that for several years now the farthest he had ventured into the basement was the back of the door where his collection of plastic bags was kept. He was deathly afraid of falling down the stairs as his mother had.

"Broke her hip, and that was the end of her. Put her in the hospital, and she never came out again," he said. "These old bones are as brittle as glass."

He had good reason to be wary of the stairs. They were very steep, shallow, open at the back. A couple of the steps wobbled threateningly under Cass and Maddy as they started down into the gloom, laden with labeled boxes.

Mr. Magnus stood on the landing at the top, giving instructions. At one end of the basement, in behind the stairs, there were rows of rough wooden shelves. They were to put the boxes there. Somewhere they would find a switch for the bare bulb dangling from the ceiling; he was not sure where. While they groped blindly through cobwebs searching for it, he groped in his mind for the memory of where it was. In the end they gave up and made do with the dim shuttered light shining through the stairs.

To get the boxes on the shelves they had first to shift aside stacks of old flowerpots, boxes of shriveled bulbs hung with earth, ancient and no doubt worthless cans of paint, and various other murky odds and ends that had sat undisturbed for heaven knew how long. On the back wall, beneath a small window covered with a piece of yellowed plastic, there were shelves of canned goods and jars of preserves. Several of the cans had burst with age, and clotted goo clung to their sides. Several more were swollen out of shape.

"Be sure to put the labels facing out," Mr. Magnus called down. "So that I can read them." He didn't bother explaining how he intended to read the labels from the top of the stairs.

"Hey," said Maddy, who had been busy poking about in the shadows. "This must be the stand for the bird cage." She carted it up the stairs with them as they went for another load of boxes.

"Well," said Mr. Magnus as they passed him at the head of the stairs, "how is it?" It was as though he were asking about someone who'd been sick.

"The basement, you mean?" said Cass. "Oh, it's fine, I guess."

Maddy slid past with the pole. "I suggest you brick it in," she mumbled. "Just in case it starts moving back up again."

Several loads later the three of them stood in the kitchen doorway peering cautiously in at the front room. Without the boxes the place looked almost abandoned. There was still the clutter, still the dust, still far too much furniture and odds and ends. But the sudden openness of the room was overwhelming. Only the corner that housed the old armchair was still comfortably contained, with a semicircle of magazines and two teetering stacks of record albums keeping the encroaching orderliness at bay.

"Well," said Cass. "What do you think?"

"I'd say it could use a few piles of old papers right about there," said Maddy, pointing to the center of the room. "Other than that—perfect."

Mr. Magnus snorted and shuffled over to put the kettle on for tea. He hid his confusion over knobs and burners now by first turning on the gas, then setting the kettle down wherever the flame happened to spring up.

Cass settled in one of the kitchen chairs, easing his finger through the door of Petrus's cage and making kissy noises as he had seen Maddy do. The bird glanced up from its millet stick and quickly skittered over to the far side of the cage. Being rejected by a person was one thing, but being rejected by a bird was a little hard to take. He took his finger out and closed the door of the cage.

Maddy was busy examining the stand she'd brought up from

the basement. It was covered with a thick layer of dust and cobwebs and didn't look like much of anything as far as Cass could see.

"Do you have a cloth I could use to wipe this down, Mr. Magnus?" she asked.

Mr. Magnus paused from heaping spoonfuls of loose tea into the pot and nodded in the direction of the drawers beneath the sink.

"Try one of those there," he said uncertainly.

Maddy unearthed a ragged square of flannel from the bottom drawer and began to carefully dust down the stand. The water came to a boil and Mr. Magnus filled the pot and clamped down the lid. He reached down the tea cozy hanging from the cupboard handle and settled it over the pot, then gathered up the cups and brought them over to the table.

Cass took the steaming cup, brushed the seed hulls from his corner of the table, and set it down to cool. While Mr. Magnus rolled himself a cigarette, Cass watched Maddy work on the stand. As it came clean it revealed a detailed design. A pattern of vines wound around the ribbed pole and formed the hook from which the cage was to be hung at the top.

"This is very old, you know," she said, standing back to admire it.

Mr. Magnus was unimpressed. "Everything in this house is old," he said. "Including me." He shook the flame from a wooden match and dropped it into a dirty saucer beside the cage.

"I think it's brass," said Maddy. "It's hard to tell though, under all this tarnish."

Mr. Magnus had lost interest. He was squinting at a corner of the newspaper that hung over the edge of the table while he smoked. The tea was so strong you could have stood a spoon in it.

As Cass sipped from his cup he watched the old man. Something about him seemed to have changed since he'd shared his war story with them. It had produced an almost physical change in him. He did not seem as stooped as he had before, did not seem to lean as heavily on the cane. It was as though a weight had been lifted from his back. He seemed younger, stronger. There was a look in his eyes that reminded Cass constantly now of the boy in the picture.

He still kept up his show of surliness, of course. That was simply part of him, something one learned to live with. But when their eyes met, Cass sensed that the guardedness was all but gone. He had said nothing to Mr. Magnus about the dreams. Somehow he sensed that there was no need to, that the old man had already understood it all himself.

He let his eyes wander freely around the room. The dusty snake plants crowding the windowsill, thriving on neglect, the dried herbs hung upside down from a slack bit of string by the door, the ancient appliances, relics of an earlier age, that persisted here still. But now he saw them with other eyes, eyes that saw past the dirt and dust that shrouded them now, to what they had once been and were still in memory.

"Bah," said Mr. Magnus as he tore off the strip of paper he'd been reading and flung it to the floor. "Now I'm reading obituaries."

He rapped his finger hard against the table edge, sending Petrus into a startled flurry.

"It's a very funny business, this growing old. A very funny business indeed. I doubt that I shall ever get used to it. There are times I find myself standing in front of my mirror, wondering who on earth that old man is staring back at me. Things I was quite capable of not so very long ago completely elude me now. I have to keep telling myself, 'You can't do it, Magnus. You simply can't do it, so stop trying.' But that's easier said than done, you see. Because there's always that young boy, locked inside this ruin, who resents this sudden loss of strength, resents this terrible tiredness that falls on top of me like a stone, that no amount of sleep will dislodge. He detests the slowness, everything taking longer and longer. He will not simply sit back and accept it, as the old are expected to do.

"It was he who let you through the door that day, not the old part of me. That part would sooner sit alone and brood. It was he who looked forward to your coming each day, to listening to you speak, watching you work, seeing you coax life back into this shuttered old house, and at the same time coax life back into me." He took one last long drag of the cigarette and butted it in the saucer. "And it is he who now needs your help."

Maddy stopped her cleaning in midstroke and looked up. Mr. Magnus was looking down at his lap, working the ring with his fingers.

"When I got back from the war," he began, "I tried with all my strength to put it behind me, to simply take up my life where I had left off and go on. But I couldn't. I was no longer the same person I had been, and I was no longer looked on in the same way. I had gone off sound and come back crippled, and I could no more put behind me what had happened there than I could make this shattered body whole again. Everything had changed, changed utterly.

"Neither could I forget Philip, nor what through some strange magic he had done for me. For broken and battered though I was, I was at least alive. This ring on my finger became a constant reminder of the debt I owed him, and by and by I found myself poring over the little book he had left me. It was, as you have no doubt already guessed, a book of alchemy."

Maddy's mouth fell open. "You knew?"

"I suspected." He poured the last of the leafy tea into his cup.

"For how long?" said Cass.

"Oh, almost from the start, I suppose." He sipped loudly at the tea. "I heard the mouse at the hole back there again after that first night. And I've seen the way you eye this ring, young man, not an ordinary eyeing, I assure you. For whatever reason, fate appears to have cast our common lots together. And now it seems we have even crept into each other's dreams.

"I have been over seventy years at this business — seventy wasted years, some would say. And in all that time I've taken great pains to keep it secret, for secrecy is the essence of the Art, the book says. But now, at last, it is at an end.

"In the beginning it was little more than a game. I was simply curious. Certainly I had no thought of discovering some magical stone. I had seen far too much blood and knew better than to believe in such fantasies. In that way I was not unlike you." He looked at Cass.

"At first I could make neither head nor tail of that little book. It was all strange symbols and secret words. But it drew me, and by degrees I came to understand that it was this that Philip had been speaking of on that last night in the trenches, and it was in this that the meaning of the ring lay. And it grew in my mind that somehow it had fallen to me to take up the task where he had left it off.

"The years passed and I continued in the Work, and slowly I began to see with other eyes. The earth about me then began to stir with secret life; the very stars in the sky seemed suddenly alive. And all things everywhere seemed to hunger after one thing: wholeness, and to strive one and all for completion, perfection.

"And somewhere, said the book, a seed lay hidden which,

when transformed by the magic of fire, possessed within itself the power to bring perfection out of imperfection, wholeness out of want, to coax gold from lead, to draw life even from the jaws of death. And it was not far off. In fact, it lay all around us, beneath our very noses, yet completely unrecognized by all.

"It was the dream that drew me on. Not the gold, no, never the gold. The gold I sought lay buried somewhere beneath the mud and slime of a field in France. I had been robbed of my youth. I went away a boy and came back a frail old man. And I longed with all my heart to have that boy back again, longed to rise up and shake off this shattered body like a slough of skin and have him reemerge.

"I have worn myself out on dreams. One could do worse, I suppose. In the end we are all dreamers dreaming dreams. And so every year, come spring, I begin the Work again. And it never quite turns out. There is always something I've forgotten, something I've left out. Something simple, I'm sure, for it is always the simple things one overlooks.

"And now it is simply a part of my life, something I do. A way, I suppose, of believing in the miraculous. And though this old part of me is convinced at times that it is all a foolish waste of time, the child shut inside me continues to dream and will not let it go. 'The next time,' he insists on saying. 'The next time we will manage it at last.'

"Well, the sad fact of the matter is that this old body can manage it no more. And that, you see, is why he let you in the door that day, why he needs, why we need your help."

From the living room with muted chimes the mantel clock struck four. It was the time when Mr. Magnus always disappeared to tend the fire. Now, as the sound faded into silence, there was a long, uneasy moment during which the three of them sat watching one another. Mr. Magnus stood up. He glanced over at the two large boxes of jars and bottles blocking the door, then turned to them.

"Perhaps you could give me a hand with these," he said.

The bottles chattered in the boxes as they made their way down the tenuous path to the garage. Mrs. Wharton's roses hung over the weathered fence and watched with wide pink eyes as the old man fumbled with his key in the lock.

They left the sunlight standing on the threshold and followed him in. He quickly closed the door on it, and for a moment there was darkness. Then a dim bulb leaped into light, and they found themselves standing at last in the witch's den.

"Set those down over there," said Mr. Magnus, motioning to a workbench near the back of the garage.

They wove their way through the clutter of broken furniture and discarded odds and ends. The floor was of bare earth, and the sharp smell of soil mingled with the odor of mildew and smoke from the fire. It was like having entered the burrow of some strange beast, its booty hoarded against the light. There was a loud complaint of glass as they set the boxes down on the lumber-littered bench.

The old man was over by the stove, feeding handfuls of charcoal from a sooty bag into its open metal mouth. The vessel itself was invisible now, hidden beneath a battered tin bucket inverted on top of the stove.

Cass found his eyes traveling instinctively to the side wall of the garage, the dusty wired window, an old wooden ladder hung on nails beneath it. And framed between two rungs of the ladder, a small knothole in the wall below the window, and a faint trace of daylight piercing through. Had he not known it was there, he would never have noticed it.

"You had better cover that over," said Mr. Magnus suddenly, standing now and staring over at him as he wiped the charcoal from his hands on a rag. "You never know what sort of creature might stumble on it one night." He turned and peered for a moment into the heart of the furnace, then closed the door with the cloth.

One of the pictures from the pile did the trick. A rather mildewed Resurrection scene: the stone rolled back from the mouth of the empty tomb, the radiant figure rising in the air. Cass hung it from one of the nails that held the ladder in place, covering the hole. The rock rolled back in place.

Outside, a screen door slapped closed, a clothesline creaked.

"That will be the enemy," said Mr. Magnus. "She's seen us all troop in here, no doubt. And she's wondering what we're up to."

The creaking of Mrs. Wharton's clothesline continued intermittently for a few minutes like the shrill cry of some carrion bird anticipating prey. Mr. Magnus stood near the door, ear cocked to the sound, finger to his lips. At last the bird took flight; the screen door rattled shut.

"All clear," said the old man. "The enemy has retreated—for the time being, at least."

He made his way over to the table by the stove, and from among the glass and metal implements clustered there lifted a leathery black thing, like the folded wings of a bat.

"Do either of you know what this is?" he said.

"A bellows," said Maddy immediately, and Cass remembered the woodcut in the book.

"Exactly," said the old man. "Then you will no doubt know that it is used to fan the fire." He set it down and hobbled over to the stove.

"To this point, all of the skill has lain in keeping the fire beneath the vessel at an even heat so that the matter inside might slowly mature, as a child flowers in the womb. But for the final stage the fire must be worked to a white heat for the transformation to occur and the Stone to be brought to birth. Someone must work the bellows, and work them long and hard. I no longer have the strength to do it; it is quite simply beyond me."

The old man turned to the stove and slowly raised the bucket from the hidden vessel. The room was washed in sudden radiance, like the radiance of the figure rising from the tomb. The glowing glass egg stood at the heart of it. This was the white radiance they had read about, the completion of the second stage of the Work.

"I am close this time," said Mr. Magnus. "Closer than I have ever been before. If I am not to fail I will need the aid of younger arms. But be warned, the final stage of the Work is most dangerous. The substance is extremely volatile. It kicks and strains against the glass, and there is always the risk that it may burst its bonds completely. One false step now, or the echo of an earlier error, will result in disaster." He turned to them.

"Knowing that, are you willing to help me?"

They looked at each other, then nodded quietly.

"In a little more than two weeks' time the sun and moon will both align in the constellation of Leo, the House of the Lion. We must consult the books to determine the exact dates, for it's then we must attempt the final phase—Redwork."

— 25 —

THE END was in sight. Redwork lay less than a week away. All their time now was spent in coaxing the fire to a steadily increasing heat. The slightest drop in temperature at this point would threaten the entire enterprise. A constant supply of charcoal was required. It was Cass who finally decided it would be wiser not to continue buying it from Magistrale's. With Maria now seeing Sid regularly, there was a good chance she might mention something about it to him. No one knew exactly how much Sid knew, but he was definitely suspicious, and there was no point in making him more so.

That meant that once every few days they had to go on a charcoal run. To take attention away from the house, they had been bringing the load in down the lane and storing it in Maddy's backyard until they could slip it into the garage under cover of darkness. Mr. Magnus's old bundle buggy, battered back into shape, had been enlisted for the task.

Today Cass was making the trip while Maddy stayed behind with Mr. Magnus. After first stopping at the library to consult an old *Astrological Ephemeris* for the exact dates of the alignment of sun and moon in Leo this year, he had ended up walking all the way to the Busy Bee. There he had loaded up with two large bags of charcoal, which would likely see them through to the end.

On the way back he passed the Palace. Though it was broad daylight, the marquee lights were on. Fischer was on top of the roof replacing the bulbs that had burned out. As Cass passed by unnoticed below, he briefly considered snatching away the ladder propped against the marquee and leaving him stranded up there. He certainly had it coming to him. He resisted the temptation, turned the corner, and started up the street.

Now that he was safely off the strip, he unzipped his backpack and took out the book he had discovered shelved beside the *Ephemeris* in the library. It was a collection of seventeenth-century English alchemical texts, mostly in the form of poems. The librarian had looked at him a little strangely when he signed it out. As he walked along the tree-lined street, he read aloud from it under his breath, the squeaking of the bundle buggy he pulled along behind him punctuating the rhythm of the words:

> Take Earth of Earth, Earthes brother
> And water of Earth that is another
> And fyer of Earth that beareth the pryce
> And of that Earth look thou be wise.
> This is the true Elixir for to make,
> Earth owt of Earth look thou take—

There was a sudden squeal of brakes directly beside him. He started, looked up, and found himself staring into the sinister, smiling face of Benny, the big guy who hung out with Sid. The mirrored shades he was wearing hid his eyes and cast Cass's own frightened reflection back at himself.

Benny humped the front wheel of the bike up onto the sidewalk in front of him, blocking his path.

"Well, well," he said with barely concealed glee, "if it isn't our good buddy Casper the friendly ghost." He made a sound that was supposed to be a laugh but sounded more like a snort, and rocked back and forth on the seat of his bike, pleased with himself. Cass had the uncomfortable feeling that he was in the presence of someone who wasn't quite all there. His stomach tightened and he felt a sick tingle run through him.

"Having a barbecue?" said Benny, taking in the bundle buggy loaded with charcoal.

"Yeah."

"Heh, that's nice. I like barbecues."

Cass searched frantically for some way out of this. They were near the end of the block. Just up ahead on the corner stood the Magistrales' store. Between it and them lay the entrance to the lane he had been about to take the buggy down. Two minutes more and he would have been off the street and out of sight. There was no point in thinking about that right now. The important thing was to try to keep calm and hope that he would come out of this in one piece.

He glanced quickly over his shoulder and down the street. Deserted. On the one hand, that meant that there was no one around to help him; on the other, it meant that Benny was apparently alone.

"Nice day for a walk, eh?" Benny's huge white hand wrapped itself around his upper arm like a steel trap and gave a little tug in the direction of the lane. When he didn't start moving right away, the hand tightened its grip a little, and Cass knew with sickening certainty that, if he wanted to, Benny could snap his arm in two like a dry twig. He started walking, and Benny let go.

He kept his eyes riveted to the sidewalk. His breath came in short, painful stabs. He could feel the blood shooting through his limbs in sudden panic. He concentrated on putting one foot in front of the other, trying to read deliverance in the cracks in the concrete, the whole world suddenly thrumming with the rhythm of fear. Out the corner of his eye he watched Benny's black boots bumping down on the pavement every few paces, pushing the bike along the curb, counterpointing the metallic titter of the gears.

The front tire suddenly loomed up in his path.

"Right here, Casper. This is our stop." The smile on his face looked like a crack in a slab of cream cheese.

The buggy bumped down off the sidewalk into the packed dirt of the lane. A bit of the broken wicker from the buggy began to rub against one of the wheels. The chafing sound it made was like a long, rasping wail of terror, the mouth of his own mounting panic. Now that they were off the street he felt utterly alone.

As though sensing he might run, Benny was riding along close beside him now, so close that Cass could smell the sharp odor of his sweat. They were walking along beside the back of the Magistrales' store. Over the low wooden fence he could see the plastic crates their milk was delivered in scattered around the dirt yard like building blocks in a giant playpen. Up against the back of the building, boxes of rotting vegetables were ripening in the sun. He could see the flies buzzing around them, could almost convince himself that he could hear them.

There was no sign of the monster dog, but the back door of the store was open a little and he could see shadows moving in behind the screen. Upstairs a window was open too and the wind blew the curtains around a little. He wanted to scream.

Just past the Magistrales' property lay that patch of ground that no one seemed to own, a sort of buffer zone between the Magistrales' nightmare yard and the golf-green lawns behind the houses along the street, with their cedar sun decks and hooded gas barbecues. Around the fringes of the lot a lush crop of goldenrod was growing and in the middle of it stood the rusted shell of the old Chevy sedan. Its windows were merely memories now, and the paint had been baked to a dull dead shade of gray spattered with pigeon droppings.

As they drew even with the lot, Cass suddenly caught sight of three bikes tucked in among the weeds around the car.

"Surprise," said Benny as the back doors of the sedan opened and two more of the guys from the pool poured out, like a couple of roaches crawling out of the wall, and came toward them.

"Hey, guys," said Benny. "Look what I found walking down the street. Say, you guys like barbecues?"

"Sure," said one of them, coming up and yanking the buggy out of Cass's hand. "Why?"

"Because Casper here's having a barbecue, and he says we're all invited. Isn't that right, Casper?"

Benny was getting off his bike. The third guy was walking slowly toward him with a sick smirk on his chalk-white face. For an instant Cass thought he might just have a chance, if he could just make it down to Maddy's yard.

He made a sudden break for it, pounding down the lane for all he was worth, ignoring the confusion that had erupted behind him, trying to run faster than he had ever run before.

He was almost down to her fence when the bike slammed into his leg. He flipped, falling for what seemed an eternity, watching the ground come rushing up to meet him, feeling the searing pain knife up his arm as his elbow came down hard in the dirt. The book skittered out of his grasp.

He lay motionless for a minute, the pain surrounding him like a shell, praying he would open his eyes and find them gone.

Hands hooked under his arms and he was lifted effortlessly to his feet.

"Hey, are you all right, man?" Benny stood in front of him, brushing the dirt off with his hand. "Look at that, you cut yourself."

The sudden concern confused him, then he glanced over and saw a guy in tennis whites standing on his sun deck staring over at them curiously.

"We'd better take care of that elbow," said Benny, louder than he needed to. He started walking him back up the lane. One of the others picked up the bike and wheeled it along behind them. The guy was still looking, but losing interest fast.

"A little accident," said Benny as they walked by. He might

as well have said "Get back in that house, you nosy bastard," because as soon as he said it the man turned and quietly retreated into the house.

"You stupid little jerk," spat Benny between his teeth as the door closed. He pulled him along, his hand wrapped painfully around his upper arm, back to the clearing and the car.

The third guy was leaning against the car door, sadly shaking his head. As they approached, he pushed himself off the car and swung the door open like a chauffeur tending a limousine.

Benny planted one of his ham hands on Cass's head, ducking him down through the door opening and pushing him into the backseat of the car. The door slammed shut behind him with a sickening finality.

The inside of the car was hot. It smelled of mildew and dirt, mildew and dirt laced with cigarette smoke. He opened his eyes. Lounging on the opposite side of the seat, staring into the curl of smoke coming off his cigarette, sat Sid.

"Nice of you to drop by," he said with mock civility. "Sit down." And when Cass did not immediately respond—"I said sit."

A hand came in through the blown-out back window, holding the book.

"He had this," said a disembodied voice, and Sid took the slightly battered book and started listlessly flipping through it, leaning back in the seat to catch the light.

Cass had hitched himself up onto the seat. His elbow was on fire. He could feel the blood trickling lazily down his arm, but as he watched Sid flipping slowly through the book, the pain in his arm was swallowed up by a far greater dread.

"Poetry," said Sid with a snort as he dived into the book here and there. He fanned quickly through to the end and was about to toss it aside, when a scrap of paper fluttered out onto the seat beside him.

He picked it up, turned it over, and furrowed his brow at what he found there.

"What's this?" he said.

"I don't know." It was a bad lie. He knew well enough what it was—the paper he'd written the dates of the alignment down on at the library. He'd stupidly tucked it inside the book, thinking it would be safe there.

"Sun and Moon conjoined in the House of the Lion," read Sid. "Eight/eight, eight/nine."

"What's all this about the House of the Lion, Casper? What lion?"

"I don't know. Really. It's a library book. Somebody must have left it there." *You're a pretty lousy liar. Anyone ever tell you that?*

Sid gave him a long, flat look, then carefully tucked the slip of paper back into the book and let it drop to his lap. He ran a hand through his hair.

"I see you've been doing a little shopping," he said, looking out the window at the bundle buggy.

Cass nodded his head.

"What do you want all that charcoal for?"

"Barbecue."

"Don't get smart with me, Casper. It's for old man Maggots, and don't tell me otherwise. I told you once, nice, that I wanted you to keep away from that guy and mind your own business, didn't I? Didn't I?"

"Yes."

"There's something going on in that garage, isn't there? You think I don't see the smoke? You think I don't see you, you and that girl? There's something up all right, and I intend to find out what it is." He flicked his cigarette out the window and slid over closer to Cass.

"Listen, kid, why don't you save us both a lot of trouble and tell me what you two are up to. Just between you and me, all right? Forget those guys out there. They wouldn't know something big if it hit them in the face. Just you and me, okay?"

"I don't know what you're talking about."

"No, not much. What's wrong with you, kid? You got a death wish, or what?" He suddenly heaved himself out of the seat and leaned forward, pushing his face close to Cass's. He had crazy eyes.

"There's money in this somewhere," he said. "I can smell it. I can smell it clear across that park, and I—"

A dog began to bark. There were two quick thumps on the hood of the car and a voice said, "Better split, Sid. Someone's coming."

The craziness drained instantly out of Sid's eyes. He straightened himself up and ran his hands through his hair. He took the book and jammed it down the back of his pants.

"You don't mind if I borrow this for a bit, do you Casper?" He got out and slammed the door.

The dog was going crazy now. There was a general flurry as they all scrambled onto their bikes and took off up the lane. From somewhere close by someone yelled after them,

"You keep away from here, you creeps, you hear? If I catch you near that car again, I'll break your faces, you hear me?"

By this point they probably didn't, but it was impressive anyway. Cass hunched down in the backseat, hoping he wouldn't be seen. There was a sudden thud as something slammed against the side of the car.

He looked up and saw the Magistrales' dog leaning in the window. The dog took one look at him and went crazy, its claws skittering against the side of the car as it scrambled to get in.

"Down, Lucifer," shouted someone, and the dog dropped like a stone. Footsteps approached the car. A muscular torso appeared in the window wearing a white coverall with red smears down the front that looked a lot like blood. The figure bent down and peered in through the window. It was Tony Magistrale.

"Hey, kid, what's happening? Someone told me you were having a little trouble with those creeps on the bikes. You all right?"

"Yeah, I'm okay."

Tony caught sight of his arm. "Looks like you cut yourself up pretty good. I got some bandage in the back of the store if you want."

"Thanks, but it's all right. I just live down the street."

"Suit yourself."

Tony yanked the door open and Cass stumbled out into the light. For the first time he saw how he looked, covered in dust from the fall, his elbow wet with blood. He brushed himself off.

Tony had the dog by the collar. Its tongue was hanging out, drooling into the dirt of the lane as it eyed his bloody elbow like a piece of beef. The buggy full of charcoal was lying behind the car. The top bag had been knifed open and the charcoal scattered over the ground. Tony started picking up the bigger pieces, stuffing them back into the bag.

"Hey," he said suddenly. "I know you. You live in that house with the charcoal guy, right?"

"Yeah, right."

"What does he do with all that stuff anyway? None of my business, right? Hey, looks like one of the wheels got broke."

He was right. The wheel Cass had managed to repair was

totally twisted now and wouldn't turn anymore. Tony pulled the buggy over to him, the broken wheel scoring a track in the dirt.

"You sure you're okay?" he said.

"Yeah, I'll be fine, and—thanks, eh."

"No problem. Jerks like that—beating up on people—it's no good. You let me know if you have any more trouble with them, okay?"

"Okay."

Tony jumped the low fence and loped across the dirt yard, Lucifer at his heels. He scooped up a couple of the milk crates as he went past and threw them up against the back of the store. The screen door slammed behind him as he went in.

Cass stood there for a few minutes, watching the flies buzz around the vegetable boxes, just glad to be alive. His elbow didn't even hurt.

He started off down the lane, dragging the buggy behind him, loose bits of charcoal popping free every time he hit a bump. Suddenly he had the feeling someone was watching him. He swung around. The lane was deserted. In the upper window of the store the curtains were still blowing around, but now there was someone standing there. It was Maria. As soon as she realized he was looking at her she stepped back and melted into the shadows.

And suddenly he knew that she had seen the whole thing happen, that it was she who had called Tony to his rescue, she who had practically saved his life.

He saw the long, weaving gouge left in the dirt by the buggy. He turned and started back down the lane. When he got to Maddy's place he paused and made sure no one was looking, then he lifted the buggy over the fence and hid it in the bushes at the side of the garage.

On the way back up the lane he kicked the loose charcoal to the side and smoothed out the track left by the buggy.

It wasn't until he passed by the lot and the abandoned car that he thought about the book again and the piece of paper tucked inside. His arm began to ache.

—— 26 ——

IT WAS FRIDAY night at the Palace. They were showing a couple of Hitchcock pictures, and as usual the crowd was considerably larger than on other nights. There were a lot of Hitchcock fans out there who wouldn't have been caught dead in the Palace normally but who thought of it as a bit of a lark to go slumming with their friends whenever one of the master's pictures came around.

You could tell them right off. They were the ones with the casual clothes that looked like they had just come out of the package, the hair that looked like it was used to staying exactly where it was told. They'd come sauntering up the stairs with their tubs of buttered popcorn and their diet drinks, talking just loud enough to be overheard, and smiling indulgently at the strip of cloth tape that held the carpet together, and the cute little usher in the funny uniform.

Meanwhile, the cute little usher was trying hard not to bash his flashlight over the back of somebody's head. It was almost a relief when some of the regulars started trickling in: the weird guy in the trench coat, a carton of cigarettes tucked under his arm, the two old ladies with their knitting, the "undertaker" looking cagey, and two old bag men looking tired.

He could have handled a houseful of bag men tonight, with pleasure. At least they looked like they belonged, and they didn't spend half their time running back and forth to the candy counter. And tonight every drink, every bag of jelly beans and box of popcorn that came up those stairs was just one more piece of garbage he was going to have to clean up when it was over. Tonight he wanted old Harry in the projection booth to skip a reel; he wanted the popcorn machine to break down and the soft drinks to run dry. Anything, just as long as Maddy and he could be out of there fast. For tonight was the night.

The first movie, *Vertigo*, whirled by. Intermission came and went. Zeke was more than a little excited. The second film was *Psycho*, and the way he told it, it was probably the best movie ever made. No doubt about it, the Palace was definitely beginning to get to Zeke. He was starting to get that wild look around his eyes like the guy in the trench coat. Another year or so and he'd be beyond help. As soon as the lights went down, he melted back into the shadows with his sunflower seeds and was as good as gone.

One thing about a Hitchcock crowd—they were quiet. It was like they were in church or something. They wouldn't dream of putting their feet up on the seat in front of them or whipping their jelly beans at the screen. There was nothing for Cass to do but relax and watch the movie.

This proved more than a little difficult. For one thing, the music in this movie was not designed for relaxation. At certain moments in the story an ominous thrum would start up, building steadily to a climax in a terrifying shriek of violins. For another thing, his mind kept wandering to the work that lay ahead of them later that night, and to sudden flashes of Sid sitting in the back of that bombed-out car, leafing curiously through the book. Maddy and Mr. Magnus had taken it pretty calmly when he'd told them what had happened in the lane. Maddy was convinced that Sid would never piece together what the note meant. Cass only wished he could feel that sure.

True to form, Zeke had already spilled the whole plot of *Psycho* in elaborate detail while they were changing. Still, by the time Janet Leigh checked into the Bates Motel in the middle of the thunderstorm with the suitcase full of money she had stolen, his stomach was completely in knots anticipating the shower scene he knew came next. Despite Zeke, nothing could have prepared him for it. The thunder of the water pouring down, the overwhelming sense of dread that something awful was about to happen, the sudden shadow of the intruder cast on the shower curtain, the shriek of violins as they were ripped back, the terrible plunge of the knife. Zeke said the whole thing lasted less than a minute. If so, it was the longest minute of his life. By the time it was over he felt as if it were he, not Janet Leigh, lying facedown on the bathroom floor.

He peeled himself off the wall and made his way downstairs to the lobby on legs that felt as though they had suddenly turned liquid. In the bathroom he splashed water on his face and took a drink from the tap. It was strange to think that people actually watched this stuff for pleasure.

When he came out, Fischer was making slow passes with the carpet sweeper in front of the candy counter. Maddy was waiting on a customer and looking a little harried. She glanced up and gave him a weak smile as he went by, an exchange Fischer did not fail to notice. Cass could feel his cold eyes on his back all the way up the stairs.

The next time he looked down, Fischer was draped all over the counter talking to Maddy. For some unsettling reason Fischer reminded him of Norman Bates, the psychopath in the movie, leaning over the desk of the Bates Motel, eyeing his victim as she signed the register. It was not a pleasant thought.

From that point on he was only half watching the movie. The other half of him was busy keeping an eye on the lobby.

Maddy, finally finding a break from the nearly constant stream of people coming down for refreshments, put the lid down on the counter fifteen minutes later and started into her cleanup. He watched her shovel the leftover popcorn into a couple of tubs for Jack to eat after everyone had left. She counted the cash and took it over to the office, cleaned out the machine, swept up behind the counter. She was taking her time, slowing things down so that just as she was finishing up, Jack would emerge from his office with the night deposit bag. Then he and Fischer would take off for the bank and she would be free to slide upstairs unseen to watch the end of the movie and wait for Cass to finish.

She lifted the hinged section of counter at the end, opened the door, and came out, crossing the lobby quickly on her way to the supply closet for the mop and pail and the wet rag for swabbing down the counter. There was no sign of Fischer, which should have struck him immediately as strange. But the music was starting up again in the movie, and despite himself he found his eyes drawn to the screen.

The private eye who was investigating Janet Leigh's mysterious disappearance had just entered the old Bates house on the hill behind the motel uninvited. That was his first big mistake. His second, if the music had anything to do with it, was starting up the wide staircase to the second floor.

As he reached the top the music peaked and the cameras switched to a long overhead shot. The violins started their unnerving shriek and a figure flashed out of a doorway. Down came the knife. Several people in the audience screamed and the detective fell backward down the stairs.

As he hit the bottom there was another scream, this one not from the screen or the audience though, but from downstairs. Or was it only his imagination? Zeke didn't seem to have noticed anything.

He listened from the top stair. Maddy was still in the supply closet. He could hear the muffled drum of the water filling the wash bucket. But then another sound, the dull thud of something banging against the inside of the door.

He didn't bother to stop and think. He took the stairs down two at a time, raced across the lobby, and tore open the door of the supply closet.

Fischer had Maddy backed against the sink. He had pinned her arms against her sides and was pressing his fat mouth against her face. The water was sloshing over the side of the overflowing bucket, bringing back all the horror of the shower scene.

Without even knowing what he was doing, Cass took a run at Fischer, knocking him off balance. He let go of Maddy, and turned on Cass.

"Get the hell out of here, you—"

He didn't get a chance to finish what he was going to say. Maddy brought her knee up hard into his groin. He gave a surprised yelp and doubled over. Maddy screamed something and pushed him face first into the bucket of water. As Fischer came up coughing and sputtering, the office door opened and Jack sauntered out with the money. He stopped dead in his tracks, taking in the scene. Zeke, who had obviously heard the commotion, was halfway down the stairs. Jack shot a glance in his direction and he turned and hightailed it back up to the floor.

"I want to see you, all three of you, in my office. Now."

Fischer, of course, lied through his teeth. He stood there with his wet head dripping all over the carpet while he ran a fistful of napkins through his stubble of hair, trying to dry himself off. The way he told it, he had come to put the carpet sweeper away after the cleanup and had discovered Cass and Maddy necking in the supply closet. When he tried to break it up, they'd done this to him. He dropped the wet wad of napkins into the garbage. He should have put his story there along with it.

Even Jack, normally a pushover when it came to Fischer, seemed to have a hard time swallowing this one. He looked thoughtfully from one of them to the other as he lit the stump of a cigar. The padlocked money bag was still clutched in his free hand as if it might run off.

"He's lying," said Maddy quietly.

"Did I ask you?" said Jack.

"No, but he's lying anyway. I went to get some water to wash down the counter, and he was waiting in there for me. As soon as I turned my back on him he made a grab for me. It's not the first time either. And I'm not the first girl he's done it to."

"You lousy liar," said Fischer.

"She's not lying," said Cass. "I heard a noise and came down to see what it was. I found him trying to come on to her in the closet."

Jack looked at him long and expressionlessly. Then he looked back at Fischer. His hair was still wet, a mass of tiny spikes. The shoulders of his uniform were stained with dampness.

"Mr. Grant, sir," he began, "they're lying. You know that I wouldn't—"

"Enough," said Jack. "I've heard quite enough. You can go, the three of you. But believe me, this is far from over."

He stayed for a long time in his office. Fischer went into the john and dried his head under the hand drier. Then he went and stood at his post by the exit doors waiting for Jack to come out so he could go with him to the night deposit and plead his case along the way.

Finally Maddy could kill no more time. She put the stuff back in the closet, got her coat, and left through the front doors. Fischer didn't look at her as she went past.

It was another ten minutes before Jack came out with the money. Cass watched from the top of the stairs as he headed for the exit doors, trailing smoke. Fischer pushed open the door for him and started following him out. Jack turned, said something to him, and left alone.

Fischer just stood there while the curtained door closed slowly in his face. Then he went to the plate glass window that looked out on the street and peered out, cracking his knuckles and shaking his head.

Jack returned ten minutes later with a newspaper tucked under his arm and a cup of coffee in his hand. It was the first time Cass had ever seen him with either. He didn't bother acknowledging the fact that Fischer had opened the door for him. He just crossed the lobby quickly and disappeared back into his office.

Shortly after that the movie ended. The lights went up and Cass took his place with Zeke against the back wall of the orchestra as the people began to file out.

"What was *that* all about?" said Zeke out of the side of his mouth.

"Fischer made a pass at Maddy in the closet."

"I figured that. But what did Jack say when he hauled you all off into his office?"

"Nothing. He didn't say anything."

"Well, something must have happened. Take a look at Fischer down there. Boy, if looks could kill. I'd steer clear of him if I was you."

Fischer was stationed at the door as the patrons filed past.

He had a definite Norman Bates look about him now as he glared up in their direction.

Cass took Zeke's advice to heart. A confrontation with Fischer tonight was the last thing he needed. He wasn't even sure how or where he and Maddy were supposed to meet now that their initial plans had been fouled up. Rather than risk going down to the change room and running into a crazed Fischer perched on one of the cans in the stalls waiting for him, Cass decided to leave his jacket right where it was for the night.

He whipped through the cleanup in double time, scooping up all the big stuff and cramming it into the green garbage bag he dragged along behind him. Zeke, fearing for Cass's safety, agreed to finish up the loges alone.

Cass hauled the garbage bags down to the back doors of the theater, in behind the screen. He pushed open the heavy metal doors and dragged the bags out into the night, letting the doors slam closed and locked behind him.

It was raining and the fire escape that the door opened onto was slick and treacherous. He hefted the bags up over the railing and dropped them into the metal hopper below. Then he carefully made his way down the stairs and into the unlit alley at the rear of the theater. The rain dripped with a desolate sound from the roof of the theater into an oily black puddle. The sound echoed off the blank back of the building along with his footsteps as he made his way slowly to the street.

He had intended on shedding the uniform once he got out of the theater, but with the rain coming down steadily he decided to leave it on. He unclipped the bow tie and tucked it in his pocket, then flipped the collar up around his neck.

He felt a little like a convict, just escaped from prison and still wearing his stripes, as he stepped out into the glow of the street lights. Fischer's bike was still parked in the lot across the road. He took a quick look back toward the theater, then another down the dark wet street. There was no sign of Maddy. She must have headed off for the garage alone rather than risk waiting for him in the rain with Fischer still lurking about.

He took one last look around, then took off down the street, his shoes slapping against the wet pavement, the rain pelting against his face. Every motor he heard in the distance took on the menacing drone of Fischer's motorbike. Twice he ducked down beside a parked car while a vehicle approached, listening to the hiss of the wheels, feeling the grope of headlights as it drew near, then passed. One of them had been a cab, the other a sports car.

He had just caught sight of the park, shining like a dream in the distance, when the hooded figure leaped out in front of him from behind a car. A sick chill shot through him and his eyes instinctively sought an escape route.

The figure threw back the hood, and standing there in the glow of the streetlight was Maddy.

"Sorry," she said—a little lamely, he thought. There was a trace of a smile tugging at the corners of her mouth.

"Fine. You just lopped about five years off my life, that's all." He could feel his heart thumping crazily against his rib cage. "Is that funny?"

"No, it's not. I didn't mean to scare you, really, Cass." She was trying hard to erase the smile. "You just look a little, uh, odd out here with your uniform on."

He looked down at himself. The uniform was fairly soaked. It looked a little like a limp sealskin with a racing stripe down the side.

"I can see your point," he said. He went on to explain his escape from the Palace by way of the back door.

"Thanks," she said. "For what you did tonight."

"Seems to me that you did most of it," he said. "I guess we may as well kiss our jobs good-bye."

"Yeah, but let's not worry about that now. It's late. We'd better get moving."

Soon they were making their way down the lane, trying to dodge puddles in the dark. They opened the creaking gate just wide enough to squeeze through, closed it carefully behind them, then stole around to the front of the garage.

A narrow frame of light outlined the door against the dark. They opened it and went in.

Mr. Magnus was standing over by the stove.

"Close that," he said without looking up. "And lock it. I was beginning to think you weren't coming."

"Something happened at the theater," said Maddy. But the room was loud with the sound of rain on the roof, and the old man did not appear to hear. Examining the contents of the egg closely, he bent down and scooped another shovelful of charcoal into the stove. The odd gleam in his eyes was more than reflected firelight.

As they stood before the stove Cass could see that the substance in the egg, though still luminously white, was now faintly tinged with red, like the light tint on the lips of the young soldier in the photograph.

The heat spilled from the open mouth of the stove in warm waves. The coals within pulsed with a red life. The room was already hot, and the sweat had begun to run in rivulets down the old man's brow. He struggled with the cord at the waist of the old dressing gown he wore and pulled it off.

"It's not too late to leave," he said, wiping the back of his hand across his brow, leaving a streak of soot. "The substance is extremely volatile now. Anything could happen."

Cass and Maddy traded glances. "We'll stay," they said.

"Good. Then get off those wet things and we'll begin."

Over the course of the next hour the two of them took turns feeding coal into the stove and working the stiff old bellows to fan the fire to a white heat at Mr. Magnus's direction. He paced back and forth in great agitation between the low table nearby spread with books and the egg on the stove. They felt as though their arms would fall off, pumping the bellows madly, like the beating of black wings struggling to take flight. The open mouth of the fire made a fearful whispered roar as it sent wave on wave of heat washing over their soaked and aching bodies.

And still the substance in the egg showed no change. The glass, the very stove itself, seemed to shimmer with the heat until they seemed no longer real, but merely ghostly images hovering in space. In his exhaustion Cass began to feel as he worked the bellows that if he pumped hard enough they would utterly disappear.

Fatigue was taking its toll. The fire began to seem to him like a fourth and sinister presence in the room, mocking them, refusing to be bound to their bidding, determined to suck them dry of all their strength. He looked at Maddy as she fed the coal into the fiery belly of the stove. Her hair hung in soaking tendrils over her forehead, her glasses danced with reflected flame, her face shone with firelight. Her strength seemed suddenly overwhelming, a goddess's, feeding off the fire like the moon. He worked the bellows desperately, with the last of his strength. And suddenly Mr. Magnus called out "Look. Look," and pointed at the egg.

The surface of the luminous whiteness was agitated now, like a sea whipped up by storm winds. Waves of light lashed against the side of the glass. And now, rising, it seemed, from the center of it, like an island surfacing from beneath the waves, was a glowing redness as bright as the heart of the fire.

He stopped pumping the bellows, and stood up to see the wonder more closely. Immediately it sank beneath the waves.

"No," yelled Maddy. "Don't stop." And she snatched the bellows from his hand and began pumping with renewed strength while he stood there dumbfounded, like someone in a dream.

The spell was shattered by a sudden muffled thud from outside the garage. He swung in the direction of the sound in time to see a hand describe a slow circle against the dirty glass, and a ghostly white face suddenly fill the frame.

"There's someone out there," he said, and instantly the spectral face vanished from the window.

He threw the door open and wheeled around to the narrow passage. The screen covering on the window hung loose like a flap of skin. Someone was scrambling over the fence at the end of the passage and into the lane.

Cass took off after him, ducking under the dangling screen, skidding on the wet tangle of weeds and garbage that choked the passage. And then he was over the fence and into the lane.

Halfway up, a figure on a bike was racing toward the street. He could hear the wheels skidding against the wet gravel, hear the splash of the water as it bounced through the puddles, hear the panting and grunting of the rider.

He took off after him. It was useless. Long before he made it to the end of the lane the bike had turned and vanished. He looked down the dark street in the direction it had taken, but there was not so much as a trace of it. The street had turned quietly in its sleep and covered it.

The rain had revived him. The events of the past hour seemed suddenly like a dream. He turned to start back, and in that instant there was a dull muffled explosion nearby, followed by a terrifying silence.

* * *

By the time he got back to the garage, lights had begun to wink on in houses up and down the street. Maddy was tearing madly around the yard coughing and crying for help. Smoke was billowing out the open door of the garage.

He shook her, shook her hard.

"Where is Mr. Magnus?" he screamed. "Where is he?"

"He's still in there. On the ground. I couldn't move him."

He pulled a handkerchief from his pocket, soaked it in a muddy puddle, tied it over his mouth and nose. Then he headed blindly into the garage.

At first he could see nothing. There was only the fury of the fire, the dense curtain of smoke. And then he saw the stove, lying on its side, the flaming embers scattered around it like deadly jewels, and lying close by on the ground the motionless form of Mr. Magnus.

He hooked his hands under the old man's arms and began to pull him backward toward the door. The fire roared like a beast being robbed of its kill, and the smoke enfolded him in its terrible arms. The few yards to the door swelled suddenly to a hundred or more. The smoke seared his lungs like gas, and for an instant he swore he heard the low howl of a shell pass overhead.

And then he was free of it and out into the night, choking and coughing uncontrollably. And now Maddy was at his side, helping him drag Mr. Magnus free of the smoke and fire.

They pulled him a little along the path, then laid him down on the wet grass. The old man lay there limp, his hands clenched tightly into fists, the moon mirrored like pearls in his wide, unseeing eyes.

Maddy took one long look at him lying there, and ran.

— 27 —

THEY STOOD together at the bedroom window looking down into the yard. The charred remains of the garage still smoldered in the early morning sunlight. A clutch of curious neighbors had gathered in the laneway to gawk at the ruins. Only the framing remained standing, like the blackened bars of some strange cage whose occupant had flown from the flames.

The rest was rubble. The old wood stove lay on its side in one corner, its metal mouth open in surprise, sections of stovepipe scattered in the ashes around it. Several sooty glass bottles lay strewn about, having survived the blaze along with the metal ends of tools whose wooden handles had been consumed by the flames.

The place had gone up like a torch, raging away in the dark uncontrollably while firefighters doused the neighboring garages with water in an attempt to contain the fire. Eventually it had simply burned itself out, until with a sad whoosh the roof had fallen in and stilled it like a blanket settled over a sleepless child. Still, the leaves of the lilac in Mrs. Wharton's yard had been blistered by the heat, and a black dust lay on the roses.

Maddy reached out, took his hand in hers, and squeezed it gently. He could feel the energy pass back and forth between them, feel her strength surge into him, his anger and exhaustion flow out.

"Vultures," he said. "Why don't they just go home. There's nothing left to see."

His eyes fanned over the curious faces, young and old, talking among themselves. Hair combed, hands in pockets—a quiet chat around the ruins. He could have puked. Here they were, all these people who made a point of walking quickly past the old red house, who turned their heads the other way when the old man made one of his rare forays onto the street. Here they all were, happily chatting, as though the danger had now been defused.

Mr. Magnus, with his ramshackle house, his strange ways, his affinity with the dark, had reminded them of something they would sooner not have seen. Here people were not supposed to limp, grow old, talk to themselves, be different. People here were supposed to be happy and whole and have neatly trimmed lawns and sandblasted façades and scrubbed, exceptionally gifted children. Mr. Magnus had been a worrisome reminder of everything they wanted to do away with. And so here they were, gathered around the ashes, as the citizens of an earlier age would have stood around the spent fire of a stake, happy to have done away with the darkness again.

He felt tired, so very, very tired. The edges had begun to blur between inside and outside, between now and then. Overlaying the sunlight and cinders he kept seeing bright tongues of flame lapping at the night sky, the sparks showering lazily down like swooping birds, kept hearing the muted explosions as yet another bottle shattered inside. Starshells bursting over no-man's-land.

He had stood at the window most of the night, numbed, watching the fire unfold, going through the whole thing time and again in his mind, trying to coax it to a different conclusion. If only he hadn't left them alone. If only he'd known what might happen, if only . . . Over and over, until finally the roof had collapsed and he with it, flopping back onto the bed fully clothed.

He had awakened early in the morning, the cover pulled up over him, the sun streaming through the window, and memories of some strange dream of lying in a hospital buzzing in his brain.

As he looked down at the lane now he saw the little girl with the tricycle come pedaling out her back gate to investigate, her father in tow. The sight of the tricycle, the sound of the wheels against the gravel of the lane, set him off, and again he saw Sid's bike racing away in the dark, turning onto the night street, disappearing.

The tricycle stopped in front of the fringe of onlookers. The girl peered in through the wide gap where the double doors had been, her mouth open wide. She said something to her father, then edged down to the side of the garage and looked down at what was left of the passageway. On her way back she suddenly swung her head and stared right up at the two of them standing there in the second-floor window. Her face said nothing, but he had the feeling that if he stood there looking at her any longer she would cry.

He turned away from the window. The room felt different, no longer wholly his. The bed was unmade. Strewn across it were the pictures he had retrieved from the box at the back of the closet. He had taken them out that morning, going slowly through them, staring intently at the faces in the photos, trying to charm the shattered pieces back together as if by magic. He took the sad-eyed soldier down now and laid him alongside the others.

Maddy and he walked hand in hand through the house. He could not keep things in focus. The rooms kept wanting to change shape, dissolve into different rooms from other times than this.

The bust of Blake was back on the mantel overseeing the front room. The room was full of light, as if somehow the spirit of the man had conjured it up. He stood in front of it for a moment, running his fingers lightly along the broad brow, the narrow flaring nose, the eyes asleep in the stone. Immediately the sunflower poem came into his mind.

> *Ah, Sun-flower! weary of time,*
> *Who countest the steps of the Sun,*
> *Seeking after that sweet golden clime*
> *Where the traveller's journey is done.*

And suddenly the tears were running down his face, tears of frustration, tears of exhaustion. He let them come.

Maddy was standing by the window, looking over at the park. He wiped his face on his sleeve and went to join her. He was still wearing his white shirt from work, spattered with ash and mud. It didn't matter.

The pool was full of children, splashing in the sun, their towels laid out like patchwork around the rim. The water danced like crystal in the light. There were no signs of Sid and the gang. For now the park belonged to the children. His gaze drifted to the bench, where Alison and he had sat that first day in the snow. Again he thought of Blake and the tree of angels, and for a crazy moment the leaves of the tree were laced with wings.

Downstairs a door opened. He heard Alison's voice in the hall along with Maddy's father's. The conversation continued on the stairs, but stopped abruptly at the top. The door opened and they came in.

Alison managed a weary smile. Dr. Harrington was carrying his black leather bag. He set it down on the chair. Last night, as soon as they had pulled Mr. Magnus free of the garage, Maddy had taken one look at him lying there and had raced off down the street to fetch her father. He had come in a

matter of minutes, ministering to the old man, thumping feverishly on his chest, trying to snatch him back from the brink.

He was still working when the ambulance crew arrived.
Together they carried the old man into the house while the
fire raged outside. He had stayed there through the night, Mr.
Magnus absolutely refusing to be taken to the hospital, and
Dr. Harrington finally convincing them to leave him.

He sat on the edge of the rocker now and ran his hands
through his hair, yawning.

"I'll put on some coffee," said Alison. "We could all use
some."

"Fine," said the doctor. He looked over at them. "You two
look dead on your feet," he said.

Cass listened as Alison turned on the water in the kitchen,
filled the kettle, settled it on the stove. The image of Mr.
Magnus fiddling impatiently with the knobs on the stove
flooded into his mind.

"How is he?" he said.

"Weak," said the doctor. "Tired, like the rest of us. Sleep
is what he needs now. But he absolutely refuses to sleep until
he sees the two of you. He's a stubborn old bird, I'll give him
that."

"But is he going to—" Maddy left the word hanging in the
air.

"To die, you mean?" said the doctor. He stood up and
looked for a long while out the window at the park, as though
the answer might be there.

"This may sound a little strange," he said at last. "But I
think he already did. When I first got to him in the yard, I
was convinced he was gone. I couldn't get a pulse, heartbeat,
anything. There was no response to resuscitation. Then just
as the ambulance crew had loaded him onto the stretcher and
were about to take him away, I glanced down at him and he
was looking back at me. I've never seen anything like it."

Cass and Maddy looked at each other.

"He looked at me and he said, 'Take me into the house.' I was stunned. I'm still stunned. One moment I was looking into the face of death, and the next moment he was talking to me.

"I had them take him inside. There was nothing else I could do. I could no more have run counter to him than I could when I was a boy. He had the same authority that he had had then.

"We put him in one of the bedrooms, the small one, away from the noise and commotion that was starting outside. His color was already beginning to come back, and his vital signs were good. It had been a heart attack, I think. There was a bad gash on his forehead, which I patched up, and a burn on his hand, but nothing needing hospital attention. Not that he would have gone anyway.

"I convinced the ambulance crew to leave, assuring them that I would stay the night to monitor him, just in case there was another attack. There wasn't, but he's not out of the woods yet, not by a long shot. The next forty-eight hours are critical."

Alison came in with the coffee and a plate of cookies.

"Wonderful," said the doctor. "You know, Cass, this is quite an amazing mother you have here. I don't know what I would have done without her last night. She even sat with our patient herself for a couple of hours while I got some sleep. Not that she's slept a wink herself since all this started, I'm sure."

"There'll be plenty of time for sleep later," said Alison. "Now perhaps you two should pop down briefly and look in on Mr. Magnus. We'll promise not to eat all of these if you hurry."

They practically flew down the stairs. The broken buggy sat on the mat outside the door. The door itself was open wide. It was strange to find it so, somehow almost sacrilegious.

As soon as they were in they closed it quietly behind them and stood silently while the room settled around them. It was as though a spell lay over it, apt to shatter if they spoke. Someone had opened the curtains. The room was bright with unaccustomed light. The figurines on the sill had been dusted. And there, with the china dog and cat, the ivory elephants, the bird perched on its crystal branch, stood the unicorn, its horn held high.

It was the same room, yet utterly different. The old flowered armchair still sat in its corner, remote, retiring, surrounded by its ring of magazines. One of them lay splayed open over an arm, as though some invisible occupant of the chair might momentarily awaken. The magnifying glass had fallen to the floor.

They tiptoed quietly through the room lest they waken the ghost. The sound of laughter from the pool laced through the stillness. The rhythmic creaking of the swings echoed the complaint of floorboards underfoot. Cass stared at the piece of shrapnel lying on the shelf.

They stopped in the small hall between the bedrooms. These doors had always been closed to them, but now to his left Cass could see into the bedroom beneath his own; the bed pushed up against the same wall as his, a single picture on the wall above it, an old phonograph on a table by the bed, a fan of records spread out on the floor below. And snaking its way eerily across the ceiling toward the chimney flue by the window, a narrow, winding crack.

If he were to walk in there now and look in the mirror above the dresser, he wondered, who would be looking back?

"Who's there?" came that unmistakable voice from behind the other door. Maddy gave him a gentle tug, and they pushed open the door to what they had come to know as Mother's bedroom and went in.

It was as unlike the room directly above it as one could imagine. No mattress on the floor, no Blake posters thumbtacked to the wall, no numbered stacks of papers, piles of clothes, abandoned coffee cups. It was a soft and ordered room, with a high brass bed and a flounced coverlet, a vanity by the window with a chair drawn up to it, muted photographs in frames against a pattern of roses on the wall.

Standing on the floor at the foot of the bed, bristling with metal bars and worn leather straps, Mr. Magnus's leg leaned against the polished brass pole supporting Petrus's cage. The bird was asleep.

Mr. Magnus lay in the bed, his body swallowed by blankets, his head propped up on pillows. A large gauze bandage covered one side of his forehead. He looked at them over the rim of his glasses.

"Come over here where I can see you, and sit down," he said. He shifted over a little in the bed. His body, dwarfed by the large bed, looked no bigger than a child's. They sat down, Maddy at the vanity, Cass on the edge of the bed.

"Don't look so solemn, the two of you. I'm not dead yet."

"How do you feel?" asked Cass.

"About as battered as I look, I should say. But"—and he propped himself suddenly up on his elbows—"I'm sure a cigarette would make me feel much better."

"Not a chance," said Maddy.

"Just as I suspected," he said. "Like father, like daughter." He slumped back in the bed and snorted, then launched into a fit of coughing.

"I suppose the garage has gone," he said when he had recovered.

"Yes," said Cass. "Burned to the ground."

He nodded. "They told me what you did for me last night. I'm fortunate to have found such friends."

The silence fell over them, a silence no longer simply his, but belonging to each of them equally now. They felt it quietly at work among them, weaving them strangely into one.

"My mother came again last night," he said at length. "I lay here sleeping, dreaming I was in England, in the hospital they took me to after I was wounded at the Front. And when I woke up she was sitting there at the vanity, where you are now." He looked at Maddy.

"She didn't speak, didn't say a word. But it was Mother nonetheless. I sensed that she'd been sitting there for most of the night, watching over me as she had when I was ill as a child. She looked very tired, and finally her head slumped forward and she fell asleep. And I lay there for the longest time just listening to her breathe.

"It was near dawn when I finally called out to her. She looked up, fixed me with her wide eyes, and in that instant she was gone." He turned to Cass. "It was your mother who got up out of the chair and came to me. She must have thought I was mad." He pushed himself up in the bed and for the first time brought his arms out from under the blankets. His left hand was swathed in bandages.

"Perhaps I am just a crazy old man," he said. "But as surely as I saw her, last night I saw the Stone."

"We all saw it," said Cass.

"And for an instant after the explosion, as it lay there glowing with heat amid the shattered glass on the floor of the garage, I plucked it up and held it in this hand." He looked down at the bandaged hand.

"Then where is it now?" said Maddy.

"Gone. Buried beneath the rubble, I suppose. Hidden again, as it loves to hide. It would be useless to even begin looking."

"Next time, then," said Maddy.

"Yes, perhaps next time. But for me there will be no next

time. My work is complete. I am content to have come this close, to have seen it, touched it. That touch alone saved my life, I'm sure."

He opened his good hand. Curled there in his palm lay the snake ring.

"They had to take this off last night to bandage that hand. I have no more need of it. The wheel has come full circle. Once again the serpent swallows its tail." He extended his hand toward Cass. "Take it," he said. "It's meant for you. I think I've known that for a long time now."

Cass reached out, touched it, took it into his own hand. As he slid it onto his finger he thought he felt the snake curl snugly about the bone.

Mr. Magnus turned to Maddy. "That drawer there," he said. "The one on the right. Yes, open it. You'll find something there."

Maddy eased the drawer open and withdrew a small parcel wound in oilskin.

"You may unwrap it," said the old man.

As she did, she uncovered a small old book bound in vellum, ribbed and tooled on the spine. Sudden understanding flashed across her face.

"Yes," he nodded. "It's the book that Philip left me, the secret book of the Art. It is yours; for without you none of this could have happened."

He settled back against the pillows and drew the silence about him like a blanket.

"It's up to the two of you now, together, to continue the search for the Stone. You must go by a dark way. And the way cannot be mine. You must make your own way in the Art. Be patient, be slow. Don't be fooled by the lure of gold, for the true gold is forged in the furnace of the heart. It is there you must go, for it is there the meanings lie."

And for the next while he spoke to them of strange and secret things, things not to be found in any book concerning the Art, but passed on only by word of mouth from master to pupil down through the ages.

Finally, his eyes grew heavy and his voice began to trail off. "You must sleep now," said Maddy. "You need your rest." "Yes, he murmured, his eyes already closed as she settled the blankets around him.

Cass got up from the edge of the bed and made his way slowly with Maddy to the door. Before he left, though, he stopped and looked back. For a moment he thought he caught a glimpse of someone sitting in the chair by the bed. Then Maddy took him by the hand and they tiptoed quietly from the room.

—— 28 ——

IT HAD TO END at the Palace.

There was still no sign of them. Cass checked his watch again by the light of his flashlight and looked down at the doors where Zeke was taking tickets from the last of the few sad patrons who had trickled in. The film had just started. It was Wednesday night and Jack was screening the latest offering in his Silents Please series, a film called *The Chaplin Revue*, which, according to the program flyer, contained three of the best of Charlie Chaplin's three-reel silent shorts.

Apparently not too many people were interested in Charlie Chaplin's shorts. There were about twenty people scattered in the dark watching, counting the Golden Girls, who peered down from their pedestals by the screen.

Jack's door was open, just the latest step in a series of trans-formations that seemed to date back to the night Fischer made the pass at Maddy.

Fischer was history now. Jack had given him the sack the very next day. It seemed he had caught wind of his stealing from the candy counter around the same time, and the incident with Maddy was just the last nail in his coffin. He promoted Zeke to head usher. Those two-tone Italian loafers were tough shoes to fill, but Zeke seemed to be doing all right with his sneakers. He still didn't have the one-handed ticket tearing technique quite down yet, but he was working on it.

Maddy was behind the counter, doing her best to look busy. With the office door open, she was right in Jack's line of sight. So far tonight she had rearranged the candy in the dis-play half a dozen times and popped enough popcorn to handle a matinee. If Jack didn't shut his door soon, they were going to have to start giving the stuff away. Cass watched her now, filling up boxes with the popcorn, lining them up inside the machine to keep them warm. She caught his glance, looked up at him, and smiled.

More than two months had gone by now since the night of the fire. The two of them had sat down secretly several times already, poring over the strange little book Mr. Magnus had given them, trying to unravel the riddle of words and meanings. It would take time, perhaps a lifetime, to pierce through the necessary darkness of words and win through to the hidden truth of the Art. But as the book itself said, patience was the ladder of the alchemist, humility the key to the garden. For now it was enough to be making their way, however haltingly, into the mystery.

He checked his watch again. What could be keeping them, he wondered. It was already seven-fifteen. Maybe Murray's pickup had finally given up the ghost. Laughter erupted from the audience as Charlie Chaplin eluded a police officer, ducking back and forth through the loose board of a fence.

Cass had given Alison the passes last week by way of congratulations on her paper. Professor Frye, her thesis adviser, had been delighted with her work. There was nothing left to do now but the final typing, which she expected to have done by Christmas at the latest. And then—who knew? She was already talking about perhaps applying for a teaching position for next fall. Alison, a teacher? Somehow it was a little hard to see, but then again, what wasn't?

He turned away from the screen and glanced down at the door just in time to see Zeke deposit a mouthful of sunflower-seed shells into his palm and pocket them. Jack's door was closed now and Maddy had pulled out a paperback and was perched on the stool behind the counter reading. Suddenly she looked up.

And there they were, coming through the door. Alison saw Maddy at the counter and smiled, while Murray handed the tickets to Zeke, who tried the one-handed tear twice before he gave up and handed them the stubs, pointing to the stairs. As he reached back to take the ticket from the person behind them, Alison started over to say hello to Maddy.

And standing there in the doorway directly behind where she had been was Mr. Magnus. Zeke gave a quick flick of the wrist and looked down, stunned, at the ticket he had just torn one-handed. He handed the stub to the old man as if it might have been made of gold. Mr. Magnus took it and smiled. Leaning heavily on his cane, he started with Murray toward the stairs.